AUGURY OF GIDEON

Book 3: The Vampire Relics

The Vampire Relics Series

Book One: *The Chalice*
Book Two: *The Blood Crown*
Book Three: *Augury of Gideon*

Augury of Gideon

Copyright © 2014 Tracy Angelina Evans
Published by Fey Publishing
www.feypublishing.com
ISBN-13: 978-0692303917
ISBN-10: 069230391X

Front Cover Artwork © Amanda Lynn Cook
(http://alcook.deviantart.com/)
Cover Design © Megan Butzin
Shriekback Lyrics © Barry Andrews and Carl Marsh
(http://www.shriekback.com/)
Edited by Jill Rosenberg and Wilma T. Evans

SPECIAL THANKS

To Aunt Tudi, for believing in me.

To my Mother Unit, Wilma Terry Manheim Evans, for editing magick and funding.

To Barry Andrews and Carl Marsh for permission to use their songs to help manifest the tales.

To Jill Rosenburg, for her priceless editing.

To TP Suhr for webular space and support.

To Sophie Childs and Kristen Duvall, for their work on the project and being patient with me.

To the Writers' Cabal, especially Heidi Bowles Ellis and Heather P. Dunbar, my sisters in the Vampiric Night.

To David Lodge, for The Terrifying Squeegee of God™

The Relics Three

Relics three sway history
In destined hands they rest
Immortal clutches hold no more
These ancient trials to test.

The Relic First of blood was wrought
Its thorns wreath'd 'bout in pain
This day still aches in Holy See

Enshrouded by its stain
The Relic Twain by Goddess blessed,
Yet cursed in magick's stead
Avails no Wight nor Man to wield

The Elf-Chylde's grail of dread.
The Triune Relic, Crimson Heart,
Bears mystery at its core
Its tales of ancient sorrow
Share both Elf and human lore

The Relics Three in history
The Chalice and Crown of Blood
Keep true within the Augury
The Veins of Time's great flood.

No sip from cup
No prick 'pon scalp
Can prophecy be fulfilled
Without the Song of Gideon

PROLOGUE

The buried harvest and the boiling wound – the College of Knowledge's matriculation. Nothing doing; while the reptile moon casts its shadow of that hooligan illumination. A long time coming, a long time gone ~ just time enough for these investigations: what is true will come to you – you might not like it. It's that hooligan illumination. Stic Basin "Hooligan Illumination"

It has been prophesied, throughout time, that an End to All Things is inevitable and that a redeemer will be instrumental in bringing about a new beginning for those whose hearts follow in that soul's footsteps. Since time immemorial, Humans have held these beliefs, in one form or other, and have taken hope and comfort in these prophecies, taking heart that the cycle of all things will bring about a renewed and better world. Vampires, too, hold these hopes close to their own secret faiths and collections of foretellings, as revealed to them by Tarmian turned Upyr, Gideon the Mad.

His utterances were treasured and passed on by rote by those who heard them until there came a time when he went silent and appeared only rarely to those he felt worthy of his secrets accursed by the touching of his insanity.

After his going into seclusion, two he graced with his madness. Two, and two alone. Both were murdered by the monster Gideon often foretold, the one with whom he seemed so obsessed in his later years. Looking back upon them, one guardian of Gideon's Augury was to keep it hidden until the time of its revealing. The other, the one destined to redeem and bring about a new age for Upyr kind, knew the Augury's song and held it as a precious melody until once more his soul was reunited with the collection of prophecies, complete and ready for revelation.

Only one prophecy, known only to the Queen Upyr, was that mortal kind would save the Vampires and that the redeemed was to bring forth the true saviour of Vampire kind, through Blood, suffering and, eventually, a kind of personal redemption that may kill or cure.

This redeemer only Gideon knew and this was the only thing he never told a soul. Only one soul knows who the Redeemer is and he is determined to bring forth the saviour told of old.

CHAPTER 1
THE HAUNTED ANGEL

"Guilt is its own reward said the martyred angel to the pleasure lord." ~ Shriekback "Loving It"

Fascination is what drew him to the incorruptible body in which his endless spirit had once resided. No sign of the Pariah's vicious intrusion upon his physical person could be seen and he was just as young and vibrant-looking as the day Rebekah and Mephistopheles paid him the bloody visit that forever altered the course of Kallum's life. In this stasis, the body of the Vampire once called Faust, rested in perfect repose, his barely-opened eyes the only indication of his death, being dried by the dust that buried him several feet below the new building that had long replaced his old apartment domicile. It was still a haven for the artistic folk who so preferred SoHo, but there was no indication whatsoever that these painters, singers, composers, actors, and comedians spent their evenings treading the ground where a saint rested, waiting.

For what was he waiting? Rosetta, his angel who had embraced his spirit during the worst moments of his misery at Cadmus' hands, never revealed to him what that might be. He cherished every moment of paradise afforded him, but he was still drawn to the place of his death and was very much enthralled with the body that carried Kallum in mortal form and then as Faust.

Indeed Kallum, mortated from the young Vampire Faust was whisked away from the mundane world which had become an immortal hell for him, had beheld the face of God and had been told that, someday, Kallum would be asked to return to this Vale of Tears to bring about a sort of redemption for those seemingly incapable of such a spiritual miracle.

His paradise was his alone and indescribable in even the simplest of terms. Heaven was indeed a unique experience for each soul and was impossible to explain not only to living beings,

1

but also to disembodied souls. When he left his special place of bliss, Kallum longed momentously for his presence in that sacred space, but he was equally as compelled to return to the place of his murder and ponder the words of Rosetta and the nature of his destiny.

Kallum studied his wan face as incased solidly in packed Earth, forgotten rubbish, and seemingly impenetrable concrete. Above his resting place was a four-story building comprised for twenty-four fairly sized, poorly built apartments, all in which resided struggling artists of every race, creed, and colour. The only thing that had changed was the building and its owners.

Sensing that he was no longer alone in the ethereality of his sainted existence, Kallum sent forth waves of unconditional love for the angel. "Rosetta, why is it you are here?"

"My dearest sainted confessor, I come to drench you with the blessedness of respite and pure love only the Creator can bestow upon the children of the universe. Your time is nigh, Saint Kallum, to redeem all that the Apostate has twisted in his unnaturally long and miserable life. You come here more and more often, I have seen you."

"I am compelled. My physical self being so immaculately preserved prevents my knowing fully the joy and contentment that the afterlife has to offer."

"You know in your heart, dear Kallum, that no afterlife will be wholly complete when the existence in this plane has been so warped in a way never intended. This realm is one of mortal understanding. The walking dead is an aberrant that only you, Kallum, can help to rectify. Touched by Gideon's divine madness, only you can complete his song and reveal to the immortal cursed what it is they must do to end the wretched blight cast upon the teachers so very long ago. Your presence will set things aright and, once you've achieved this miracle, your heaven will be complete and eternal."

Kallum thought back upon his last days on Earth, bound by a variety of *geasa* and tortured in ways that would immediately have

2

killed a mortal, he felt that all-too-well-known dread boil up from the pit of his spiritual stomach.

"Rosetta, I will not have to be near...him...will I?"

"Kallum..." Rosetta said softly, wrapping her rainbow arms around the indigo-eyed saint. "Cadmus Pariah is why you must go back."

Kallum's dread manifested itself in diamond teardrops that fell to the pavement below, becoming tiny quartz crystals picked up by the delighted passersby. He left the joyous pedestrians and Rosetta behind, moving to the place wherein Cadmus slept.

Cadmus Pariah was woken by the presence in the bedroom in his hidden castle stronghold in the West Country of England. He cast his all-absorbing eyes about the darkened room, looking for the intruder.

"Who are you?" Cadmus hissed, but Kallum did not answer. "Show yourself or begone from this place."

Still, Kallum did not answer. He simply drifted in the peripheries of physical reality, studying the monster that tore his flesh asunder.

Cadmus Pariah... He sat straight in his luxuriant bed, cocking his head to and fro, trying to locate the position of the intruder. His giant black eyes took in every centimeter of his room, questing and curious, but not fearful in the least. Cadmus never feared. He could not quite hone in on where Kallum was, but he knew there was a spirit quite near to him.

"I haven't the patience for psychic tag. Go away and let me sleep."

Cadmus turned his head away from Kallum and lay back down. He was still exhausted from his sojourn into the belly of the Vatican. The weight of the memory of the Blood Crown still rested heavily on his brow, despite Kelat's gentle and insistent healing.

Before long Cadmus was asleep again, but he dreamt. In his dream, Faust stood watching him, a dusty bowler hat propped

3

askew on his curly-locked head.

"Hello Cadmus."

"Why do you plague me in my sleep, Confessor?"

"The time is close for us to be reunited," the Confessor said.

"And what should I call you when this most auspicious time arrives, if it ever arrives at all?"

"Kallum, Pariah. Call me Kallum or Saint Kallum. Because when I return, I will be mortal."

"Good, then I will get to kill you again."

"Not if you want the Augury of Gideon."

"The Augury of Gideon is a myth. It does not exist except in fragments of crazed prophecy."

"No, Cadmus. It does exist and we have to get it in order to reunite the relics and resolve the Vampire curse."

"The Vampire curse is of no interest to me. Let someone else deal with them. They're nothing but food to me."

"It is your destiny, Cadmus. Once you have all three relics, everything will change for you."

Cadmus opened his eyes to this. He hated it when someone he had murdered visited him in his dreams; it rankled him beyond comprehension. There would be no more sleep for him on this day, so he rose and walked to his computer.

Opening his online journal, Cadmus began to write:

> I am the Angel of Death for so many in this realm of existence. What I find so amusing is that I am haunted by an angel in my dreams. Can angels be haunted? Yes, I think so. They most definitely have the power to haunt.
>
> Many years ago, long before many of you who read this were born or were even a thought in your parents' minds, I encountered what could have

4

possibly been the most pure soul known to humanity, discounting the blessed presences of the Tarmi at the time of their rule on the planet. I entrapped him in his own abode and baptized my new identity inside his body cavity...repeatedly. That month was one of my most treasured times in this, the eternity of my existence but, had I known I would be plagued by his disembodied sanctity, I think I may have just left him alone in his Disco-soundtracked silent film.

Then again, I would not have known about the Blood Crown, for all the good that did me. Eventually it will, though. I need only get stronger, prepare for the inevitable rise to power when Kelat can no longer control my rampant energy.

For now, I'm collecting Pets again. I have two now, but they've contributed no new philosophical apices for me, only blood for the chalice. I will continue to collect Pets until my chambers are full again, but I'm perplexed at my inability to glean anything new from taking their souls whilst, at the same time, experiencing apices on an almost daily basis without having to access them before expressing them.

I could achieve this when in close proximity to Kelat, the Mother of Memory, because of our connection within the chalice. Further away from her, emotion became an alien expression to me. But the philosophical apices are more frequent even with Kelat far away from me and they seem more like emotions than the apices I've always called them. Perhaps it is because of my donning of the

Blood Crown for the short period of time it rested on my head. The scars from its thorns are still quite apparent.

But, I digress.

I need more Beautiful Pets. The chalice hungers, as do I, and my home echoes from emptiness rather than the occasional exquisite moan of trapped animals. I will travel to London tomorrow evening, to the Poison Rose, and hold court. Perhaps I shall be able to harvest two new additions to my collection. The youth of today are just so eager to relinquish themselves to the holy or the prurient. So many of them believe the two are interchangeable. Who am I to instruct them otherwise when I am all too eager to encourage such misguided faith?

Cadmus read what he just wrote, dipping his head down, studying the computer screen. He wondered how many responses he'd get begging to be his next Pet. The phenomenon of the Internet opened up a world of possibilities for Cadmus, but he never took advantage of them. He preferred to hand-pick his Pets and that meant going to the Poison Rose, or a place like it. It was like grocery-shopping. You can't thump the melons in a virtual reality.

CHAPTER 2
THE SHROUD AND THE JEWEL

Sometimes we're only the action figures of ourselves. This is the sort of thing you couldn't make up. Banality is the camouflage that God wears to walk unseen. It's a very funny dream, sometimes we wake up. ~ Stic Basin "Downthere"

"I put on this shroud just last month, after I woke up one morning and the dream continued to play out in my mind. It was a revelation that I knew I had to share with others...the truth of who we are and what we're doing here."

The middle-aged woman barely moved underneath the fine linen draped over her head. Her interviewer was Agatha Crawford who was not much younger than the shrouded woman.

Her interviewer was Agatha Crawford, who was not much younger than the shrouded woman. She held up her finger to pause the proceedings as she made sure that her tape recorder was running to her satisfaction.

"This is the interview with Shirley Manning, who claims to already be dead," she spoke into the recorder, then politely nodded and placed the recorder on the table between them. Agatha looked at Shirley, straining her eyes to see the woman's face behind the shroud. "You say that a dream gave this revelation to you ~ that you're dead and had have always been so?"

Paine Bryerson would have been so much better at this kind of interview. It pained Agatha in her solar plexus, thinking back to what happened to her Vampiric partner in journalistic crime. Agatha could barely see Shirley's lips move as she replied.

"Not just me. Everyone. You too. You're dead and you don't know it. I've accepted it. I just want them to know that I know.

Agatha, just a little perplexed, waited for Shirley to elaborate on her comments. Just another crackpot for the teeming public to gawk at as they stand in line at the supermarket, she thought as she grew impatient with the veiled woman. *Why, oh why can't I ditch this tabloid gig and be a real journalist?* When she saw that Shirley was apparently finished with her statement, Agatha prompted. "Them, who?"

"God, the Devil, whatever they are. Those who put us here. The ones who keep us here.

"You see, we don't belong here, not in this world, not in these bodies. All we do is walk around and decay because we're already dead. It's a punishment. For what? I don't know. But the dying, we know," and Shirley raised her fingers in sarcastic quotation signs. "The dying. we know is just the last leg of a long decay that gets worse after the body ceases to move. Only then are we made aware that we have been dead all along, trapped in a capsule of carrion. But, see, it's too late then. The vehicle doesn't work anymore, so we can't warn the others. We're either burned away to nothingness or we're placed in crypts to savour every nuance of the slow rotting process."

Her words chilled Agatha, who was beginning to wish she hadn't encouraged Shirley to explain her mysterious intro. "You don't have a very pleasant view of the life/death cycle, do you?"

"No, I don't because there is no cycle. It's just a long process of carnal degradation from which we never escape."

Changing the subject just a little before she got too nauseous, Agatha said, "So, what were you like before you put on the shroud?"

Shirley's voice was filled with bitterness. "My two children are in college and avoid me, even though I think I was a good mother. My husband, Frank has moved out of our house. He says he can't take the way I am now. I couldn't stay there alone, so I rented this apartment. As you can see, I had a normal life before the revelation. Married, kids, middle class home. I've worked off and on in department stores, but really didn't need to as Frank did very well in his business consultation firm. I had friends who would get together to clip coupons and discuss the latest fashions. All of that's gone now, but it was all an illusion anyway," and her voice grew progressively louder. "So tell me, have I really lost a thing?"

The tirade took Agatha by surprise, and she turned off the recorder. "Mrs. Manning, are you okay?"

A soft sound of sorrow wafted out of the shroud. "I'm sorry, Ms. Crawford. It's just that...I can tell you don't believe me. No one does. If they would only put on the shroud for just a few moments, they would see. This shroud has the vision woven into it, it seems. It's a constant reminder to me...and a revelation to others who dare see for themselves. I wish I'd never picked the fabric up at the thrift store."

Agatha felt pity for the woman and, in a rare moment of charity, said, "I'll put on the shroud, if that would make you feel any better."

Pausing, Shirley cocked her head to one side. "Are you sure?"

Agatha nodded. "What can it hurt?"

And so Shirley lifted the white linen from her head, revealing a handsome, matronly face with wide brown eyes. Her expression was that of resigned terror, that of the mouse looking into the mouth of the snake, unable to move and avoid the inevitable. Utter acceptance of the horror of it all. Upon seeing Shirley's face, Agatha hesitated only slightly, then took the shroud and placed it over her own head.

At first, Agatha saw only the milky outlines of her interviewee seated calmly in her chair, watching and waiting. But soon, her surroundings changed and a vision was before her. Agatha saw the whole of the world and all her exquisite cities, and for each monolithic high-rise, instead rose an equally tremendous tombstone. The cities were graveyards! And every person was nothing more than a prison of carrion, subconsciously screaming for release where there was none. Agatha sensed watchers.....Nephilim they were called, and they merely observed the goings on of the prisoners ~ prison guards for lost souls. And the closer the dead thought they were to God, the further away from the truth they really were. The landscape was that of futility and hopelessness, while the masses struggled eternally in hope of a better place in their long dead hearts.

Agatha could hear the others, who had entered into the Second Death, walled up in their tombs, wailing warnings that there was no respite when the body stopped; just darkness and the revelation of decay.

No wonder humanity seemed bent on destruction! What prisoner didn't endeavour to tear down the prison in which he suffered?

An overwhelming sense of desperation washed over Agatha. No matter how many gouges man scooped out of the earth, or how many poisons he poured onto her surface or scattered into her atmosphere, the prison would prevail and prolong the sentence with greater depths of misery.

The dead adapt.

It was all about the breaking of the Spirit in a body locked in death. There was no hope of salvation ~ only the emptiness of an eternal death under the cold stare of the Watchers.

Agatha scrambled to get the shroud from her head. She looked frantically at Shirley.

"What kind of trick is this, Mrs. Manning? Do you lace this shroud of yours with some kind of hallucinogen?"

Shirley's eyes welled up with tears. "This interview is over," She said, returning the shroud to her own head. "You've seen the truth. You've heard my message. What you do with it is up to you."

Shirley stood and walked to the front door. "Good day, Ms. Crawford. May you gain peace where none can be found."

Agatha gathered up her gear and stepped from Shirley's dark apartment into the hall of the dingy building. For a moment she thought she saw catacombs, with corpses rotting all around her. Agatha's skin crawled. Steeling herself against the onslaught of horrors, she turned to face Shirley Manning. "Thank you for speaking with me today, Mrs. Manning. I wish you the best of luck."

Agatha turned and left the wraithlike woman looking after her from behind the shroud and she exited onto the busy streets of Boston. Everywhere she turned Agatha saw life, rising and swelling under the panoramic blue sky. Shirley Manning is insane, she thought as she hailed a cab. But this is gonna make a great story for the paper.

The agents of futility watched Agatha smile as she climbed into the cab, and they laughed collectively at her choice of blissful ignorance.

In her apartment, Shirley clamped her hands over her ears in a futile attempt to impede the Nephilim's cackling. Her shroud shimmered with her movement as Shirley rocked back and forth in the torment of her Knowing.

Agatha thought about the shroud and remembered something Paine had told her – that the Apostate and the Vampires had placed magickal treasures (or cursed objects) throughout the world. She was certain that the shroud was one of these items because, honestly, she couldn't bring herself to believe that a world that had once harboured the holy presence of the Tarmi was a prison for rotting flesh. That message stunk of the Apostate's influence.

She had to know for sure.

As soon as she got home, she rifled through her rolodex for the phone number she thought she would never call. Juggling the round garnet in amongst the fingers of her left hand, she dialed the number with her right, then propped the phone on her shoulder.

"Hello?" answered a sleepy voice . It was Noon in California. Oops.

"Hello. Is this...is this Orphaeus Cygnus?"

"Yes. Who is...this?"

"I hope you remember me, Mr. Cygnus. This is Agatha

11

Crawford."

"Orpheaus, please! Oh dear, oh dear, it's been years since I've spoken with you. How are you, dearheart?"

"A little distressed," Agatha said. "Would it be okay to come visit you? I've been given some information that I'm not certain what to do with it."

"Of course!" Orpheaus gave Agatha the address to the opera house and made arrangements for her to arrive in two days' time. He and Genevieve would pick her up at the airport. In the meantime, he would make it very clear to his family that Agatha was a guest and not dinner.

Two days later, Agatha was riding along the hills of San Francisco with Orpheaus and Genevieve, going to their performance theatre and part-time home. When they arrived, the theatre was closed, but they entered and went below the stage to an expansive apartment that housed Orpheaus, Genevieve, and their children, Hercules and Lolita.

"We had a third child..." Orpheaus said bitterly. "But she fell victim to Cadmus Pariah."

He all but spit the name.

"It seems like a lot of people have fallen victim to Cadmus Pariah."

"You have absolutely no idea," Orpheaus quipped, thinking of Faust the Confessor.

They sat and had a standard dinner to honour their guest; waiting to rip their own dinner apart after Agatha went to sleep.

"So what seems to be troubling you?" Orpheaus asked.

Agatha told them about the shroud and the visions she had seen. Genevieve trembled violently as she heard the story.

"You cannot print that," she said. "It would throw thousands of people into a pit of despair where they do not belong. This shroud, it is a lie, a mechanism of the Apostate, may his rotting ash forever blow in the dead air of the Roman catacombs."

Agatha looked askance to Genevieve and Orphaeus told her the story of the Blood Crown and the state of the Apostate once he and Cadmus reached the depths of the Vatican catacombs. The one thing that interested Agatha the most was the story of Faust, particularly his interaction with Gideon the Mad.

"You know Paine was Gideon's last child," Agatha said. "The final thing he did before sacrificing himself to the sun was to give him this jewel."

Agatha reached into her pocket and pulled out a black-red stone about the size of a small robin's egg.

Orphaeus reached out his hand. "May I?"

"Of course." Agatha handed it to Orphaeus who closed his eyes and clasped the jewel between his hands. After a time, he opened his eyes and looked earnestly at Agatha.

"Has this stone ever given you visions like that shroud did?"

"I can't say that it has. Paine just gave it to me before he died. It's the only thing I have left of his."

"Hm...Maybe mortals can't access the visions. Then again, I got nothing either. Maybe only Vampires to whom Gideon actually handed the stone can access the information it contains."

"What are you talking about?"

Orphaeus leaned in to Agatha, who steeled herself so she wouldn't cringe in his Vampiric presence. "Agatha, I think you are in possession of the greatest treasure known to Vamipire-kind. I think this," and he held up the stone, "is the Augury of Gideon."

"Isn't...isn't that supposed to be a book or scroll of prophecies the mad Vampire wrote?"

"It was never indicated for sure that it was a written thing. What prophecies we know were always passed on by rote, so it was assumed that Gideon only spoke his prophecies. Some thought there might be a written account. Others thought the whole thing was a trick, mad as a bag of cats."

"But you think this rock actually contains Gideon's prophecies."

"As much as scientists believe a single cell contains the whole of the human genome. Leave it to someone like Gideon to encode his word in the Blood of his people. The problem is, no one alive can access the prophecies contained in the stone. He only gave it to Paine and Faust the Confessor. No one else would have the ability to read the genetic memory, so the Augury could very well remain a mystery. A shame really. The Augury of Gideon is the third relic known to Vampiredom. Brought in the presence of the cup and the crown, its knowledge could help remove the curse from those of us who want mortation."

"So, we're screwed as far as that's concerned. As for the shroud, I think I'll take that story to my grave. It doesn't belong to the Collective Conscious, being yet another lie by the Apostate."

"Screwed?" Orphaeus said. "Not necessarily. If I'm right, Faust is waiting for us in the dust of his old SoHo home, eager to come out and tell us all about the Augury of Gideon, or at least what he knows. I've got the sneaking suspicion that he didn't tell Cadmus Pariah everything, despite the torture he underwent. Torture is never the way to go to get the information you want anyway. Cadmus knows this, but he's too intent on inflicting pain to care about what he's told."

"So, it's off to New York then? Are you going with me?"

Orphaeus nodded. Ever since my trip with Cadmus a year or so ago, I've been curious about what we might find in SoHo."

Genevieve chuffed and Orphaeus nuzzled her throat.

"Now, now, kitten. Don't be so upset. I'll be back before you can say 'it's about bloody time.'"

"It's about bloody time," Genevieve teased and they giggled together. It was bizarre to see such a functional relationship between bloodsucking fiends when there were so many dysfunctional arrangements amongst mortals.

"Let me make a phone call and then we'll make arrangements."

Orphaeus excused himself and walked into the adjacent room where the phone was. Dialing the number, he waited for an answer and was soon graced with the voice of the Mother of Memory, Kelat.

14

"Grandmother, the mortal Agatha has brought the Augury of Gideon to me. I know this is the final relic that's foretold to break the Vampire curse, but I don't know how to crack the code. It's a Blood jewel that only two Vampires have been able to read, and both of them are apparently dead. Paine, for certain...Faust, most probably."

"Faust..." Kelat echoed Orphaeus, her voice laced with regret. "No, it's not over for him, at least his mortal form. Faust is indeed dead, but Kallum waits for you. Go quietly. We can't let on that the Augury has come to light. Cadmus would surely get involved."

When Orphaeus came back into the main room of the Cygnus' apartment, he shrugged his shoulders nonchalantly and looked at Agatha.

"Wanna go to New York with me; maybe find out what secrets this jewel of yours holds?"

"Sure, when do we go?"

"I'll book the flight and we'll head out at sundown tomorrow. In the meantime, Lolita will show you to our guest room where you can get a little rest. We'll bring you some food. Word to the wise, Agatha: whatever you hear outside your guest room, don't come out to see. We are Vampires after all and Beasts at that. We'll need to eat too, but you don't need to see it."

A chill spidered down Agatha's spine at the thought of it, but she agreed with Orphaeus' suggestion and went with Lolita to the guest apartment deeper into the Cygnus theatre. There she remained, trying to ignore the pleas for help and the subsequent wet noises and sounds of delight made by the Cygnus family.

CHAPTER 3
THE DHAMPIR

There's a philosophy, don't mean a lot to me – "the value of anything is how much it hurts." I'm nearly but not quite almost incinerated, I can't see anything for digging in the dirt. ~ Shriekback "Achtung"

Sydney Tenin thought about her parents. In fact, she thought about them quite a lot, especially since one was an absentee father with a penchant for aching in churches and the other was confined to a padded room raving about how Sydney's father was a Vampire.

Sydney was raised in the system, bounced from one family to another, never really loved or made to feel wanted. She had always been a strange child and no wonder; her father *was* a Vampire. She didn't need her insane mother to tell her, she knew by her very nature.

There was a name for this, she learned. The Romany nation called mortal children of Vampires Dhampiri. They were strange children, inclined to eating rare meat and mixing the blood with milk. They were psychic and could tell when Vampires were near. They were prone to becoming Vampires themselves upon death. The Romany both honoured and feared the Dhampiri, employing them to be Vampire killers, but fearing to have the Dhampir dwell amongst them.

But Sydney had never been in a Romany family, so her inherent abilities were never fully developed or encouraged. The families in which Sydney had been placed feared Sydney's strangeness and always gave her back to DCS for placement elsewhere.

Sydney had never had a home. Now that she was an adult, she didn't need a home or a family. But she had reconnected with her father Vasily Thiyennen and his caregiver, a woman by the name of Eve. Both of them were Vampires and desperate for a mortal or quasi-mortal to help them.

16

At the age of 18 Sydney entered into an arrangement with her father Thiyennen and his Redemptor caregiver Eve. Thiyennen had been sorely injured by Eve's Vampiric groom, Cadmus Pariah. He had been left starved, crucified, and tortured to the point of death. Had it not been for Eve, Thiyennen, the king of the Great Hive, would have died and taken many of the Redemptors with him.

The Hive of Redemption was considered the conscience of Vampiredom. Despite some of their bizarre behavior such as entering churches or temples to suffer the pain eternal sin experiences in the presence of sanctity, they worked diligently to bring a sense of holiness to a state that seemed beyond redemption.

It was Eve who sought out Sydney. Unable to do it all herself, being intentionally weakened by Cadmus so that she would always be available to him as a "garden of Blood," Eve came to Sydney and revealed to the mortal woman why it was she had always been different. The story behind her conception was one of desperation, sadness, and insanity.

Her mother, Wendy McCurrie, was the abused fiancée of banker Gordon Parkinson. They shared an apartment in downtown Charlotte, North Carolina. The couple near them was Vasily and Anna Tenin. They were quiet, kept to themselves, and polite when encountered. They were also Vampires, Gordon found out. The revelation gave Gordon, who was a control freak, a freakish sense of purpose. It was his quest to reveal to the world that Vampires actually did exist.

As events would have it, and the events of that time were sketchy at best since Wendy was out of her mind, Gordon and Anna both perished. Gordon killed Anna in front of a task force of law enforcement. When he raised the killing stake to show the mortals what he had done, the police shot him dead.

Vasily had taken Wendy to thrall months before that because he didn't trust Gordon's insistent nosiness concerning himself and Anna. The act of thralling a human female always involved impregnation. So, was Sydney conceived. By the time she was

17

born, Vasily had moved on to Asheville, North Carolina and become a religions instructor at UNCA and Wendy had been involuntarily committed to Patrick B. Harris Psychiatric Hospital where Sydney was born.

It had been a sad and confusing life but, now that Sydney knew why, she was truly involved in her father's life and her visits with her mother went much more easily now that Sydney knew her mom wasn't nearly as crazy as people believed.

Sydney McCurrie-Tenin was a statuesque woman, being almost six feet tall and extremely well fed, although she was not overweight. She was truly big-boned and her coppery red hair gave her away as a woman of pure Nordic/Celtic descent. She had her father's dark brown eyes and full lips, and her mother's womanly curves and upturned nose. She had always gone by Sydney McCurrie while she sought her way through the labyrinthine DCS system but, once she met her father, ill and almost beyond healing, she took on his name as well.

Her conception was one of necessity, this she knew. She just wished her youth had been a happier one. Sydney had the most incredible capacity for forgiveness, which she gave to both her parents. Eve was in awe of Sydney's ability to forgive and sought to learn the skill for when she was forced to encounter Cadmus Pariah.

Eve and Sydney became the best of friends as they worked on healing Thiyennen. Living in a loft in downtown Asheville, Eve worked on Thiyennen's immortal wounds from his crucifixion and Sydney worked on his psychic wounds, having a bond of enthrallment all Dhampiri possessed with their Vampiric parent. They spent three years together in the apartment until Thiyennen was able to hunt for himself. By then, they had become a family of sorts, but one that Sydney still felt a certain exclusion from, still being a mortal.

So it came that one night she asked her father if he would transform her.

"No, Sydney, I cannot do that. I can't propagate a curse that

18

only God can end for good and true. My transforming you would damn me further and ensure your own damnation."

Eve would have transformed Sydney, but did not have the strength to do so. Cadmus had made it so that her existence was awash in weakness and personal sacrifice.

So it came to pass that, one night, Sydney spied a bearded man walking his white dog down Lexington Avenue. It was none other than Thanatos, Kelat's soul mate and husband in the Blood. Sydney approached him, looking him directly in the eye without any sense of fear in her demeanor.

"You're Thanatos, aren't you? Or Dmitri, possibly Thaddeus Brannon? What name are you currently using?"

The Vampire was taken aback by surprise, but was also delighted by this woman's moxie. "You may call me Dmitri and who might you be?"

"My name is Sydney Tenin, the Dhampir daughter of the Hive King. And I want to be a full Vampire. Being a half-breed is a kind of misery to me and Thiyennen," she said, using the King's Tarmian name. "He won't do it because it offends his religious convictions."

"You do realise what you're asking of me."

"Yes. I've never fit in anywhere and I don't want to be a Gypsy Vampire hunter. It looks bad on a resume."

Dmitri laughed.

"I've tended to my father for the past three years. I've learned the ways of Vampires from him and his nurse and bride to the Pariah, Eve. I want to seal my fate, to put it a certain way. I want to be a Vampire."

"You do realise that you'll be my Blood daughter and no longer subject to the inclinations of Thiyennen."

"I do. I know much about the Hive of Redemption. They have their purpose, but that path is not for me. My sense of freedom and adventure won't allow me that path."

"Let me think about it. I'll be in town all week before going back to Jerusalem to be with Kelat. In three nights, meet me at

19

the Octopus' Garden.

Sydney was so eager, she found herself at the Octopus' Garden before the sun had set. Nervously looking at all the doo-dads available there, not to mention every shred of paraphernalia one might need to enjoy the Ganja. She didn't have to wait very long. Dmitri found her staring at the fiber-optic lamps.

"They're beautiful, aren't they?"

"Yes," Sydney said.

"Just like you."

A silence grew between the two of them. Sydney had never been referred to as beautiful. In fact, she was in her mid-twenties and still a Virgin.

"I thought about your request, Sydney, and I want you to be certain this is what you want."

"I've never wanted anything so badly," Sydney said. "I no longer want to be the half-mortal Sydney McCurrie-Tenin. I want to embrace my Vampire nature and I want you to help me do it."

Dmitri sighed. "You realise that, since I am an Incubus, I must take you sexually. Are you prepared for that?"

"Yes. Will my aunt Kelat accept such an arrangement?"

"Kelat knows full well what I plan on doing tonight and she gives us her blessing. After your transformation, she will be your grandmother by the Blood as well as your aunt. Eventually, you will have to meet her. Be prepared for a beautiful experience when you do."

Sydney swallowed. "So, what do I have to do?"

"Come home with me," Dmitri said. He took Sydney's hand and led her out of the head shop. They took a cab to Dmitri's Charlotte Street apartment and entered into his comfortable bachelor's domain.

"I must admit to you that you are only the third person I've ever transformed. The first one perished many years ago and the second became a Beast, so I had to give serious thought to ever doing this again."

About that time, the large white dog padded into the living room where the two people were.

"This is Dare. That's one thing you'll need to learn about me. I'll always have a white animal named Dare. When the time is right to tell you why, I will. Just bear in mind that it's very important to me and I'm deeply connected to the animal kingdom. Are you okay with that?"

"Of course," Sydney said, ruffling the thick mane on Dare's neck. "She's a beautiful creature."

Dmitri again took Sydney by the hand and led her into the bedroom. A plush King size bed rested Feng Shui style with the head pointed north. Sydney began to shake, but Dmitri had a calming effect on her, easing her onto the bed and kissing her lightly on the lips.

He continued this, a repetitive hypnotic kiss, barely touching her lips, but getting more insistent with each kiss. He rested her hands in his, which lay in her lap.

"How do you feel?" he murmured.

"I...I feel good."

"Good. Now kiss me." And Sydney did. When Dmitri leaned in to kiss her again, she met his kiss with her own, shy, but insistent.

Their kissing became deeper. Sydney placed her hands on the back of Dmitri's neck and pulled him closer to her as he began to remove her clothes. Soon she was naked, this lovely Amazon of a girl with creamy skin and Celtic locks cascading down her shoulders. Dmitri was smitten with her already and knew her Vampiric beauty would rival many of the most ancient and wondrous of their kind.

He lay her down and began to remove his own clothes as he kissed up her legs. By the time he reached her sexual center, Dmitri was also unclad and highly aroused. He placed his tongue against her and she bucked uncontrollably. Her body became a sacred entity that moved and functioned beyond Sydney's capacity for thought or control. She grasped onto Dmitri's thick black hair and pressed him against her as he moved his lips and tongue.

21

At the moment of her climax Dmitri bit deeply into the femoral artery and drank the orgasmic blood that gushed into his mouth and down his throat. Before he drank too much, he closed the wound with a few swift flicks of the tongue and moved up the length of her body. She was weak from blood loss and from her explosive orgasm, so she let Dmitri have his way. He sank deeply into her, taking her maidenhead with the loss of more blood.

The girl cried out, but only from the pleasure of the pain. She weakly moved her hands up to run her fingers through the hair on Dmitri's chest as he began to slide in and out of her. The pace was slow at first, rhythmic like a drum in the night. Then that rhythm began to speed up as Dmitri caught his stride. He moved inside Sydney with fervour and it was all he could do to speak, but speak he must.

"When I tell you to drink, you do it, or you will die."

"I'm ready," she said breathlessly, moving toward orgasm again.

Dmitri took her hands and pulled them over her head. Lying prone upon her, Dmitri exposed his throat to her.

"I'm coming...now! Bite me NOW!"

Sydney was surprised to find the teeth to bite into him and even more surprised to know where to bite him. The Blood spilled out of him and into her mouth and throat. It tasted like pleasure made manifest and it stopped Sydney's heart from its intensity. She knew she was crossing over. She felt the transformation moving from her toes up, and she knew that she was Darkblood from moment Dmitri's Blood coursed over her tongue.

They made love the entire night, exchanging Blood back and forth in a trade of passion and delight.

Before the sun rose, Dmitri turned to the newly-formed Vampire and said, "I get to name you now, give you your first Vampire name. Just as Kelat named me Thanatos at the time of my transformation, so do I give you a name at the time of yours. You are so incredibly beautiful and I can already tell that you're going to be a Vampire of uncanny power. So I'm hearkening to the realm of myth and naming you Ishtar. Over time, you may go by any name you wish, even your birth name as I'm doing now. But, for now, Ishtar you are, the Dhampir turned Vampire. May your father accept you for who you are.

With that, they slept and Ishtar dreamt the dreams of Vampires. She saw the world in a nighttime of technicolour, graced and blessed with such terrible and beautiful things, it was enough to make souls weep. And weep they did. Throughout the aether, she could hear the souls of the dead and the souls about to be born weeping with joy at the creation this world had been, was, and would be.

But one soul stood out. He did not weep but simply smiled, and the smile was a song in itself. He waited to be reborn not as a Vampire, but as a mortal. She could hear him as clearly as she could hear the whisper of the crickets miles away. Ishtar needed to find him. It was in her Blood to find this smiling soul and kiss the lips of the person who possessed it.

CHAPTER 4
THE DREAMS OF MADNESS

He is paralysed; he is sanctified by the god of nails and splinters Certainly knows his way around at this murder scene (hid the bloody shovels in the outhouse). Chastity and insomnia are a lousy mix. His nights are long. ~ Shriekback "Ronny"

Incandescent was the word that came to mind when Cadmus' vast eyes opened from the dream that danced around the peripheries of his consciousness. They were bright and brittle, making no sense, yet poetic in their immaculate presence. He had seen a man in the dreams, blonde and filthy, rocking back and forth spewing forth a flood of words that meant nothing and everything all at once.

In so many cultures, the mad were the shamans, the holy ones who spoke the words of God. Was this, this Gideon the Mad, an agent of God Cadmus wondered? Surely it was him in the dreams Cadmus had been having over the past few weeks. It was as if the donning of the Blood Crown opened up Cadmus' psyche to the presence of sacrosanct insanity.

He was not getting much sleep because of the dreams that plagued him. Cadmus would awake in the depths of his West Country home and hear the muffled moans of his Beautiful Pets. When he was disturbed psychically, so were they, even though they were simply empty vessels that contained the blood he needed for the Chalice. The souls he harvested still somehow connected to their bodies, making the Pets rock in distress, the iron collars chafing their frail throats.

Cadmus stood and exited his bedroom to find himself in the long corridor lined with wooden doors. His harvesting of Pets had afforded him six occupied rooms. Once his herd was back to optimum levels, all 26 rooms would contain a vessel of blood for the chalice. For now, Cadmus subsisted on his six Pets and only occasionally went out to hunt Vampires. After being reduced to a powerless child by the Blood Crown, Cadmus' healing took much

24

longer than he'd care to admit.

A year out from having the crown removed from his brow and spending several months in the Veiled Sanctuary being tended by his mother, Cadmus was not in any mood to think about the embarrassment of his attainment of the Blood Crown. It sat in stasis in Kelat's stronghold, waiting for whatever magickal miracle Kelat thought may someday transpire.

Needless to say, Cadmus felt tricked. Kelat knew that he was not capable of handling the Blood Crown's power. It essentially killed the Apostate over a very long time of misery for wearing it. The relic was deadly. He never saw Kelat don the crown herself. She told Cadmus that he would wear it again when he was stronger and when the time came for him to fulfill his destiny. Cadmus grew sick of Kelat's promises of destiny and hints of prophecy she had perhaps heard from the lips of Gideon.

Thinking of Gideon, it seemed to Cadmus that his dreams were haunted by the blonde madman. He kept having visions of burning conifers and of being tied to a wheel while having his crimes read in monotone. He saw bands of Vampires running through the streets of some unidentifiable city, stakes and knives in their hands. None of it made sense.

And always there was the madman at his side, muttering incoherencies like the one that roused him from his bed.

My dearest
The dusty mortal and the beautiful daughter of
insanity
Carefully shall they tread the paths to eternal love
For that is the only thing that endures.
Faith fades.
Love endures.

What did that even mean? It was gibberish. The madman spoke gibberish. But what else could he speak really? Only the prophecies that foretold the Pariah made any sense at all. Cadmus was fairly certain that Gideon's prophecies meant nothing

25

whatsoever save for his foretelling of the Pariah. He simply got lucky with seeing Cadmus. The rest was simply insanity.

He wondered what the Augury was like, if it even existed. Was it a great tome filled with written gibberish? Or was it a rote tradition carried on by faithful Vampires enamoured with Gideon's madness?

Cadmus strolled down the corridor, deciding which vessel he would tap tonight, trying to erase the madness from his mind. He needed more Blood because his sleep was interrupted by the words of a crazy man and the visions of violence and horror. The Pariah would not allow this madness to turn him into the modern version of Gideon the Mad. He would wallow in the blood of his Pets, grow drunk from the ingestion of Blood, and he would banish the thoughts that plagued his sleep. Cadmus would overcome this crazy bout of insomnia and he would do it with grace.

Opening the first door on the left of the corridor, Cadmus entered the bare cold stone cell. On a cot, staring off into a distance so timeless yet depthless, sat a young man who was the epitome of dementia. "Hello Jacob," Cadmus said flatly. Jacob did not respond since his essence was enslaved inside the fathoms of Cadmus' spirit. Cadmus retrieved the young man's soul so that he could see what was about to happen to his body. Some may call that cruel. Cadmus did not care.

When he felt Jacob drift forward to look out of Cadmus' deep, dark chocolate eyes, Cadmus said again "Hello Jacob."

A sob was his only reply.

Kneeling before the empty body of Jacob, Cadmus took out his dragon claw knife and the chalice. He then took Jacob's right arm and placed his hand inside the chalice.

"Sometimes, watching the blood trickle into the chalice entertains me," explained Cadmus to the disembodied Pet. "So little in the Vale of Tears amuses me, but this shall surely put a slight smile to my lips."

Taking the knife, Cadmus cut into Jacob's arm from the crook down to the wrist. Blood bubbled forth enthusiastically before beginning to clot to save the young man from losing too much of the life-giving elixir. But Cadmus cut again, deeply and precisely to open the vein from the elbow to the wrist. The blood trickled swiftly and sweetly down Jacob's arm and hand, and into the sacred chalice.

Cadmus smiled as Jacob began to slump. He wouldn't last long, this one. One more milking and it would be the tombs beneath Cadmus' home for Jacob's body.

Inside Cadmus' soul Jacob screamed and wept and plead for mercy. But there was no mercy here. Mercy was inconceivable and indefinable in Cadmus' world. Mercy was something Faust the Confessor might have given if Cadmus hadn't ripped him limb from limb in the end. Mercy was synonymous with weakness and that was something untenable to Cadmus. Mercy was a word associated with God, and Cadmus was about as far away from God as one living creature could be.

He watched the blood slow and thicken, then Cadmus removed the hand from the chalice, bringing the cup to bear in front of him as he sat with his legs crossed on the floor, not bothering to make Jacob's body comfortable as it slumped awkwardly upon the cot.

Cadmus rocked and chanted, his immense eyes closed, his eyelids fluttering from a kind of hypnotic ecstasy. His meditations on the chalice comforted Cadmus on these days when the mad man haunted his dreams. This particular meal would be most welcome as Cadmus listened to Jacob wail with helplessness in the catacombs of his spirit.

He then lifted the chalice with both hands to his lips and took a sip of the ambrosia. It had transubstantiated into Kelat's holy Blood and Cadmus drank fully and enthusiastically, leaving only a small amount to wait for the next time he must feed.

"Blessed art thou, O Cup of the Queen, blessed and holy, ye vessel of sacrosanct Blood," Cadmus said after drinking. Never before had he ever said such a thing about the chalice. What did this mean? Cadmus cocked his head and looked at the chalice. He felt no different than usual upon feeding and he wasn't one for prayer or utterances of exultation. This came as a surprise and a mystery to him.

Getting up, he left Jacob's limp body where it had fallen, and he returned to his bedroom. Opening his laptop, Cadmus sat on the bed and began to write.

On many occasions, I will chant over the chalice as it transforms the unpalatable human blood into Vampire Blood. My chants have to do with the sacred transformation and how fortifying will be the Blood. They are also conversations with the spirit whose body is providing the blood. I speak to my Pets because I want them to maintain some semblance of sanity so that I might harvest their personalities to add to or enhance already present philosophical apices.

Never once have I truly prayed to the chalice or given thanks for its bounty until today. I am not certain what this means, but I am close to deciding that this turn of events borders on being distressing to me. With every encounter I have with Kelat, including drinking her transfigured Blood, I feel myself changing. Into what? I do not know. I have the feeling that the outcome will be more to Kelat's benefit than my own. I refuse to let it happen, whatever it turns out to be.

And these dreams... They must go away. I had no contact with Gideon the Mad. Yes, he foretold my rise to power and my eventual rule over Vampiredom, but I never met the madman and I was not affected by his suicide. The prophecies he shared with Faust were the first I'd ever heard. Faust is dead, along with his memories of the night he spent chatting with Gideon. Come to think...I should have harvested Faust's spirit. That way, I would have had access to all those wonderful confessions. Gideon's only surviving child is dead by my hands. Paine should have known better than to challenge such a power as mine. Like his maker, he was crazy and had no sense of judgment. So these dreams should not be haunting me as they are. If I could remember more about them, like what Gideon is truly trying to say, I would absolutely encourage them and harvest them in my spirit, but they mean nothing to me and I want them gone from my sleeping soul. The insomnia the dreams are causing do not amuse me.

CHAPTER 5
REMEMBRANCE

Those dark eyes conceal their life within them. Buried secrets – the flesh won't keep. ~ Shriekback "Evaporation"

She opened her eyes, all silver-blue and awash in alien resplendence. Kelat, the queen of the Great Hive, looked up at the waxing moon and reflected its lunar loveliness to grace the night sky and the world that revolved within it.

"Gentle Kessilon, ye in the dust of whose feet are the hosts of heaven, whose body encircles this Universe and all the verses that have been and are yet to be sung, I call upon thee to witness this, my offering of honour to thee."

Kelat extended her ivory arms and, out of a pitcher, poured crystal clear water into a marble basin. The light of the moon was captured by the water, making its reflection shimmer and undulate with the movement of the liquid.

All was silent as Kelat poured wine upon the ground, her lips moving in silent reverence to her patron Goddess, She Who Wrought the Stars of Heaven.

It had been at least a century, maybe longer, since Kelat had visited the Canopy Ruins, one of the last untouched natural circles of Tarmian worship. The only other one she could think existed that was still diligently tended and pristinely kept was Avebury. Avebury was well-known by the Goddess peoples of the world, but no one save Dmitri knew about the Canopy Ruins. It was kept hidden by layered *geasa* to where only Kelat could find it and enter into that hallowed existence. Even though Dmitri knew about the Canopy Ruins and had, in fact, been transformed into a Vampire there, he could not find it or enter therein without Kelat guiding him.

And so she was here, acting out the ways of worship so old as to make the ancient look young, yet using the modern language of the spiritual children of the Tarmian Ways.

Kessilon and Rhyllhyn, the Star Goddess and the Messenger God, ancestors both to Lhihlhishian Kelat'Menan, the Mother of Memory. She called their names and felt their essences move through her in mourning at what she had become, but still they moved through her, reminding her that she was holy in her state of being, that all things happen for a reason, even those things that threaten to break your heart for good.

She connected to Dmitri, who was bringing Sydney over to the Ways of the Upyr as Kelat scryed the act. Once before had they done this with Thiyennen's other Dhampir child. Thiyennen seemed to have a bad habit of thralling humans because he was loath to create more Vampires, but thralling humans always resulted in the conception of a half-breed child who suffered because of their misunderstood nature. Kelat could not abide such behaviour, so she had always taken the adult Dhampiri and pulled them into the Vampire fold, or had someone do it for her.

Over time, there had been six Dhampiri, but only one survived into these modern times: Rebekah. There had been literal hell to pay for that transformation. Instead of becoming a Redemptor like her biological father or a Darkling like her Vampiric mother, Rebekah had become a Beast...the first Beast. And she almost immediately took to her bosom her Ethiopian lover who was to become Mephistopheles. Single-handedly had she run a crusade from Africa through Europe, transforming souls nightly and creating what was to be soon known as the Hive of the Beast or the Beast Tribe. The Hive of Purity and Redemption were both scandalized* by this turn of events, but Kelat was always accepting of this new breed of Vampire, even the worst of them, known as Vrakshatha. To her they were the most honest representation of the Vampire, embracing the beast within and celebrating it to its fullest. Not even the Darkblood Hive was as purely honest about their nature as was the Hive of the Beast.

In a strange way, Kelat found it refreshing, if not a bit gory and unseemly. But the Beasts brought to the Great Hive a message that, even in the worst state of being, a certain poetry could be

31

achieved and that, when a Vampire thought he or she was beyond wretched, they could always take heart that they were not a vicious and heartless killer like a Beast or a walking invalid in death like those in the Tribe of the Tomb.

There was always a reason for everything that ever happened. This was Kelat's reasoning, and the logical basis to her own sub-hive, the Darkblood Hive. Acceptance, not resignation, was the message she felt compelled to bring to her people. Never resign yourself to your fate. Accept it and embrace it. Do the best you can with what you have. The Beasts certainly did this, albeit with abandon and a certain terrifying glee, and Kelat was certain that it rankled and horrified Thiyennen that he was the unwitting father to the whole of the Hive of the Beast.

Staring with an unblinking gaze the colour of the Atlantic Ocean, Kelat scryed the pools as her lover took Sydney and initiated her into the ways of the Vampire. The entire night she watched Dmitri give Sydney Blood, then drink it away as he moved in the rhythms of desire between the virgin's legs. Kelat rocked back and forth in time with her soul mate, making love to them both with the workings of Dolman, the magick of her people.

As the sun rose over Asheville and Ishtar slept her first sleep as a full Vampire in the arms of her Blood father, Kelat breathed a kiss across the surface of the water and let the contents of the basin spill back into the small creek that split the Canopy Ruins in twain. She was content with this outcome, although she was curious about the spirit that had brushed against Ishtar as she began her first sleep. It was a spirit not unfamiliar to Kelat and it had known both mortal and Vampire lives. When the time came, Kelat was sure she would remember him and his story would be told.

But this was something all her scrying could not tell her ~ his story had already been told, and there was more tales yet to tell. His seemed the most important of remembrance for, in his fateful hands once rested the destiny of all Vampires and his death at the hands of another made certain a kind of redemption yet to fully manifest. Kelat could not let the mystery alone. She psychically drew the cradling trees of the Canopy Ruins around her and closed her Elfin eyes in transcendent meditation.

Who are you who touched the peripheries of my new granddaughter? Who were you? Who are you yet to be?

A rainbow image of a female appeared first. *Rosetta have I been called and a voice of God is a role I have played.*

A child of Rhyllhyn the Messenger, known also in these times as Gabriel, the angel of God?

The spirit nodded and smiled. *But I am not the one for whom you seek. It is my companion and my student whose sweet spirit you did feel.*

Tell me about him, Kelat prodded, her soul quivering with fascination.

He awaits you in New York, Kelat'menan. There shall you know all things.

Kelat opened her eyes and shuddered with an inexplicable joy. The sun in France was beginning to kiss the West and Kelat hungered mightily from her magickal work of the morning and afternoon. Her skin prickled with discomfort from the sun, but her many sun trails had enabled her to endure time beneath the great star of Htanna.

Standing, she picked up her knapsack and slung it over her shoulders. Tying a loose shoelace on her left hiking boot, she settled comfortably into her functional outfit of cargo pants and flannel. Raising her arms in thanks to the gods and her ancestors, Kelat exited the Canopy Ruins, leaving it sheltered and concealed from all eyes with her layered *geasa*.

It was time to hunt in Carcassonne for the first time in several hundred years. And then Kelat would return to the United States, this time to seek out the spirit who was so strong as to reach out to Kelat from Asheville to the *geasa*-cloaked Canopy Ruins, nestled in the forests of France.

CHAPTER 6
THE PERSISTENT SPIRIT

"Syndication and sympathy might work for you, but not for me. I love you best when it's all a mess. Will you lie for me, cry for me, die for me, will you please?" ~ Shriekback "Malaria"

It was Noon...and Cadmus Pariah was awake. There were dark circles spinning in misery around his dire eyes.

"Leave me in peace, wight," he said aloud.

You know that I'm not a wight. If anything, you're the wight.

"I grow weary of your presence in my dreams. I am sickened by the songs of yesteryear and the ridiculous comic antics that line your memories."

You are simply experiencing all the good that you thought you snuffed out of existence when you left my body behind in 1977.

"That was an age ago. Sleep now, restless spirit. I banish thee from this place, my refuge in the sacred forts."

I am not a restless spirit, Cadmus. I am not a residual memory left to wander an endless road of deathlessness like some sad ghost in a deserted mental hospital. I am an angel come to you in persistence.

"No angel dares to plague me. Be gone from this place, I command thee."

You have no power over me, Cadmus Pariah. You lost that power before we ever parted company the last time.

"WHAT DO YOU WANT FROM ME?!" Cadmus said, then stopping short. Did he just...lose his temper? "Just tell me and let me sleep."

But he got no answer. Cadmus closed his eyes and took in a deep breath, Willing himself to sleep. Sleep came quickly to him, thankfully. If he believed in any power higher than himself, he would have lifted his sleeping voice in praise to that avatar who blessed him with sleep.

Cadmus slept dreamlessly for a brief period, and then he found himself in New York City, watching the police press the Son of Sam's head down as he was placed in the back of the police car. An air of relief washed over the scene in Cadmus' head, but it wasn't his to enjoy. David Berkowitz looked directly at Cadmus and said, "Dogs like you should never be listened to."

Cadmus was affronted. He was not a dog, even though he knew the Son of Sam may not be capable of discerning a demon from a dog. And Cadmus was indeed a demon, or he fancied that he was one. That, or a sacred angel of suffering. He much preferred that title, "the sacred angel of suffering."

"You're not what you think you are," said the Son of Sam, but he spoke with a different voice. It was...*him*.

Suddenly, Cadmus was in Faust's apartment, its walls lined with bookcases and its tables dotted with doo-dads from years gone by. Hatred welled up in Cadmus' throat. It was pure hatred, not some distant idea like a philosophical apex. It was hatred.

"Stop bringing me back here."

This is where you have to come.

"You are dead, buried, long forgotten. The only thing left of you is the bloodstains on my mask. Die, for the last time, I command thee to just...*die*."

NO.

Cadmus sat up in his bed, his eyes wide open, his teeth gritted and grinding. He never thought that, when he engaged in the torture of Faust the Confessor, the act of it would haunt him; rather, the victim himself would natter at him over thirty years thence. He felt imprisoned by this entity that suffocated him from sleep and chatted aimlessly in his waking hours.

He wanted to go hunt, but the sun was out and his lack of sleep had weakened Cadmus' resistance to even the paltriest of dangers to Vampires. Besides, the Pariah had gorged himself on Blood in the past few nights, trying to make up for the sleepless days and restless mind. Cadmus got up and paced, his bare feet finding their way in the dark bedroom and making a well-worn path in the carpet.

Stopping, he looked at the laptop sitting on his desk. No, he did not even want to write. He would end up writing about Faust and he refused to allow the spirit even that small victory over him. No and no and no. Walking out of his bedroom, Cadmus trailed down the long corridor to his front chamber, all viridian and obsidian in shading. Perhaps if he sat and read for a while, the inclination for slumber would come and Cadmus would find some semblance of respite from the unquiet spirit that plagued him.

Pulling a book from his extensive collection, Cadmus piled into his easy chair, resplendent in the dark robes in which he often slept, and he opened the book. But what he read gave Cadmus no peace.

> It is from this singular situation that the notion of guilt and of sin seems to be derived. It is before the Other that I am *guilty*. I am guilty first when beneath the Other's look I experience alienation and my nakedness as a fall from grace which I must assume. This is the meaning of the famous line from Scripture: They knew that they were naked." Again I am guilty when in turn I look at the Other, because by the very fact of my own self-assertion I constitute him as an object and as an instrument, and I cause him to experience that same alienation which he must now assume. Thus original sin is my upsurge in a world where there are others; and whatever may be my further relations with others, these relations will be only variations on the original theme of my guilt.
>
> But this guilt is accompanied by helplessness without this helplessness ever succeeding in cleansing me of my guilt. Whatever I may do *for* the Other's freedom, as we have seen, my efforts are reduced to treating the Other as an instrument and

to positing his freedom as a transcendence-transcended. But on the other hand, no matter what compelling power I use, I shall never touch the Other save in his being-as-object. I shall never be able to accomplish anything except to furnish his freedom with occasions to manifest itself within directing it or in getting hold of it. Thus I am guilty toward the Other in my very being because the upsurge of my being, in spite of itself, bestows on the Other a new dimension of being; and on the other hand I am powerless either to profit from my fault or to rectify it.

Cadmus' face was blank as he turned the book over to see what it was he was reading. He already knew from the passage read, but he just couldn't believe it was this book he had pulled from the shelf and this page to which he had turned by chance.

Being and Nothingness by Jean-Paul Sartre rested in Cadmus' pale hands. Slamming the book of philosophy shut, he placed it back on his bookshelf and turned to the veiled window. Peeking out, he surmised the sun still had six hours, maybe longer.

Did you like my joke?

"Go away," Cadmus said aloud seemingly to nothing, but he knew the spirit was there.

Didn't that passage just bowl you over, though? What a gas!

"I have no time to translate your crude slang into actual English."

C'mon Cad, don't you wanna play? Besides, Jean-Paul's philosophy had to be translated into English and you seem to like him. Or you did.

"I played with you sufficiently in 1977," Cadmus said, ignoring the comment about Sartre. "Begone."

I'm not leaving you alone, Cadmus. Not until you come see me.

"So that's what you want. You want me to return to that squalid little SoHo dive and lay a wreath of flowers where your body was finally laid to rest once that dilapidated building collapsed?"

The spirit chortled laughter that echoed throughout Cadmus' West Country home. Cadmus could feel the Pets startle at the sound and it angered him.

*Something like that, Cadmus. Yeah, something just like that. Bring flowers if you want. I haven't been on a date in **ages**.*

Cadmus returned to his bedroom and opened up his laptop. Going to the Virgin Air website, he booked himself a flight to New York City for the following night. Knowing he wouldn't be able to sleep until he was on that airplane, Cadmus busied himself with packing his bag, making sure the Chalice was nicely tucked away. He would hunt tonight, taking a Vampire life, which was always his personal preference anyway.

If Faust wanted a proper funeral, Cadmus would be more than obliged to give him one. He was sick of the ridiculous tin pan comedy that was keeping him awake and making him age, if only in increments felt and seen by the most aged of Vampires.

Before he closed the laptop, Cadmus made one short entry to his growing collection of journal entries.

By the scarab and the scorpion shall I exorcise thee from my sleeping hours.

He didn't care about the dozens of responses that almost instantly flashed back inquiring what this meant or begging to help in some way, in any way. He cared not for these people who glimpsed into his life like it was a book or he was a character that someone was creating for fun on the Internet. Let them think what they wish and say what they wanted. Cadmus knew the truth.

And the truth of which he was the most aware was that he would find resolution in New York City.

CHAPTER 7
KIDS THESE DAYS

Waiting, working up an appetite, the crows among the corpses, all panaceas out of sight. The cannibals we know are always sorry till the next time. ~ Shriekback "Big Sharp Teeth"

They enjoyed the barracks so much more in the days of the First Great War. The blood and piss and the heady sense of apocalyptic paranoia and psychotic breaks. Men broke like kewpie dolls from the inside out but when their insides were ripped out by rusty bayonets, Rebekah was always a little disappointed that fine porcelain didn't spill out instead. Barracks these days were office jobs for the most part and the men were pre-medicated so they'd leave the war addicted to the high of the medication instead of addicted to any perversion that would keep them from screaming out into the inky night because they'd just been visited by their eviscerated buddies from last year's tour of duty in Iraq.

Or take Vietnam for instance, when mankind first began to really explore the connection between physical and mental horror and the complete meltdown that so often happened when the two were intermingled. Only a handful of men weren't diagnosed with PTSD after having their spirits pissed on by their "great leaders." These men were great men indeed, for they proved beyond a shadow of a doubt to have no soul whatsoever. They could say, do, or have to done to them anything and they may show physical distress or a certain distaste for the occasional activity, but they slept like babes swaddled in granny's knit blanket every night without one bit of issue taken with the activities of the day.

These were the men and women that easily embraced the Way of the Beast. Sought it out, they did, having heard in back alleys of the shithole town in which they were stationed or sitting in the galley eating the swill afforded them by the what was told to them was the greatest nation on Earth. And these were the men and women Rebekah and her beautiful mate Mephistopheles hunted, tortured, ate alive, and left for dead on an almost nightly basis. It was a shame that the Muslims were being blamed for a spat of gruesome murders throughout the war-torn desert streets of Iraq but no... Rebekah and Mephistopheles are gorging on the blood of the soulless and enjoyed the fact that they were actually saving more lives than they were taking.

They found four of the Soulless alone in their rec room joking about the days of Abu Ghraib and the games they played with the bodies stretched too far and the sacrilege they made these unfortunate people suffer. "And what's so funny," one of the soulless said. "He had no idea of what was going on. He just wanted to find his wife and son. Well bow to the East 22.5 times, take this broom stick up your arse and proclaim yourself a Catholic priest, and I'll putcha out of your misery."

The room rang with laughter, the kind that makes you want to make it the cackling of the damned. And so Rebekah did. With Mephistopheles, they entered the rec room and opened each throat before anyone could even really move. Drinking the blood they needed, they then opened the viscera to play a kind of ring-a-round the rosy with the jar-head's bowels. They left the room bloody, happy, and pleased with the fact that the four marines still had a few more minutes of sentience to realise that their bowels were tied in a knot in the middle of the room and they were slowly bleeding out after having been visited by what the locals called Jinn.

The more blood there was, the more justice. At least Rebekah thought so. Mephistopheles had to say he agreed. He adored his beloved Rebekah and made it a habit to agree with her on matters, especially important matters of the blood. It was her idea to transform artistes ~ musicians, painters, clowns ~ those proficient in the arts of the world. She wanted the Way of the Beast to be enacted tastefully and, perhaps, with a certain sly message behind the carnage. In Orphaeus, her vision was made manifest so beautifully, Meph had witness Rebekeh weep and come close to introducing herself after all these years. But that was a rule they would not break. They left the artiste to his or her art after they transformed the child. What came after would be a message to the world someday. There is death and horror in everything we do. If you eat you are propagating the horror of the plant or animal into which you bit. Do you have any purpose other than hunger? Is it wrong to want to make preying on one another an art?

Rebekah walked out into the hot desert night and shook herself with glee at the vision of those four soulless goobs taking their last breaths. It was indeed a beautiful message their commander would surely find amusing even if he buried the image deep inside his psyche wrapped in a kind of ghastly mirth.

"Meph, why can't all our children be like us? Why are some of them so very clumsy with their bloodbaths whereas others just refuse to succumb to what should be their natural inclination?"

"Why do you ask, Rebekeh?"

"I had this dream this morning about that fellow in the tacky spats, the one we did during the Great Depression?"

"Faust?"

"Yeah. He came to me in a dream, all holier than thou in a way, telling me that my other kid Orphaeus would be needing our help. It was so real."

"Did you ever think it might *be* real?"

Rebekeh shifted her head and her abundant black Semitic hair weighed on the left side of her alabaster face.

"He didn't come out too well, helping all those retarded little Tomb huggers and never drinking until the Bloodlust took him."

"Well he did come out as a Darkblood, not one of us, if you remember correctly."

"He's not even alive anymore, is he?"

Meph wrapped a beautifully-sculpted arm around his lover of two thousand years. "No, Becca, I'm afraid not. He ran afoul of the demon seed Cadmus Pariah a few decades ago."

"Then why am I dreaming about him?"

"Maybe he's dreaming you. Maybe he's still hanging around in

41

some weird way. The sun will be up soon. It's time to go spin ourselves some desert hammocks and sleep the day away. Maybe he'll come back and say what he wants to both of us."

"Kids these days, Meph... That one was a real disappointment. It was like an ancient great Truth was presented to Charles Chaplin and the Little Tramp decided to trample it under his oversized feet instead of bringing out the absurdity of existence. I swear, if I could have, I would have killed Faust myself for being such a...sweetheart."

Rebekeh rolled her eyes and walked with Mephistopheles into the desert, wondering what dreams would come.

They spun into the mealy desert sand, making cradles of protection from the uncharitable Arabic sun. Almost immediately the dream began, this time for both of them.

"Hello muddah, Hello faddah," Faust began singing, his face cocking to the right in a sidewise smile. "I asked Cadmus Pariah about the two of you. He told me very little before he tortured and killed me. Just thought you should know that. I'd like to get to know you better soon."

"Uh...how...?" Rebekeh said, her hands splayed in impatience.

"Come to New York. This war will be going on for a while so I'm sure you can get back to your Great Work after you tend one of your own. I'm asking as your son to be there. I'll need you more than I ever thought I would once I caught my stride as a Vampire."

"And if we don't come?"

"I'll keep asking in the dreams and messing with your psyche with my endless collection of bad jokes from the 1930s. It's your choice."

"We'll be there in three days, wherever there is."

"Don't worry, you'll know. Love you guys. The four corners bloodbath back there...uh hum...just brill."

They didn't wake until the sun went down. When Rebekah climbed out of her protective sand pod, she looked at Mephistopheles.

"What was I saying earlier about kids these days? Even when

42

they're dead, they find a way to make your life a misery. Am I right Meph?"

"Rebekah, you are always right, lover. Always. Let's go to New York City and see what sort of trouble we can cause."

CHAPTER 8
PROPHECIES AND PARIAH

We could wobble in the golden haze, We could contemplate this riot of sensation, Feel the thunder as the boilers shake, Could be a moment of that Hooligan Illumination. ~ Stic Basin "Hooligan Illumination"

Kelat rested her head on the tea-bag-sized pillow the airline provided and waited for the airplane to take off. There was a layover in England, then it was nonstop to New York City. She had called Dmitri to bring Ishtar and meet her at JFK at the time her flight was due in. All would be revealed, she felt, regarding this entity, once she was reunited with her soul mate and came to know her new granddaughter.

She knew it had to do with the Augury of Gideon, that mystic relic most believed to be the imagination of the supposed author and his faithful followers, those who didn't burn when he sacrificed himself to the sun.

Kelat smiled, thinking back on Gideon before he was driven mad by the transformation the Original Ten endured. He had been beautiful. Long blonde hair, a rarity in the Tarmi, cascaded over his shoulders and down his strong back. His eyebrows were deep black and his lashes were a combination of black and blonde. Almost chiamsa in colour, a hue that was invisible to human eyes and most precious to the Tarmi.

In his Tarmian incarnation, Gideon was known as Gamtha Nurin Aradhel and he was well-loved by his family, friends, and the community at large. Being Tarmian had its otherworldliness to humanity, but Gamtha was so down to Earth as to be human. He worked building homes for Tarmian and human alike; working with wood like it was an entity unto itself. And indeed, Gamtha claimed that each tree had a story to tell and the wood could speak if only the woodworker would listen. 'Twas Gamtha who began carving spirit faces into pieces of wood, bringing out the face of the spirit of the tree, a practice that lived on in human circles to this day, particularly among the Native American cultures.

He was a loner, never joining with one mate and creating a family of his own. He always said his family was the trees and that he could love many women, but could never truly love one as much as his beloved trees. Women understood this and loved Gamtha for who he was. He bore no children, consciously making it to where there would be no abandoned dependents. He was a good soul, Gamtha. He just had an odd way about him.

The night of the Apostate, Kelat'menan asked Gamtha to come be in the Circle because they were going to a grove of particularly important trees, ash and oak, and she wanted his magick present in the witness of these ancient harbingers of the Earth. When the Apostate attacked, these trees averted their attention from the Circle, thus creating a way to kill the Vampires, by using wooden stakes made of either ash or oak. Gamtha was psychically linked to the trees when this happened and was overrun by their ancient knowledge, mingled with the perversity of the Apostate's magick. It twisted his mind and pierced his spirit with a kind of divine insanity.

A tear drop fell from Kelat's chin. She didn't even realise she had begun to cry, thinking about that horrific night and how terrible it had been, especially for-- Gamtha.

Soon after the night of the Apostate and the subsequent Vampire attack on the Welas, Kelat heard about the prophecies Gamtha was reciting. This was unprecedented in that day and age. The women were the prophets of the people, scrying the pools and the message of the Moon. But Gamtha could not be quieted. He saw what he saw and he communicated it the best way he knew how in his state of madness.

The Vampires and humans began calling him Gideon, after the Hebrew's name for 'tree feller.' There was also a story where Gideon made his presence known much larger than expected by the sounding of trumpets. Gamtha surely sounded trumpets with his prophecies, uttering them in the night to those who did not become his victims. And they would pass the words on to others, thus creating the Rotes of the Augury of Gideon. Kelat knew them well. She ran through many of them in her mind, letting the urgency of madness run across her soul so she could touch the memory of her long-time friend, Gamtha.

Sanguinem mittat – Let Blood be sent forth, inscribed upon the sacrificed.

The desert shakes with the footsteps of the Jinn, ascending for the perishing sun, Owl and Serpent alike.

And it shall come to pass that an abomination be born out of a forbidden union unknown even to the Regency by way of profane alchemies wrought by the Magus of our doom. It shall stir in the belly of a she-Wyrm, feeding on her form from within and taking her very nature into itself until the dark night of its rising.

OUTCAST shall be his cognomen and he shall be known and his name be uttered as a curse among those of the Great Hive. Death is the pathway of the Abomination's Dominion! All shall keen with lamentation at his behest and his song shall be the utterance of the damned.

He gathers them in dreams and visions. He gathers them the players of the game. He gathers them in grace by grace. Gathering, they come.

Ŭ sa dorken na'aaŭlor kenropfehli

And I remember well in the distant realm of memory.....

The dread progeny shall bring us from every corner of the globe, desiring of us the life that stirs within... Its venom shall burn and brighten the night and its voice shall summon sorrow. Woe until the Darkblood! Woe unto the Flagellants! Woe unto the Bathers in blood and the Crippled in spirit! The Bride most

46

pure shall pave way for the Beast, her garden of Blood come to harvest. And yon Beast shall tread forbidden paths and whisper songs into the Basin of Life. His voices shall summon sorrow.

Child of Blood, Thralled in the flood, she sees the saint and holds his heart like he holds the ruby.

His destiny is mortation and the sanctification of flesh. Immortality in death shall be his repose. Sainted in suffering, blessed in the bliss of dread and dissolution. This vessel of secrets, this child of wisdom. Utterances of crowns rest upon his lips. Compelled ye shall be to bring him forth in the belly of the Spirit of Creation, he waits. Pools of indigo will carry ye Home. Redemption in the song that goes before us...

Woe and destruction meet and follow him, He who follows eternity with the dove at his side. Tears fall. So many tears as to flood the ocean blue. His planet will be devoid. The dove's planet one of respite.

She finds him again, takes him, and he drifts away into the mist of time, leaving her bereft. But she knows they will meet again. Destiny made manifest is their union. They will walk into the End of All Things, hand in hand. In a place of perfection.

My dearest, the dusty mortal and the beautiful daughter of insanity...carefully shall they tread the path to eternal love, for that is the only thing that endures. Faith fades, love endures.

These were just some of the strange utterances Gideon made in his life. Some she understood as prophecies come to pass, others were still a mystery to Kelat. As time wore on, Gideon grew quiet and the tales of the written Augury began to spread throughout the Great Hive. It was rumoured that Gideon had resorted to writing down his prophecies and the Augury would someday become the

Vampire Bible for God himself spoke to Gideon. The Hive of Redemption in particular held close this rumour, believing in it desperately.

Kelat reached out to her wounded brother and, as always, hit a psychic wall. He never wanted to talk to her, she who had embraced sin so readily. Or so he thought. He was in good hands with gentle Eve, who was safe from Cadmus whilst in the presence of Thiyennen and psychically linked to Kelat. Eventually, though, they would reunite. It was unavoidable and so tragic that a child who belonged in Meybhelahn could be so soiled and degraded by a child who belonged amongst the Tarmian clan in grace.

Giving up on trying to connect with Thiyennen, Kelat closed her eyes and let her spirit fly with the airplane that just took off. It would be a short trip, as they were landing in Heathrow to drop off some travelers and pick up more. Kelat would sleep through most of it. She enjoyed the feeling of slumber on a giant monster of a machine like the airplane. She drifted and thought and touched the souls of those she loved, including Cadmus who was in flux. Despite his dislike of her touching him in such a way, she did so. He was, after all, her only son. Kelat fell into a deeper sleep, ignoring the speed of the plane and its eventual descent in England. She dreamed of when he returned to her Veiled Sanctuary, in full thrall to the Blood Crown. It had not been his to wear. Not yet. It took her weeks to remove the wretched thing from his brow and put the relic in a kind of stasis. He remained with her for over half a year, depending on her Blood and her inexplicable love. With every expression of love Kelat gave Cadmus, he responded with spite, but she knew he was softening in ways he could not yet begin to comprehend. When the time came, emotion would be his and he would blossom into an entity unlike anything anyone had ever seen. This was her hope and her faith. She dreamed deeply this Great Work in progress.

But she was brought to full awareness when she heard a familiar voice.

"You..."

Kelat opened her eyes to see her son, the one about whom she was just dreaming. Cadmus Pariah stood with a small black denim sack.

"You!" Kelat exclaimed. "What are you doing here, Cadmus?"

"I'm flying to New York, Mother Kelat. I'm guessing we're going there for the same reason."

"The dreams?"

"The dreams of Faust the Confessor..."

"Yes, it seems you left a job unfinished," Kelat said, unable to resist teasing Cadmus. He gave no reaction to her taunt, but she sensed his body tense from toe to powdered blue head.

"Why did I have to end up on an airplane trip of eight hours with you?" Cadmus said, a hint of agony drifting along the edges of his comment.

"Sir you need to sit down, please, we're about to taxi out," a flight attendant politely requested of Cadmus. When he turned his eyes in her direction, the flight attendant seemed to melt with adoration. It never failed to fascinate Kelat, Cadmus' natural glamour.

He placed his sack underneath the seat in front of him and sat down next to Kelat, reclining his seat to a comfortable position. First Class was always so much better when it came to getting rest.

"So you're going to try to sleep, son? You don't want to catch up?"

"I've hardly been gone from your wretched little triple helix hole. What is there to catch up on?"

"I just want to know how you are, son," Kelat said sadly.

Cadmus turned to her, his eyes not just dark and absorbing, but also dark with poor health. He looked a little older too. Perhaps a man in his 40s with dark circles around his eyes.

"I'm tired," Cadmus said. "These dreams plague me. I cannot sleep. The insomnia is driving me to distraction. Is that satisfactory for you, Mother dear, or shall I fall into a rhapsody of how badly I truly feel?"

"I'm sorry, Cadmus. Perhaps now that you're going to New

49

York to resolve whatever you may have left undone, you can claim slumber as yours again. Until then, I hope you're able to capture Morpheus during our journey to the New World."

"Yes, that was my hope, but I'm not certain I can sleep with you sitting right beside me. I do not trust you, Mother Kelat. Look at what you did to me with the Blood Crown."

"Just as with the dragon fire, you did yourself in with the Blood Crown. I didn't place that crown on your head. You chose to do that yourself."

"But you knew...you knew I would do that. That is the true reason you wanted that paltry little bone collector to go with me, so he could bring my unconscious body back to you. Why didn't you go get it yourself?"

"You came to me, if you remember, keen on retrieving the relic, probably for nefarious purposes you chose not to share with me. I was happy to let it rot on the Apostate's dusty head."

Cadmus fell silent and stared at her sidewise. Kelat was again stricken with how truly beautiful Cadmus was. "So are we to argue for the entire eight hours we're in the air?"

"No, Cadmus. I won't argue with you and I promise, I won't touch you or your belongings should you choose to sleep before we get to New York. I am your mother and, whether you like it or not, I love you, Cadmus. I want the best for you, if that's even possible. I want to see this end well for you because I love you very much. Never forget that, no matter what happens in this new adventure. Never forget that I love you."

"This concept of love is something I believe that I will never understand."

"I hope before the end that you do. Love is the one that that anyone should be allowed to understand."

Cadmus gave Kelat that sidewise look again and raised his eyebrows. "This bag is mine and it's held tightly between my feet. Don't think of looking in it or taking it. I don't care that you're the Queen Vampire, I *will* kill you if you make any overture of taking what is rightfully mine."

Guessing the chalice was in the bag, Kelat shook her head. "I will watch over you and your belongings while you sleep. I hope you rest well."

Narrowing his eyes, Cadmus glanced at Kelat, then turned away from her, making a scene of settling in and ignoring the flight attendant who asked him to put on his seatbelt before take-off. He placed earbuds in his ears, carefully adjusted his iPod and slipped it into a pocket hidden in his many cloaks. He closed his tired eyes and was soon breathing steadily, indicating that, for once in what seemed a great while, Cadmus was getting some sleep.

CHAPTER 9
THE ANGEL AND THE VAMPIRE

"I've done dubious things alright, wandered far from the cosy light, and now I wanna go home." ~ Shriekback "Now I Wanna Go Home"

Ishtar put it off for as long as she could but, after a week, she told Dmitri that she had to return to her father and Eve. He let her go without incident, hoping against all hope that Thiyennen wouldn't turn his face away from his half-breed daughter. She was, after all, following her nature, even though her path was Darkblood and not Redemption.

Eve caught the night bus across town to Biltmore Village where Thiyennen and Eve were staying. The minute Eve opened the door, her Spanish eyes welled with tears and she turned away, letting Eve let herself in.

"Eve, please don't cry," Ishtar said. "Please. You know I was never happy as a Dhampir and I could never be truly human. This was the only option for me."

"I know that, Sweetheart. I do. Thiyennen won't be as understanding. Since his tribulation at the hands of Cadmus Pariah, his intolerance of Vampiredom has reached an insurmountable level. I just hope that he can come to grips with what I know you had to do."

"Where is he?"

"Outside looking at the moon," Eve motioned to the back door of the large apartment.

Ishtar nodded and moved toward the back door.

"Sydney..." Eve said, and Ishtar stopped.

"What did he name you? Dmitri? I know it was him because I smell his Blood in you. What is your name now?"

"Ishtar."

"That's beautiful. Go child. I won't be here when you come back in. It's time for me to hunt."

A chill ran through Ishtar at those words. Eve was made a very

52

weak Vampire, almost to the point of being rated a member of the Tribe of the Tomb. But she did not subsist on animals and the blood of the freshly dead as did most of that sad hive. No, she was a child killer, made so by her maker, Cadmus Pariah. She fed on Innocence and made Blood to be harvested by her husband and sire. It was a horrible existence and one she barely tolerated by being a member of the Hive of Redemption. Being Thiyennen's nurse was a good match for them both.

Ishtar opened the back door and walked out on the expansive deck covered with all manner of potted plants.

"Hello Father," she said quietly.

No response came from the man sitting in the porch swing gazing up at the waxing moon. His vast Elfin eyes twinkled magickly with the special light afforded only the Tarmi and the Original Ten. His black hair was a little shaggy and needed cutting. The scar on his throat was barely visible now, but would never fully go away. When a Vampire was crucified, it was usually a killing action. How Thiyennen survived it and for how long he survived such a state, God only knew. At least that's how Thiyennen saw it, embracing the Christian God, forgetting his days as leader and shaman of his essentially Pagan people, the Elef'therosi.

"So you ignored my wishes and went ahead with it, I see," he said sadly, not even looking at her.

"I'm sorry, father, but I had to. Being stuck in the middle of something so large and never having a place in the world was driving me mad. Surely you didn't want that. I was resorting to self-harm because of my non-place in this world. It was time to make a choice."

"And you made the wrong one. How strong is your need to feed? Are you a Beast?"

"I'm a Darkling, father. Kelat's mate brought me over."

"Thank God above you're not a Beast, like that ungodly entity Cadmus Pariah."

"Cadmus isn't a Beast, father. He isn't anything. He's an

53

aberration."

"Don't argue with me, child. What's done is done. What am I to call you now?"

"Ishtar."

"A Pagan goddess."

"An ancient Tarmian, if memory serves. And my memory is long now, being your child and being a Vampire now."

Thiyennen stood and walked over to his daughter. His strong chin quivered only a little. He took her face in his hand and turned it to one side, then the other, studying her china doll face. With his other hand, he stroked long red hair which accentuated her face with its coppery wonderment. Quite suddenly and unexpectedly, Thiyennen pulled Ishtar to him, hugging her tightly.

"I love you, Ishtar. From the moment you were conceived, I loved you..."

"I love you too, Father," Ishtar said quietly, her heart pounding.

"Have you experienced any strangeness since you crossed over?"

Ishtar thought before thinking. Yes, she had. Quite a bit, actually. Should she tell him, she wondered? Ishtar swallowed, then spoke.

"A spirit brushed against me as I transformed. And he's been speaking to me in dreams."

"Kallum?"

"You know him!" Ishtar exclaimed, relief washing over her.

"I have been dreaming him too. As has Eve. Is he summoning you to New York?"

"Yes, but I wasn't going to go"

"You must."

"Are you going, father? Are you able?"

"I can travel now. With the help of Eve...and you and Dmitri."

Ishtar had not mentioned Dmitri except to reveal him as her Blood father. She wasn't sure Dmitri would want to travel with two Redemptors all the way to New York. Talk about the Road

Trip from Hell...

Dmitri had mentioned the angel and Kelat's intention to go to New York for several reasons having to do with this restive spirit and the Augury of Gideon. She believed it existed. Ishtar wasn't so sure. But one thing she did know: Kallum was very real and she felt that she already loved him despite his being a disembodied mortal.

Every night, he visited her and talked about his time on stage, singing and dancing in an age when live performance was of great import. His knack for language and his comic timing were eerie in perfection and his knowledge and ability to sing all the songs of that beloved age made Ishtar shine from within. Many a night now had Kallum sung her to sleep and rested quietly with her in her dreams. She had no choice but to fall in love with him, whoever he was. He had mentioned that his place was in New York and that she should come. Only Ishtar knew exactly where he was. If she could find him, he would sing and dance for her in person.

How could an angel be embodied? Was he one of the Nephilim Thiyennen had mentioned, the fallen ones who embodied themselves so that they could mate with humanity? Then again, he was talking about his own people, he who had abandoned the Old Ways and forgotten who he was. How was Thiyennen going to go to New York when Kelat was going to be there? If they laid eyes on each other...all Hell was going to break loose. Death would abound across the world. It would be the end of Vampiredom, that was for sure.

Maybe that's why Kallum was summoning everyone, if he was indeed summoning everyone. He wanted to end the great sin of Vampirism. Only an angel or God himself could do it. Cadmus had tried, but failed, probably much to his great chagrin.

"Dmitri is talking about driving up. Are you able to do that, Father?"

"I'm stronger than I look or sound, my sweet. Go and speak to Dmitri about it. I am certain he will acquiesce to my wishes. It is time to give this sweet soul the rest he deserves. Kallum is a restless angel and his song has been sung. It is now up to us to finish the show."

"I agree with you, Father."

A silence grew between them as they stood on the deck listening to the katydids and frogs sing their own song in the night. The sweet smell of honeysuckle filled the air promising the bloom of magnolias soon. The honeysuckle always preceded the magnolias ~ it was a Southern rule.

"I have been building a place..." Thiyennen began. "Or rather I've been having it built. The angel said it was necessary so, over the months, I've been preparing. I pray that my actions are understood by God and that I will be forgiven..."

Ishtar almost asked what sort of place, but she held back for some reason. A mote of fear began to spiral in her Vampiric spirit.

"Go to Dmitri and tell him we want to ride with you the two of you. Eve and I will make preparation to travel."

"I will Father," Ishtar said, stepping away from him. She paused. "Father?"

"Yes, Ishtar?"

"Do you still love me, even though I crossed over?"

There again was that silence and it weighed heavily on Ishtar. Then came the answer.

"Ishtar, I will love you until death takes us both and beyond."

Ishtar smiled and opened the back door.

"Thank you, Father..." she said, and she was gone.

Thiyennen sat back down on the porch swing and began to weep quietly. His little girl, his little girl... She had taken the sin upon herself. He wondered what sort of life she would have now that the end was almost near. The place he had prepared, he hoped was not for her. It was a place for inquisition and suffering, a place foretold by the madman Gideon. The Redemptors would have holy regret. It would come on the great wheel and the tears he shed right now would be nothing compared to the great

56

suffering Thiyennen's place of preparation would reap.

Kallum had spoken of it. He who had suffered so greatly at the hands of Cadmus Pariah, he who had mortated as a reward for his suffering, he had spoken of the prophecy that the Hive of Redemption would have prepared a place where the worst of the Vampires would pay his debt to the world and receive the spirit of God into his life. Thiyennen was merely trying to bring about prophecy. That was his reasoning, no matter how dreadful that reasoning was.

He would road trip to New York, and bring back the embodied angel and the bound demon Cadmus Pariah. Then shall the prophecies of Gideon the Mad be fulfilled. It was foretold. It was foretold and it shall come to pass.

Ishtar took a taxi back to Charlotte Street and ran into Dmitri's arms when he opened the door. She was as tall as he was, but felt very small in his arms at this moment.

"How did it go, Innochka?" Dmitri asked, using a Russian name of affection closest to Ishtar as he could remember.

"Well, I think, but..."

"What?"

"Father wants to ride with us to New York, him and Eve both."

Dmitri pulled away from Ishtar and gave her a shocked look. "Really?"

"Yes really. Is it all right?"

"Of course. I don't mind. But Thiyennen seems to have an aversion to anyone not a Redemptor. How can he possibly tolerate us?"

"I don't know. He seems to be on a mission. Kallum has been visiting him too. And..."

"And what?"

"He spoke of a place that he's prepared. I don't know what he's talking about, but it struck a chord of fear in me Dmitri. I fear this will end badly."

Dmitri laughed. "I've come to the realisation that any quest involving a Vampire Relic ends badly, or at least not as good as it could have or even should have. Probably Cadmus' involvement in every little thing having to do with it."

Ishtar frowned. "I can't imagine Kallum wanting to have anything to do with vengeance or exacting some holy punishment. I hate to say it, but I fear my father is treading that path, and it breaks my heart. I think that what Cadmus did to him has done something to his sanity."

"Can you blame him, Ishtar? The man was crucified and raped by his own son. That's enough to rattle anyone's sanity."

"I don't see how more pain can heal a pain that is likely unable to be quelled. Eve and I have done our best to nurse Father back to health and, really, he's physically healed completely. He has gone out to hunt and his resting pattern is back to normal. But his mind...his thoughts...I'm just afraid for him and for us all."

"Well...only time will tell. I'm planning on our trip to New York tomorrow night. We should be there within two nights. By then, Kelat will be landing at JFK. You and I will meet her there. Eve, too, if she wants. Thiyennen, of course, will likely pass on that meeting, which is a boon to us all, considering."

"I'll let them know. I'm sure they'll be ready."

CHAPTER 10
THE SWAN AND THE WRITER

"What about those days we make up a secret pact to splash and paddle into the dark and back. No hesitation, never a shadow of doubt." ~ Shriekback "Hand on My Heart"

"I can't believe I'm doing this," said Agatha to herself as she paced outside the great room of the underground of the Cygnus Theatre and Opera House. "I just can't believe it. Does it make me complicit in murder? Am I gonna be arrested if it's found out that I waited outside a room where an unconscious woman is being ripped to shreds by four Vampires? Arrested or taken into custody before transferred to the loony bin? I just can't believe it..."

Soon the door opened.

"We've cleaned up," said Lolita. "You can come in if you wish."

Sighing heavily, Agatha walked into the great room for the fourth time since she flew out to talk to Orphaeus. The room had a palace-like feel to it, with a high ceiling and a large expanse of floor. *I guess it would have to have a lot of floor space, given what goes on in here,* Agatha thought to herself grimly.

"Aggie!" Orphaeus said with a happy voice. He was removing something from his mouth and, to Agatha's horror, it was the first bone of the dead woman's right index finger. He placed it in a bag that hung from his belt. Agatha followed the movement of the bone, then looked back up to the merry Vampire. Curly red locks hung loosely on his forehead and around his face. Orphaeus really was a handsome man with deep brown, expressive eyes, an aquiline nose and smiling full lips. His forehead sloped back, giving him a bird of prey profile that Agatha thought was irresistible. "So good of you to join us. Are you ready to head out to the Big Apple?"

"More than ready!"

"Given any more thought to what's going on with that jewel of yours?"

"Not really. I don't see how anyone or anything could decode it. A scientist maybe, but not any scientist I know of. How about you?" She asked, sitting down to one side of the pile of Vampires of which Orphaeus was the center. Beside him rested his mate Genevieve, who was very amicable toward Agatha, if not a little standoffish. Then there was the teenager Lolita, who obviously loved Orphaeus with a passion. She was to his left, looking longingly into his big shiny eyes. And lying with his head in Lolita's lap was Hercules, the twenty-something surfer dude. His bleach-blonde hair spilled out across Lolita's Gothic thighs and down past her knees. This was the strangest family Agatha had ever seen. She would have been scandalized, though, if she'd known that her opinion was shared with Cadmus Pariah.

Orphaeus kissed Genevieve, then stood. "Well, you said you'd eat at the airport and I've already eaten. The sun is down, so I guess it's time to head out."

The entire family got in their Chevy Impala. Agatha was squeezed between Lolita and Hercules in the backseat, her bag lying across their laps. If she weren't so paralysed with fear, she'd be laughing at the comedy of it. For certain, she'd be writing about it. She'd already started a novel, officially fiction, even though she knew it all to be true. The story of the chalice had already been written and she'd heard that a monumental occurrence in Vampire history had transpired about a year ago. Orphaeus had been a part of that and had told her some of the story, but not everything. Now this, this whole weird disembodied spirit calling people to his resting place and had a connection to the Augury of Gideon, if that was indeed what Agatha had.

But it seemed feasible. Based on what Orphaeus knew, the jewel Paine had passed on to Agatha before challenging Cadmus was indeed the Augury of Gideon. He never knew the importance of the jewel, but he kept it to honour his Blood father, the madman who had brought him one crazy Woodstock night.

Before she knew it, they were at the airport bidding the family a fond goodbye. As the Impala drove off, Orphaeus looked at

Agatha and smiled, charm dripping from him in great waves.

"Well, off we go then," he said, leading her into the Delta terminal. Their flight was nonstop and was scheduled to go in an hour. They stepped into the terminal and had their boarding passes confirmed and their luggage checked. Moving on to the gate, Agatha stopped and got herself a gigantic Cinna-bon and a coffee. She really didn't want to fall asleep next to a Vampire, even if he'd already fed for the night. Thinking about that bag of bones on his belt made her shiver a tad and her coffee splashed on her hand, burning her a little. It didn't matter. That discomfort should help keep her awake as well.

Orphaeus watched all this with not a small amount of amusement. He knew what Agatha was doing, but it didn't offend him. If he were in her shoes, he'd probably do the same thing, even though Orphaeus had been nothing but helpful and downright chivalrous to Agatha. She had had Vampire experience for years, working with Paine, but she didn't realise it until he came out to her right before he was killed. So everything was still relatively new to Agatha, and Orphaeus respected that. He didn't comment on the overload of sugar and caffeine; instead, he offered to carry her carry-on luggage along with his. She gratefully accepted and began wolfing down the cinnamon bun on the hoof.

They got to the gate just as their seat range was being called for boarding. Orphaeus and Agatha trundled aboard and took their seats on the wing. Agatha passed the empty Cinna-bon container to the put-out flight attendant with a polite smile, and began gulping down her coffee.

"Comfy?" Orphaeus asked

"Snug as a bug in a rug," Agatha said nervously. "I'll be good for the entire flight. How about you?"

Orphaeus held up two books, *The Lost Road* by JRR Tolkien and *The Golden Bough* by Sir James George Frazer. "I've got my reading to keep me warm."

"That's quite a combination."

"Gotta pass the time somehow."

"You could pass some of the time telling me about the Blood Crown and your time with Cadmus Pariah. It'd be nice to know what I'm going to be facing if he shows up because of the Augury."

Orphaeus rubbed his chin carefully. "Do you want to wait until you get sleepy and that way I can keep you awake?"

Agatha appreciated Orphaeus' thoughtfulness. "You wouldn't mind?"

"Not at all," Orphaeus said, smiling wolfishly. "I can't think of any better way to stay awake than to listen to scary stories about a terrifying fellow."

"You said he'd mellowed out some."

"Yep, seemed to. Looks can be deceiving though. If he shows up for this round of good times, I guess we'll see firsthand."

The reporter in Agatha took hold of her. She took a long swallow of coffee and said "Orphaeus, tell me, what kind of situation or abuses create a thing like Cadmus Pariah?"

"Hm. That I can't tell you. Only Kelat knows that story and she may not know everything. I know that his conception is pretty fucked up, being the result of an alchemical mix of Kelat and Thiyennen's issue, and the Apostate and dragon DNA."

"And dragons actually do exist?"

"I saw one. The rest are sleeping. From what I understand, they'll awake when humanity most needs them. I'd say that's proof enough that they were allies to the human race; another creature that got the lesser of the deal when encountering humankind. Why they seem to think that the human race is worth the help the dragons may be offering when they rise is beyond me. But that's just me."

"Not much faith in humanity, eh?"

"Well, it's like this, Aggie. I know that I'm a monster. I know that I tear into people and bathe in blood." Orphaeus shook his bag of finger bones. "I'm essentially a supernatural serial murderer. But at least I'm honest with myself and others about it. I try to make my prey as comfortable and unaware as possible. I have come to grips with whom and what I am and I behave accordingly. Humanity as a whole is comprised of murderers, rapists, abusers and killers of animals and their lesser man, polluters, pillagers, and poor tenants on this, the only planet we have. Which is worse? You are doing everything you can to stay awake around me but, I daresay, you're safer with me than you would be with any human being and that's a bet I'd be willing to place my entire fortune on. And my fortune is vast."

Aggie looked down at her giant coffee with a peevish eye. But her need for knowledge prodded her forward.

"Vast fortune? Is that typical of Vampires or are you unique?"

"It's a byproduct of many of us. I'd say that all the Darkbloods are wealthy depending on their age. One tends to acquire riches over time. The Darkblood Hive are comprised primarily of Incubi and Succubi who absorb the riches of their prey because they almost always kill when feeding. They don't have to feed every night, but many do and end up with quite the *'inheritance'* as a result.

"The Hive of Redemption will take the fortunes of victims only out of necessity. Vampires also must deal with cost of living issues, just for your information. When they kill, and kill they must for the absorption of the life force, they will take that person's equity and make it their own. Their process takes longer so young Redemptors are often, as you might say, Middle Class or maybe right above the poverty level. It won't take them long, though.

"We Beasts often become rich very fast," Orphaeus said quietly, his face expressing a vague shame. "Many of us succumb to the Bloodbath and will later, after the effects of our indulgence has worn off, take the victim's money and investments. But a lot of Beasts also go on spending sprees, buying shit that no one, especially Vampires, would ever need. I think it's a monetary expression of the Bloodbath. Sometimes I think the whole of my Tribe is bipolar, for we certainly behave that way. Because of this, Beasts will fluctuate between being fabulously rich to incredibly destitute in a matter of weeks. There are those of us who keep our instincts in check, though, and we enjoy a life of luxury for decades, even centuries.

"The Hive of Purity, consisting of the Original Ten and their progeny, are all rich beyond your wildest dreams. Well, the remaining nine and their Darkling children... Gideon's children were certainly wealthy, even your Paine in case you didn't know. Gideon himself? Who knows? He was thought to be a raving mad man who was barely aware of this reality. When he was seen, he often looked disheveled and dirty. That could have been an indicator of homelessness and a state of poverty, but who knows? Gideon was a mystery. The rest of the Puritans...well, they've been walking this Earth for so long, the mere inkling of poverty is not in their comprehension.

"The final hive, the Tribe of the Tomb, every last one of them is poverty-stricken. They are disabled in some way, unable to feed properly, barely able to function in any basic human or Vampire way. We don't know what happens with these Unfortunates. There aren't many of them, thankfully, but I can guarantee you won't encounter an Unfortunate that isn't homeless and destitute.

"Does that satisfy your curiosity regarding Vampire finances?"

Agatha laughed with amazement and mirth. "More than. Will you be this forthcoming about anything I ask, Orphaeus?"

"M'dear, I have nothing to hide from you." Orphaeus tucked away his books and grinned at Agatha, flashing his white fangs like a flirtatious wolf, then he looked up and around, his curly red hair moving back as he did so. "The airplane has already taken off and we missed it. If this is any indication, our trip will seem like it flashed before our very eyes as if we were dying. I should have worn one of my Dia de los Muertos tee shirts in honour of this quickly perishing journey, eh?"

Orphaeus laughed and patted Agatha comfortingly as she laughed along. Orphaeus was such an odd bird, she thought, but thoroughly engaging and enchanting. In just this short time, she'd totally forgotten about the bag of finger bones the Vampire had fastened to his belt. It was going to be a wild ride indeed.

CHAPTER 11
CADMUS' JOURNAL:
DIVINE INTERVENTION

"Well all God's children got their dubious side, and it's deep and dirty and it's real real wide." ~ Shriekback "God's Gardenias"

I am astonished that I'm sharing a plane ride to New York City with my Mother, Kelat'menan. If I believed in the chattering of priests and shamans, I might attribute such an occurrence to one of fate, of destiny. What do the Christians call it, a kind of divine intervention?

There is no such thing, no matter how the unwashed masses hope for it, preach about it, depend upon it. It simply not *is*, and I will hold to that assertion until the sun burns itself out and takes us all into the Abyss of its final resting place in space. I refuse to succumb to the trappings of religion to explain a simple coincidence. That is all this is, a coincidence.

Kelat wants to talk, to discuss the matters that find us on this aeroplane heading for New York City. I have nothing to say to her. For months she left me in her Veiled Sanctuary to suffer the effects of the Blood Crown while she supposedly tried to remove it. O Queen of the Night, wrap your fingers in amongst the thorns of the crown and pull it off my head! Stop the suffering! It is my suspicion that she was gleaning information of how the magical Crown had come in to being and what secrets it may hold in regard to the Great Hive. She used me as a biological computer to get this information from me. There were too many strange dreams and

65

visions during my so-called healing from the Crown.

I lay in stasis, listening to the endless Tarmian chants Kelat uttered over my prone body. When she fed me her own Blood, the visions grew more vivid and I could hear Kelat whispering what I saw as if committing by rote the images to memory. There was no respite for me, no shred of healing. The Mother of Memory would tug at the crown only to make it dig deeper into my wounded scalp.

Her intentions were to pull from the crown all magickal lore that she could. She cared not for her only son, whom she sent to be sacrificed to this dreadful artifact.

The Vampires of the Great Hive may see her as a queen and a deity to be loved and perhaps even feared. I see her as a person in a long line of people whose only intention was to administer suffering. I am a vessel of suffering and I will absorb every shred of abuse you could imagine and wish to enact. Give me your abuses, just as Kelat did. I will eat them like the sin eaters of Welsh yore. I will take it and turn it into dread tenfold. Then shall your intentions be revealed, for you shall be screaming your guilt at my wise hand. Where will your divine intervention be then? Read carefully, little ones. I am your divine intervention. I will intervene with lacerations, tears, and the hurried whispers of the damned. The Great Hive will see their Goddess devoured in spirit and body and their lamentations shall echo through the halls of creation. That is the only divine intervention there is in the great dark world, the kind you make for yourself and impose upon others.

She is looking at me in the peripheries of her vision. I can see her watching me as I type this out. Our journey is still quite young, so I may eventually acquiesce to a conversation with her, but not right now. Now is my time, ordering my thoughts in this, my journal. I find it interesting that the disembodied spirit of Faust has had the rash intestinal fortitude to enter Kelat's dreams and summon her to the New York ruins where his body supposedly lies, incorruptible as ever. I expect to go to SoHo to find a small pile of bones that was once the Confessor followed very quickly by a group of dismayed Vampires. I then expect to surprise them further by cutting all their throats in short order and drinking until I am about to burst. I grow weary of these theological meanderings and the most powerful creatures on Earth being guided by portents and omens. I'll show them what Gideon saw, their own miserable little deaths as their spirits are absorbed into the Abyss of my soul. Let them have faith in these so-called sacred artifacts. Let them tremble with hope or fear that these relics will somehow save or condemn. They'll be so busy fawning over the relics, they will not even realise I've killed them before their empty bodies fall over in a dead heap and I hear their spirits crying for release within my infernal soul.

Cadmus closed his laptop and turned his head to Kelat, who had sat quietly knitting what looked like a simple blue scarf. If she wanted to engage him in conversation, he would certainly let her, now that he had vented in his journal. In fact, being close to Kelat had stirred even more emotions than what he had been experiencing. He'd have to admit that he was thoroughly annoyed by her presence on this plane and that he would have to sit and share this long trip with her whether or not he liked it.

Smiling like a snake in a bird's nest, Cadmus took the initiative and said to Kelat, "I've finished my journaling, Mother Kelat. Do you want to speak of anything in particular or simply catch up since I left you at the Veiled Sanctuary so many moons ago?"

Kelat looked up from her knitting.

"It's up to you, son. I'm simply glad to see you and would enjoy any kind of conversation you feel like having. Do you want to tell me more about Faust, anything Orphaeus hasn't already told me, that is?"

Gritting his teeth as he continued his smile, Cadmus made a mental note to visit certain special acts of suffering upon Orphaeus for his disclosure of Cadmus' Summer of Sam with Faust.

"I've nothing to hide, O Mother of mine. Let the games begin."

CHAPTER 12
THE DREAMS OF ANGELS

"Quote me no more Horace, swat me no more flies. Don't rely on what we try to symbolize. The walls like tissue – it's a mean design. God's Gardenias rain on me." ~ Shriekback "God's Gardenias"

He wasn't sure if people believed angels could dream or not. Something inside him wanted to shout from the minarets of the east to the steeples of the west that angels did indeed dream, and their dreams often shook the very earth in their envisioning.

Of course Kallum wasn't an angel, not truly. He was a spirit blessed with the presence of angels. One in particular, his saviour angel, Rosetta often bathed him in the rainbow light of her undeniable existence. She would speak to him of things and sing in the holy tongue to him. Once she revealed to him that she was Ophanim in nature and that, when she was with her charge as decreed by God, she was at the throne of creation guarding it with many eyes and tongues, singing songs that were of such beauty, they would strike a human dead from their very intensity.

Kallum was spending all his time now in the basement of the new building that stood where his old apartment building once swayed and sagged. Sometimes he grew restless and poked about the corridors upstairs, but mostly he remained in the basement and slept. The dreams he had been having were of import to what was his coming destiny, thought Kallum. They consisted of his meeting with Gideon the Mad and the nightmare sessions he spent with Cadmus Pariah. Oftentimes, he would awake in a cloud of terror only to be comforted and surrounded by the holy spirit of Rosetta, who always came when she sensed her beloved Kallum was in distress.

But he had recently been having different dreams. These he did not understand, but they weighed heavily on Kallum's consciousness for he seemed not to be himself in the dreams, but someone else. He thought he might even be Gideon the Mad himself, seeing the ages to come and interpreting them the best way he knew how. It would seem that Gideon did not just foretell the ages of Vampires, but he also had seen the future of humanity, of the planet herself. It had always been assumed that Gideon's inability to accept his Vampiric self combined with his ability to see the future drove him mad. From what Kallum had seen of the human prophecies, he was beginning to think that it was humanity's possible destiny that had been the end of Gideon's sanity.

So far in the dreams, he had seen a wall of water so tall as to be a fish's staircase to heaven smash into the east coast of North America, a volcano emit fire, ash, and lava that covered the west in utter destruction. The cloud encompassed the Earth and the beasts of field and forest perished for lack of sun. Humanity resorted to cannibalism and found new and more horrible ways to make one another suffer and die. It was like they decided to, instead of helping one another, punish one another for simply being. All was wet grey ash and the sounds of suffering that went on from damp, dim day to black night.

Was this something preventable or inevitable? If Gideon went mad from it, one would think that the destiny of this planet was inevitable. But Kallum did not embrace insanity from beholding these things. Instead, he accepted them and considered them in his heart and mind. There had been times in the past that the Earth went through great changes and, as a result, many horrible and untenable things occurred. But something always was the same throughout these global gauntlets: life persisted. It may not be the life that once walked this blessed ball of creation, but it was life nonetheless, and it would go forth and create its own destiny in this symphony sung by God.

Humanity, too, had survived so many catastrophes. Who was to say that, should this horrible thing happen, they would not carry on in some wholly new existence? It may be hell on Earth for them at first, but humans were wired to survive despite seemingly insurmountable obstacles. This was proof to Kallum that his species was special in some way, touched by God each and every one. The children of today lived because their ancestors had the fingerprint of god on their foreheads. Every last human child was the offspring of survivors. That had to say something.

And, if humanity had run its course, that was okay too. Kallum rested his spirit in faith in God. They were simply being called Home. Some may linger in the destruction before realizing it was time to move on, but move on they all would and must. And then they would see that everything was always going to be okay. They would see the face of God and move on to their own paradise, awash in the grace of creation. Kallum knew this and believed it with every fibre of his being. Knowing and believing were different things and, combined, they created a mighty fortress of faith.

So, either way, Gideon's vision of a broken and battered Earth only brought Kallum hope that tomorrow would be better. This kind of outlook had always rankled some people. It certainly had rankled Cadmus Parish, much to Kallum's unfortunate chagrin. But he couldn't help how he saw the world, or creation for that matter. Kallum simply was *Kallum* and he would continue on his merry way as long as God would let him. He was cradled in the arms of an angel and, if his dreams were nightmares for a while, he had faith that these dread visions were things he needed to see not to degrade his spirit but to eventually lift it up in glory.

With that, Kallum closed his spirit eyes and drifted in the sleep of the holy, to and fro in the basement of the New York apartment building.

Almost instantly he was in the dream, or what he perceived to be a dream. In front of him was Gideon. He was dressed in dirty jeans and an olive-coloured tee shirt two sizes too big on his bony frame. His feet were bare and he stood in the mud of a giant field. His hair was a tangle of frizzy dread locks and tiny braids creating a blonde bird's nest on his head. Gideon's face was clear and beautiful, devoid of any madness whatsoever. His large blue eyes studied Kallum intelligently, and his mouth was curled in a friendly smile.

71

"Hello there, Kallum."

"Gideon?"

"Yes, it is me. How are you doing, camping out over your own grave like this?"

"I would rather be back in my heaven."

Gideon smiled wider. "I understand. But you have such an important job to do, this is necessary right now. I hope you realise how important you truly are."

"I am doing what I must. I don't care about my importance. We are all important in the eyes of God."

"You are such an incredibly wise person, to be so young," Gideon laughed. "No wonder you mortated from Faust back to your human self."

"It was either that or continue being used as a human bowl of blood for Cadmus Pariah."

"Indeed."

"Absolutely."

"You've summoned the people here and they're on their way now. Soon, you'll be fulfilling your destiny and the destiny of others. This is why I wanted to talk to you."

"I hope you're here to give me some guidance, because I have no idea what to do when Cadmus and the others get here."

Gideon nodded. "After the group of people assemble here and bring your body back to the light of day, you'll tell them that you're all to travel to Kelat's Veiled Sanctuary. There shall the Augury be unlocked. You'll be the one to unlock the Augury, Gideon. It's by the Blood you'll do it."

"Do I have to be the one to do it? Why?"

"Because you're the only one who is alive who was freely given the Augury by me. It's the act of passing on the genetic code. There's a part of the Augury in you because I gave you the Augury early in its forging, just as there was part of it inside Paine when I gave the completed relic to him before passing from the living realm."

"But I passed from the living realm too. How am I supposed to get back? Just enter the body? I tried that already, but maybe it's because I'm buried I can't do it. I don't know, Gideon, I'm just so confused."

Gideon's spirit hugged Kallum's and said, "It will be your guests who get you to where you need to be. Just watch and wait. One thing you may not like..."

Gideon's pause lasted longer than Kallum felt comfortable with. "...like what?"

"You'll be partially Vampiric in your new form. You will need Blood to survive, but not much and it will not mean that you're cursed. You will still be mortal, human, and blessed in the sight of God."

"Gideon, no!"

"It is necessary, Kallum. Do not worry, everything will be revealed in its time, and you'll know it to be good and gracious. There is one coming, a youngster in the realm of the Vampire. She will be your friend throughout all of this, your dearest and most-cherished ally. Do not squander her beauty or take her for granted in any way, Kallum. Your path back to paradise depends upon this one young lady."

"I'd never take her for granted, I promise. I don't make brodies like that."

"Good... Now there's another thing..."

"Oh no. What, Gideon?"

"You'll be interacting with Cadmus closely and there will come a time when you can either curse him for his crimes or bless him for his being. The choice will be yours and the fate of Vampirekind rests upon your decision."

"That's it?"

"Yes."

"Well what kind of applesauce are you handing me here, Gideon? I don't know if I'm gonna be able to get behind this caper."

"Kallum, you have to. I can't force you to do it, but my visions definitely show you as the key to all of this. You just have to do it of your own free will; otherwise, nothing will change and the Vampire world will continue to degrade and become something much worse than it already is. Cadmus is a powerful entity and his Will will overcome them all over time. Until the day of the Rapture, his rule would be absolute and humanity would writhe in the fear and dread of it all. This, too, have I seen in my visions of possible futures. I've beheld the Pariah in every way known to the Great Ancients and his role is not so small in my embracing the safe-haven of madness. I'm hoping that you choose wisely so that my madness would have been for nought."

Kallum pondered and groused, but eventually said, "I'll do as you wish, Gideon. Hell, I tolerated landlords during the Great Depression, I can tolerate rubbing elbows with Cadmus and giving him my blessing whenever the time comes. How will I know, Gideon?"

"You'll know... Kallum, my friend, you will know."

Kallum came back to consciousness only to find the building's superintendent messing around with the furnace.

"Goddamn, blasted piece of shit. What the hell is wrong with you anyway?"

"Maybe it's tired from working all season," Kallum said aloud to where the man could hear him. He felt every hair on the man's body go straight out with pure fright. It tickled Kallum to play with the occasional mortal visitor to the basement, especially the superintendent, who was course and unkind to the building's tenents.

As early English speakers might have said, the super hied he thence, leaving Kallum chuckling alone in the basement. He thought about his dream of Gideon and a smile came to his spiritual self. This was going to be interesting.

CHAPTER 13
THE ROAD TRIP

"Nous entendons ta voix d'argent, tu nous appele, Une fois pour toute sur l'chemin éclair, La lune si pleine - nous la poursuivons - cette belle lumiere, Nous baigne doucement sur l'chemin éclair" ~ Shriekback "The Shining Path"

Dmitri put his and Ishtar's bags in the trunk of his blue 1989 Nissan Sentra. He looked tired, but in good spirits, Ishtar thought. His elderly neighbour was keeping Dare while Dmitri was out of town but, right now, Dare trailed every step her human friend took, faithfully resigned to the fact that he was going to be gone for a while.

He looked up at Ishtar who had been standing in the doorway of his apartment, just out of the setting sun's unpleasantness, sipping on a box of grape Kool-Aid. "You ready to do this, kiddo?" he asked amiably?

"Yeah, I'm ready ~ more than ready. How about you?"

"Yep," Dmitri nodded. "As soon as our dynamic duo arrives, we should hit the road. We'll have about nine hours of night, so we should be able to get to New York just as the sun is rising. I had Bessie here equipped with tinted glass years ago, so even the rising sun won't bother anyone for at least an hour or two. You'll all be safe until we can find shelter in the city."

About that time, a taxi pulled up and out stepped Eve and Thiyennen. Eve immediately rushed to Ishtar and the blessed shelter of the apartment. Thiyennen got the baggage from the taxi, paid the driver, and turned to Dmitri.

"Good evening Dmitri."

"Your Highness," Dmitri replied respectfully.

"Don't be mad, boy. Thiyennen is fine with me," He stuffed the two bags he and Eve had brought into the trunk with Dmitri's and Ishtar's luggage. Dmitri shut the trunk lid easily.

"Fair enough then, Thiyennen. Are you ready to head North to meet our appointed destiny?"

"You have no idea!"

"Well, let us go then. The sun is almost gone and we have to make the miles while we can so we can make this trip in one night. I'm to meet your sister in twelve hours."

They all piled into the car. Ishtar sat up front with Dmitri and clicked her iPod into the FM tuner. "You guys don't mind a little traveling music, do you?"

"No, not at all," Eve said. "Just as long as it's not Magnificat, I'm okay."

Dmitri nodded his approval.

The first song to come on was "Glastonbury Song" by the Waterboys. Dmitri started the car and it hummed merrily along with the happy song as Dmitri began their journey by making a couple of turns to get them onto highway 19.

"Inama Nushif" set the tone for their journey, peaceful and hopeful all in one package. Ishtar sang along, her beautiful voice ringing in the car like a bell wrought from the purest crystal.

Dmitri eyed her. "I didn't know you could sing like that."

"I don't often sing, but I like to sound good when I do."

After "Inama Nushif" came "Puttin' on the Ritz," which left everyone in silence, just listening to the song. Song after song came on and everyone just listened silently, enjoying the music. There was also an awkwardness that existed. The King Vampire was sitting in a car with the bound mate of the Queen Vampire, his immortal enemy. In some strange way, Dmitri felt like he was betraying Kelat by bringing Thiyennen; then again, how could he not agree to take him along to New York City? Does one ever say no to such an ancient and magickal being? It was a Catch-22. Dmitri shrugged it off, knowing that Kelat would know Dmitri was merely doing the best he could, given the circumstances presented to him.

"Up on Hi" by Lighterthief came on Ishtar's iPod, the dizzy wonderful vocals of Andy Partridge and Jen Olive filling the car with musical birds and pure happiness.

Ishtar looked back at her father and Eve and smiled widely as Dmitri took exit 9 to I-26. They'd be on this road a while and she wanted to make sure they were both comfortable.

"Will either of you need to feed tonight? We can stop for that whenever you wish."

"Your father fed last night and I can skip a day. I'm not exactly eager to be a bounty for Cadmus if we do, in fact, encounter the Pariah in New York."

"Dmitri fed earlier and then he fed me, so I'm good, too."

Silence settled between the carriage riders once more. The music sounded far away and did nothing to ease the unspoken tension. But Ishtar seemed mostly oblivious to this and continued on.

"I know you won't want to hear this, Father, but so far I've loved being a Vampire. The blood...I never knew that blood could taste so incredible, especially Vampire Blood! I can understand why you didn't want me fall under the same curse as you, but you have to understand that I was already halfway there as it was.

"It was hell being a Dhampir. I made hardly any friends in school because people naturally sensed that I was strange, I was *other*. I was picked on and derided by my fellow classmates. The teachers behaved in pretty much a disinterested manner, happily passing me along from one to the other; just happy they didn't have to deal with me in their class anymore.

"And then there were the eating quirks. I can not count how many times people would watch in disgust as I'd mix the blood of my meat with my milk and drink it. Needless to say, I didn't make many friends like that either."

"I'm sure you hated both your mother and me for your unfortunate circumstances. Sydney...Ishtar, I am so sorry."

"No-no Father, that's not why I'm telling you about the hard time I had as a kid. I'm telling you so you'll understand the decision I made and won't be mad or hurt at me. Please, Father, can you forgive me?"

Thiyennen leaned forward and put one olive hand upon Ishtar's own pale one. "Child, there is nothing to forgive. I'm just glad you feel you've found a place in this hateful world gone wrong."

Unable to resist, Dmitri asked, "Why do you think it's gone wrong, Sire?"

"So much murder, starvation, rape...unkindness virtually dripping from wounds cut into the Earth by the heavy machinery. This is not the world that was intended. People need to embrace Christ and one another in these final days, and pray for healing from the very young to the ancient."

"Why Christ? I ask because I grew up in the Church...the Church that fell early on under the influence of the Apostate, and I remember the abuses I suffered at the hands of the priests. Wouldn't you say that unkindness begins in the heart of a child and, since most children are made to go to church, they learn their meanness there?"

"It's possible, Dmitri, but so much good also comes from the Church and, now that the Apostate's influence is dead and gone, perhaps the Church that was meant to be, Christ's church of kindness and forgiving, can flourish freely and share the beauty with any seeker willing to listen."

How did Thiyennen find out about the Apostate? Dmitri wondered. There were only two ways. Kelat told him in one of their many one-sided conversations where Kelat tries to get Thiyennen to respond to her and Thiyennen ignores her, or at least pretends to, at any rate. Or Cadmus told Eve during one of his visits to her in the coldness of her nights. He was betting on the former because Eve's living with Cadmus had been a detriment to Cadmus' terrorizing her. Dmitri shrugged to himself. Either way, Thiyennen knew, not that it really did anybody any good.

"But why does it have to be Christianity, Dmitri? Why always Christianity? That path is only one of so very many on this planet. Christianity can't be the only path to goodness."

"It was the path of our last great Magus," Dmitri said quietly. "In him we had tied all our hopes for humanity to understand the magick of this place."

"You could have stuck with the ancient teachings and done just as well."

"We did fabulously with the Apostate, didn't we?"

"Touché."

"Guys can't we discuss something a little more lighthearted," Eve said, her voice the edge of a razor. "Like how funny it is that Vampirism has enjoyed a boost in pop culture lately?"

Ignoring Eve's plea, Thiyennen continued on, his lovely brow furrowed in a zealous expression.

"The magicks of the Last Magus were the first wholly human magick. Through him you would have tapped into your own natural power and been able to communicate with the high ancients. This world would be a very different place, the one that was intended, had the course of events that surrounded the Magus been different."

"So you follow Christ in the hope of restoring his teachings that he learned from your people of old."

"Something like that...in part."

"We Darkbloods faithfully follow the ancient Pagan, or Tarmian, ways. Doesn't that make us closer to Christ than what you do to yourself, going into churches to suffer and pay penance for something that was never your fault to begin with?"

"You Darkbloods embrace the abomination of this state of existence while still following the Old Ways faithfully. It's a perversion of sanctity and one we've all paid for over time. Look at the chalice. We're all bound to its fate as long as Kelat's living Blood inhabits it. What sort of dreadful magick is she performing that the accursed are influenced by a cup that's now held sway under the power of Cadmus Pariah? You know there's a better way of 'living' so that you can control your nature instead of it controlling you, but you choose instead to embrace the chaotic power of the Vampire and forget that goodness once walked this Earth."

"You are so full of it!" Dmitri exploded. "I think you're confusing us with the Beasts. Our very nature is one of control.

79

We manipulate the magicks afforded us and live according to our power without it controlling us. Embracing who you are is the most freeing moment in a Vampire's life. It allows us to work with our nature and control it accordingly. We live a happy life, fulfilled in every way, in tune with whatever religion guides us and working in harmony with our Vampiric nature. To deny who you are is to eventually let that thing control your life on a dangerous level. Look at the Holy Inquisition. Those people punished and tortured others because they denied their nature to the point of madness; so they inflicted the pain and misery upon their fellow man as a kind of release from their own denial. Whatever you deny, Thiyennen, only grows bigger and meaner until you finally succumb to its power."

"Can we please just not talk about religion?" Eve said in a raised voice. "We've got hours to spend with one another. Fighting about why we do what we do and how we cope with what we've done after the fact will bring us all nothing but unhappiness. Let's just try to get along while we're together, okay? Please?"

Dmitri nodded and ruffled his nearly-black hair until it looked like a rat's nest resting on his head.

"You're right, Eve. I'm sorry."

Thiyennen said nothing for some time. The music filled the car again. "World on Fire" by Sarah MacLachlan, "Lady in Black" by Uriah Heep, "Deliver Us from the Elements," by XTC, "Who Wants to Live Forever," by Queen, "I Have a Dream" by ABBA, "I Wanna Be Loved" by the Andrews Sister. By the time they turned onto I-81, Eve, Dmitri, and Ishtar were all singing along to "Nowhere Man" by the Beatles whilst Thiyennen nodded thoughtfully to the music. Ishtar was happy everyone was enjoying her playlist. She thoroughly believed that music could bring the worst of enemies together if they would just listen. It certainly seemed to have worked in this case.

Once they settled in on I-81, Dmitri shifted in his seat and prepared for the long ride. Almost 100 miles on this one road. It was going to take an effort to keep things light and easy when all he wanted to do was grab the King Vampire by the collar and

80

shake him to and fro whilst saying "Can you snap out of it already?" But that would be a bit rude and unseemly, so he tried to focus on the music.

Then Thiyennen spoke over the music and said, "Ishtar, did I ever tell you about how and why you were conceived?"

"No. I've asked in the past, but you never would tell."

"If you all don't mind my telling this story, I feel Ishtar is ready for the truth of her conception."

"Not at all, Dmitri. I could use the conversation while I drive."

Into the night the Vampires rode and Thiyennen began his tale.

Ω THIYENNEN SPEAKS

Anna and I had just moved to Charlotte, North Carolina to begin a new life. Anna was my lover and wife of over 300 years. She was incredibly beautiful in her Vampiric perfection. Long dark waves of hair fell about her alabaster face and her dark Slavic eyes never missed a move I made, she took everything in...my Anna. Her lips were prim and pink under a small upturned nose. And her carriage was that of the most noble of Europa. She loved me unconditionally and the feeling was quite mutual, I assure you.

We were coming from Virginia Beach, after spending a good 50 years there Charlotte was to be our new home, our haven from being exposed for what we really were and thus exposing the entire Great Hive. Take this as a lesson, Ishtar. You can only spend so much time in one place without humans twigging on to your secret. Being a Vampire means being a nomad of the night

We settled in a nice condominium not far from downtown right across from businessman Gordon Parkinson and his lover Wendy McCurrie. We were polite neighbours and were gracious toward Gordon and Wendy.

But Gordon fell immediately for Anna, wanting her badly. He made no effort to quell his desires or attempt to keep them secret. The man treated Wendy badly and he treated her even worse when

Anna and I came onto the scene. Every chance he got, he arranged to "bump into" Anna and aggressively woo her. He watched her using binoculars and telescopes. I think he once actually broke into our apartment in the hope that Anna might be there, but we were hunting at the time. It was as if Anna's presence drove Gordon crazy.

One night, though... It was the night that changed everything for us. I was away at my night job at the community college and Anna had brought home a man to feed from him. She forgot to close all the drapes on this one night and Gordon was home scoping out the object of his obsession.

When he saw Anna bite into the man's neck and drink him dry, then shriek out in agony over what she had done (Anna was a Banshie), Gordon did truly go quite mad. On that night, he became a Vampire hunter. He studied up on Vampirism and how to kill us. He carved out stakes and bought cloves of garlic. Wendy asked him what on Earth he was doing one night when he was stapling the strings of garlic up around their condo. He slapped her and told her to keep her mouth shut, it was none of her business.

A few weeks after spying Anna feed, Gordon came to our condo, again while I was away. When Anna answered the door, her pristine beauty shining like a sun in the blackest of space, Gordon paralysed her by placing a cross on her chest and he took her off, whisking her away to a place where he could have his way with her and then kill her.

When I got home and saw Anna was gone, I sensed something was wrong, so I went to Gordon and Wendy's home. I knew that Wendy, too, often spied on us and I would know what she had seen if she'd seen anything at all.

"Hi Wendy," I said. "Is Gordon home?"

"No..." she said grudgingly.

"You wouldn't happen to know where he's gone would you?"

"I have no idea."

I looked around the apartment from the door. At the nearest

window was Gordon's collection of spy gear, all pointed in the direction of my home. I was going to have to leave Charlotte sooner rather than later.

"You sure? Because Anna isn't home either. I was wondering if maybe they went somewhere together."

"No..." murmured Wendy. It was then I knew that Wendy knew what happened to Anna, but she'd never tell out of loyalty to her abusive boyfriend.

So I brought out my glamour and suddenly kissed Wendy on the forehead. When she looked at me, tears of passion welled up in her eyes. She was seeing me in a flourish of Vampiric beauty and that beholding made her want me without question. I stepped into the condo and held her hand. Hopefully the glamour would be all I needed to get my question answered.

"Wendy, where did he take her? Where is Gordon and Anna?"

Stuttering shyly as she gazed at me with love and lust, Wendy said, "I – I don't know. I didn't see anything."

I then kissed Wendy on the lips and felt her melt gratefully in my arms. I asked again, but her loyalty to Gordon was strong. I ended up making love to Wendy on the living room floor, biting her breast as she came and taking in a long draught of blood and milk, which I then fed to her. I then gave her three drops of my own Blood to Thrall her, which she drank enthusiastically, wanting more. But I couldn't do that. I had a mate and I needed information. I didn't want to thrall Wendy, but it was the only way to find out what was going on with Gordon and Anna.

Again, I asked.

"Wendy, where are Gordon and Anna?"

"The zoo. He arranged a place at the zoo for him and Anna. Iron bars he said would keep her pliant and compliant."

I raced off into the night, heading for the zoo. What I saw there I will never forget. Gordon was raping my Anna, who was paralysed by the iron all around her. As he came inside her, he also drove an ash stake through her heart and into the dirt floor of the iron pen. Soon after she had been staked, Anna turned to ash and blew away into the sacred night, taking her spirit with them.

Sorrow and rage over took me and I entered that cage where Anna met her fate. Taking Gordon by the throat, I ripped out his esophagus and drank his blood until he fell like a bag of beets at my feet. I returned to the condo and took only what I could easily carry, leaving behind the trappings of mine and Anna's long and happy life together. Sensing that I was being watched, I looked up to find Wendy watching me, so I went to the apartment and gathered up some of Wendy's belongings and took Wendy with me. It wasn't long before we settled here in Asheville. I set Wendy up in an apartment and took care of her and her unborn child in every way.

It was only when she began telling anyone who listen that she had given birth to a Vampire's child that I had to distance myself. I still paid for everything until Wendy was institutionalized for her obvious schizophrenia, leaving you, Sydney, out in the world alone. There are so many regrets I have regarding the thralling of Wendy and how much more I could have done for my child if I had just been able to control Wendy's so-called flights of fancy. I've been in Asheville for over twenty years taking care of the child I conceived the night my mate was murdered.

"And I will take care of you, my Ishtar, for as long as I can because I have loved you from the moment Wendy and I made you on that grim night."

Ishtar looked at her father, tears streaming down her face. "I'm so glad you watched over me, Father. I'm grateful to you for never giving up."

"And I never will, Ishtar. As long as you want me in your life, I will be there."

A much happier silence developed between the travelers as the music, now "I Live in a Suitcase" by Thomas Dolby, chimed lonely in the deep Vampiric night.

CHAPTER 14
THE ART OF EMOTION

I have nothing to promise but the hope of demise and the sorrows of living again. I have nothing to show but the world in my eyes and its bitterness, sadness, and pain.

Cadmus stared at Kelat in expectation.

"How are your emotions coming along, Cadmus?" Kelat asked, jumping right into the silent fray into which the two of them found themselves.

"Why are you always so interested in my so-called emotions, Mother? What could it possibly matter to you?"

"Everything that affects you is of import to me, Cadmus, because you are my only child and I love you."

"Love. A Vampire's love is like quicksand. It surrounds you and engulfs you but, ultimately, it kills you. Blood isn't the only thing you Darklings drink."

"Blood is the only thing we need, though. We aren't walking around with hundreds, perhaps thousands, of souls trapped in the prison of our spirits."

"Ah, you speak of my Beautiful Pets. Most of them would already be dead by now had I not afforded them a kind of immortality within me. I have tended toward taking the bereft, anti-social, and the waif and orphans of this failed Western World. If I had not killed them...eventually...they would have done it themselves. And that is just a waste of good blood and philosophical apices. Can you blame me for trying to clean up the streets of London while assuring my own survival?"

"I can blame you for perverting your own inner magick when you know you don't have to. Cadmus, you know that you never had to create a herd of humans to milk for the chalice. You did so because it amused you in some vague way. It was gratifying to tour the long hallway that held your Beautiful Pets as you tormented the souls you entrapped."

"I'm not one to amuse easily, if at all. You attribute to me emotions that I simply do not have."

Kelat sighed. She needed Cadmus to admit to himself that he had experienced some emotion so that he could open the door to more emotions. There had been a prophecy that Gideon had told her as they stood, back-to-back in a lonely Grove in Europe a thousand years ago.

He who feels not will embrace them and open up the ways to the hidden isle.

Kelat had long meditated on this and other strange statements Gideon had shared with her. She was now certain that the term "embrace them" meant the embracing of feelings. Cadmus was the only person she knew who was actively, enthusiastically, even aggressively emotionless. Since so many of Gideon's prophecies pointed to the existence of Cadmus, Kelat had to believe this was yet another one of those prophecies. And, if she could get Cadmus to actually experiencing emotions, the way to Meybhelahn would once again be revealed. She could go home and be healed. She could take Dmitri with her and they could live in blessed immortality on the holy isle. And Cadmus could finally find some peace with himself, experiencing emotion on a level he never dreamed, not since having such frivolous notions beaten out of him.

"Cadmus, someday, and I promise it won't be long before it happens, you'll embrace your ability to feel emotions. You can't say you haven't already experienced some of them."

"Indeed, I have experienced anger, perhaps even hatred. These emotions I don't believe I ever lost during the cleansing process enacted upon my person and soul by my teacher Nissius. I certainly feel them when in the presence of Orphaeus Cygnus. And you tend to raise my ire with your endless pontifications and revelatory statements. It's enough to make anyone a tad testy."

He was baiting her, Kelat knew it. She would not go down that path by taking the bait, though.

"There are more to emotions than anger and hatred. There's

humour, which I've noticed you dancing on the edges of that one during my encounters with you. Yours is a dry humour, rarely used, but there nonetheless. There's love and affection. Frustration is one you have exhibited too. And regret. You've had your regrets."

"I've had no such thing."

"You forget, Cadmus, you keep an online public journal. I read it and I know that you regretted what happened between yourself and Mary Magdalene. You can't say it was a philosophical apex. Those words were yours."

Cadmus turned his head away from Kelat in an act of disregard. He thought back to the morning that he had killed Mary Magdalene, and how all she wanted was his love, the one thing he wouldn't...*couldn't* give her. Even with her spirit safely imprisoned within Cadmus' being, Mary Magdalene pleaded for his love and all she got was the void of his spirit.

"The words were mine, yes. But they are merely words and I often embellish my tales for the sake of my readers, nothing more."

"Wouldn't that mean that you care about your readers then?"

"No."

"Cadmus, you have softened since our time in the desert. I can see it so clearly and I hope that you might someday see it too. In many ways you are an artist, being a songwriter, a poet, and a writer. I can see the emotion spilled out across a song or a journal entry. It's right there, glistening like mica on a wet autumn day. All you have to do is touch it and it will be yours, Cadmus. You could lead a so much fuller life if only you'd break down that wall around you. As your mother, I want you to embrace these feelings, allow your philosophical apices to become true emotion. After that, you'd have no need for your Pets' spirits. You could release them and be your own self instead of an emotionless facsimile."

Cadmus listened to what Kelat was saying and he felt a bubble of hatred well up within him. Why was she so intent on his emotions? Why did she even care? He was her hateful alchemical son who had killed so many of her children, not to mention his rape and torture of her brother, he would think that Kelat would be out for his Blood. It distressed him that she cared so much, when it would be so much easier to not care at all. He posed these questions in so many words to Kelat, who said,

"The love a mother has for her child is unconditional. There is nothing, absolutely nothing you could do to me that would stop my loving you, Chylde. You are the product of my own issuance and, even though I didn't carry you to term, I'm attempting to psychically carry you now in order to help you be reborn in a new light, one that will hopefully be both healthier and happier."

"What if I told you that I am happy just the way I am?"

"You would be lying because you can't feel what happy is yet. Then again, I could say my job is done because you're now experiencing the emotion of happiness and you slipped up and accidentally told me. Either way, you have me for the duration as I make sure my child is okay and...*happy*."

Cadmus didn't like Kelat's logic. It was too much like his own, which meant an argument between the two of them was like banging two very large stones together repeatedly. It gave him a headache most times. This was one of those time.

"You have to learn the art of emotion slowly, Cadmus. It was painstakingly abused out of you so it will have to slowly be introduced to you. If I were to open the floodgates of the emotions you've tucked away over the years, it could very well mean a death sentence to you."

"I'm surprised you aren't working toward that very goal."

"I don't want to see you dead, unlike most everyone else in the Great Hive. I am your ally and I will do any and everything within my power to protect you, if fate would have it that I must."

Cadmus leaned across the aisle to Kelat, his sloped Elfin brow smooth with neutrality, his eyes heavily lidded as he spoke. "Just for the record, Mother, if the shoe were on the other foot, I'd be the first to want my hand at you. Nothing would please me more than to rip you asunder and collect every last drop of your blood in the chalice. The wailing of the Vampire Hive would be a threnody of joy to my ears as I watched while your life force faded away from your vision and into mine. I am *not* your ally. Never forget that Kelat of Thessalonika. Once the relics are gathered and the mysteries are revealed, you'll come to understand that I am here for one thing and one thing only; the total eradication of the pestilence that is Vampirism. Are we quite clear then?"

"Unequivocally," sighed Kelat. "But I want you to remember this conversation at a later day, either when you need to look back to a moment when someone was unconditionally kind to you or when you're walking these lands unfettered from the trappings set upon you by the Apostate and his infernal agents. I want you to remember that you mother was not only your ally, but also your friend, despite it all. I was, am, and forever shall be a friend to you, child."

"The likes of me neither needs nor want friends, Mother."

"Everyone needs a friend. Even the 'likes of you.' I can promise that you'll understand that before the end."

CHAPTER 15
DIGGING IN THE DIRT

*"We fall in love almost every night. We're quite ridiculously tight." ~
Barry Andrews "Mousetrap"*

"I dunno Meph, what do you think we're supposed to do here?"

"Other than reminisce about the good ole day we were here before, I haven't a clue Becca. Didn't the dreams say more were coming?"

"Did they? I'm a bit dodgy on parts when I wake up. Maybe I should start keeping a dream journal."

"There's always that."

"Well, it's only been three hours and I'm bored already. When do you think the other 'candidates' will be here?"

Mephistopheles laughed. "You make it sound like a game show!"

Rebekah joined Mephistopheles in the laughter.

They poked around the basement a little. There were two ratty washers and their dryer mates, obviously second hand. A furnace that looked like it came straight out of the heady days of the early 1980s sat near the far wall of drab area. One of the walls sported art and graffiti. It was the only portion of the basement that exhibited any life. There was a painting of a large parrot in a rainbow of colours. Underneath it was graffiti that said 'awaken you dreamers.'

"Savvy folks here," said Mephistopheles. "The parrot there, it's referencing that XTC song that mentions parrots and lemurs."

Rebekah cocked her head and looked closer. She wasn't as abreast of the music scene as Mephistopheles, so she took him on his word about the art. She plopped down on the concrete floor and offered up a bored "harrumph." Mephistopheles moved over and sat down across from her, taking her pale hands into his chocolate brown ones.

"It's been a day since we've been here and it doesn't look like anyone is going to show up tonight. At least, that's how I feel. I think we got here early. Maybe we should hunt. I know I'm hungry, so you must be starving."

About that time, a man behind them said, "What the fuck are you doing here? I'm getting so sick and tired of homeless people trying to hole up in the fucking basement. Get outta here!"

Rebekah gave Mephistopheles a look, and that was all it took. They fell upon the superintendent with enthusiasm, ripping, clawing, and biting into him everywhere. Before he could scream, Mephistopheles tore a hole in his throat and drank deeply of the gouts of blood that poured out. Rebekah joined Mephistopheles at the fountain for a moment, then returned to her joyous clawing at the superintendent's body. She drank from the bends of his arms and legs, bit off his penis and drank from there, tore at his thighs to find the femoral artery and vein. Mephistopeles took blood from the man's tongue and then clawed his way into his chest cavity to find the heart, which was miraculously still beating, albeit slowly. He ripped the heart loose from its cage of protection and he and Rebekah shared it equally, drinking the heart blood and eating a portion of it.

They both sat back and looked at the broken body of the superintendent, breathing heavily and smiling. Both were in full Bloodlust and it was always a beautiful feeling for a Beast to experience this often mind-altering experience.

"Meph," breathed Rebekah.

That's all it took. Mephistopheles was on Rebekah, kissing and licking the blood of their victim off her face. She returned the favour, growling her approval. Mephistopheles reached down between them and loosened their pants. Soon he was inside her, moving frantically as he bit deeply into Rebekah's throat, drinking her Blood. She bit Mephistopheles and bucked against him in the passion of the Bloodlust and Ambrosciata. They came together, moaning in harmony as the Blood flowed faster between them.

Rearranging their bloody clothes, they both lay flat on the basement floor, enjoying the afterglow of their feeding and making love. They lay there for a few moments when Rebekah suddenly said,

"Do you hear that?"

"Hear what?"

"I don't know, but do you hear it anyway?"

"Can't say as I hear a thing, Blood-droplet."

"Listen…"

After a minute or so, Mephistopheles said "I don't hear a th –"

Then he stopped. He did hear something, but he wasn't sure what. It wasn't quite a heartbeat, but it possessed rhythm.

"What the hell is that?"

"A beacon maybe?"

"Faust?"

"Has to be. His body is sending out a signal where it can be found."

"But it's coming from everywhere, how are we supposed to know where he is?"

"I guess we start digging and hope for the best."

Mephistopheles stood up and helped Rebekah to her feet. "Before we begin anything I need to dispose of this unpleasant man. I noticed some dumpsters out back, so I'll only be a quick minute. Then we should go back to the hotel and change clothes before we start the dig."

The dead superintendent was a large man and there's nothing heavier than dead weight, but Mephistopheles had no problem picking him up and throwing the body over his shoulder. He strode up the stair to the exit while Rebekah scoped out that rhythmic sound, trying to pinpoint its origins. It seemed to be close to the furnace, so she decided that would be where they'd dig.

Cloaking themselves from the public, Mephistopheles and Rebekah quickly made their way back to their nearby hotel. When they got into their room, they shed the bloody clothes and put them in a plastic bag. Beasts went through a lot of clothes thanks to their feeding habits. Rebekah joked that they were giving back to society by keeping textile mills in business making clothes for Beasts.

In fresh clothes and freshly fed, both Beasts felt like themselves again and ready to tackle the mystery of their dead Blood child buried somewhere in that dingy old basement. Before going back to the basement, they dropped by a hardware store and bought a mallet, pick and shovel. They then returned to the apartment building and placed a *geasa* on the basement so they'd have no more rude interruptions like the superintendent. Neither wanted another mess to clean up and they already had to take care of the blood on the floor. While Rebekah worked a charm over the blood on the floor so it would never be seen by mortal eyes, Mephistopheles scoped out the basement floor.

"You say you heard it stronger around the furnace, Bek?"

"Yep, sure did. Almost done here, I'm hurrying."

"Take your time," Mephistopheles drew back the mallet and slammed it into the basement floor. The concrete cracked into pieces. Removing the pieces, Mephistopheles began a pile of concrete in the corner nearest to the furnace. Rebekah joined him and the removal of the concrete went more swiftly. Underneath the concrete was dark brown New England dirt. Rebekah placed her hands on it and cocked an ear in the direction of the bare area.

"Well?"

"Meph I don't know. It doesn't seem that strong now. Tell me what you think."

Mephistopheles listened quietly, taking his time to be sure of what he was hearing. "Maybe the other side of the furnace?"

Rebekah said, "Could be. I'll dig here while you break up the concrete there."

They worked in silence for several hours. Soon all the concrete was gone, in piles against the walls of the basement. A few holes had been dug to no avail. After all this work, Rebekah sat down in a fret.

"This is ridiculous. Everywhere we dig, the beacon seems to move. Maybe we aren't supposed to find Faust."

"If we weren't, then why the dreams?" Mephistopheles said. "Why the beacon we're hearing now?"

"Well, my theory is that everyone will hear the beacon, but maybe we can't pinpoint it until the people who have been called get here. Surely we aren't the only ones who've gotten the call to come here. There has to be others. Does that make sense?"

"You always make sense, Bek. So why don't we call it a night and head back to the hotel? The sun will be rising soon and I really don't want to spend my down time lying in the dirt.

They left the basement and headed back to the hotel with the plan to return to the basement after sundown to wait on the others, whoever they might be.

CHAPTER 16
IN LEAGUE WITH BEASTS

"Comes the monster in his season, and he won't calm down. You gotta reason with the beast." ~ Shriekback *"Reason with the Beast"*

Orphaeus eyed the screen that showed the progress of the trip. They only had two more hours before touchdown he reckoned. Agatha was nowhere near sleepy. She asked Orphaeus about the strengths and weaknesses of Vampires.

"You aren't going to publish this are you?" Orphaeus asked, concern lacing his voice. "I'd hate to be the one who unleashed any Vampire killers out there on the unsuspecting Vampire populace, if you get my meaning."

"If I publish it, it will be in a fictional setting. Besides, no one really believes in Vampires anymore and, if they do, they're fascinated with you and want 'the gift' of being one. I think you're more than safe with what I'm going to write and how I write it."

"Very well, then..."

ORPHAEUS SPEAKS

Vampiric abilities and weaknesses are as many and as varied as the stars in the sky. What dictates who is in possession of what is not really certain. One might say it's genetic, but how does that explain a Beast whose Blood parents are both Darkblood. The best thing I can do is give you the most basic abilities and weaknesses for each Tribe. This is by no means a guide that's set in stone. I'll start with my own Vampiric traits. I have the Anubis ability, which means I can shape-shift, usually into a wolf. I have been known to shift into bird form, almost always the crow. I can move at extreme speed, which helped when Cadmus and I were traveling to Rome to take the Blood Crown. I possess the Glamour, which means I have the ability to attract people. Most Vampires have this ability because it's necessary for the way we feed. That whole drawing flies with honey instead of vinegar mentality should be had when thinking about the Glamour.

As for weaknesses, the sun is a big no-no for most Vampires. I can't tolerate it at all, and must take strong refuge from its killing rays. Dmitri, or Thaddeus as you know him is immune to the sun. This is a very rare trait. Oak and ash stakes can kill me, but the stake has to be pounded through me and into the ground, not just through my heart like you see in movies.

Kelat, the strongest Vampire by far, can tolerate the sun even though it can eventually kill her if she stays out long enough. She is Anubis, taking the shape of birds, cats, the hound, among many other animals. Her Glamour is exceeded only by Cadmus Pariah. She possesses telekinetic ability and can also read minds and achieve empathic links with both Vampire and human. She can communicate with the animal kingdom, particularly big cats and birds. She has otherworldly speed and can go long periods of time without feeding; however, the longer she goes without feeding, the more likely she is to kill when she does feed.

Her weaknesses are iron, which is an old curse placed upon the Tarmi by the Apostate. Iron can imprison them because they are unable to touch it. The sun, although of minor concern to her, still remains a discomfort and, as I said, it can eventually kill her. She had a clash with the local Jewish Patriarchy an age ago, which produced a charm against her that parents place over the cribs of their newborns. It's said to possess the names of three angels that helped banish Kelat and keep her from harming innocent children. The names of the angels are Sanoi, Sansenoi, and Samangelof. Even hearing those names makes her extremely uncomfortable and not a little sad. I'd suggest not even asking her about that period of time in her life, if I were you.

In general, Vampires have the gift of speed, Glamour, and the Beasts have the gift of Anubis. Basic Vampire weaknesses include religious objects and symbols, not just the Christian cross, but any religious icon displayed by the offending human. Everyone in the Hive of Redemption has a serious allergy to sacred objects. The stake is big, as is the iron rod. Again, though, the killing lance must pierce the heart and go through into the ground. This is harder than expected to do. The heart is a strong muscle and you are often fighting an entity that is much stronger than you and fighting for his life. The stake is rarely successful because of this and it only serves to piss the Vampire off.

There is one phenomenon that is characteristic only of the Tribe of the Tomb; millet seeds. If you think you're being harassed by a Vampire from this Tribe, which is highly unlikely since they can barely care for themselves, much less harass humans, you can spread millet seeds outside your door at night. If an Unfortunate happens to come across these seeds, they have to count them, every last one of them. I can't tell you how many Unfortunates have been caught by the rising sun because they've spent all night counting millet seeds they chanced upon. It's funny, but really kind of sad too.

"So there you have it. A short compendium of Vampire characteristics. What do you think?"

"I think I can't be more fascinated with you guys. I'm half tempted to ask to be transformed myself."

"Well, if you decide you want to, I'll do the deed," joked Orphaeus. But he was also being serious. He liked Agatha and wouldn't mind having her around forever. It'd be nice to have a writer as part of his family, but Orphaeus wasn't certain that Agatha would leave the East Coast for the wild and crazy West. If they discussed the possibility of Agatha joining his family with any shred of seriousness, he'd pose the question and make the offer officially.

They touched down, got their luggage, and hauled ass to the hotel in SoHo Orphaeus had booked. After a long rest while the sun stood guard over the object of their fascination, Orphaeus and Agatha found their way to the SoHo building to snoop around and wait for Kelat. Soon, they'd know for certain if the stone Agatha had was indeed the Augury of Gideon and they might achieve some revelation about Vampirism and the world in general, since Gideon after all was a prophet.

They sneaked into the building and took the stairs to the basement. When they walked in, they found Mephistopheles and Rebekah digging a new hole. Rebekah looked up and hissed, showing her long fangs. Mephistopheles immediately moved in front of Rebekah in an action of protection.

"Orphaeus?!" he said.

"You!" Orphaeus exclaimed. "Mephistopheles and Rebekah!"

"Son! How you doing?"

"Don't 'son' me! You transformed me and left me for dead."

"But look at you now," Rebekah said. "Flourishing and being your wonderful self. We knew you'd do okay. Why else would we leave?"

"Who is the mortal?" Mephistopheles asked suspiciously.

"Agatha Crawford. She may be in possession of a holy relic. It drew us here. We're waiting on Kelat."

"Auntie is coming?" Rebekah asked delightedly. "It'll be nice to see the old gal."

"Excuse me, who are these people?" Agatha asked fearfully.

"Oh," laughed Orphaeus a little bitterly. "Where are my manners? Agatha, meet Mephistopheles and Rebekah of the Hive of the Beast. They are my Blood parents. Mother, Father, meet Agatha Crawford. She's in possession of what could be the Augury of Gideon."

"Well, alright then," Mephistopheles said. "Let's kill her now, have a nice feast from her warm flesh, and take the Augury for our own, shall we?"

Orphaeus moved in front of Agatha and Agatha she peered over his shoulder, her eyes wide with fright. Were these Vampires really going to rip her asunder and drink her blood right there? They seemed so nonchalant about it, like she was nothing but food to them. Orphaeus introduced them as Beasts. Why did she keep ending up in association with the most dangerous Vampires in the

Great Hive? Why couldn't she have been associated with the classier Darkbloods or even the Redemption Clan, who usually possessed too much of a conscience to kill. No. She had to be in league with beings that discussed eating her flesh like it was a Sunday picnic outing to the local park.

"Why don't we find someone else to sacrifice their life for our subsistence," Orphaeus said. "Aggie is off limits, being a Vampire friend. And the Augury must stay in her possession until Kelat arrives to see what power it holds. It was given to Agatha by the last child of Gideon the Mad. From what I understand, it must be passed on willingly from one person to another. Paine trusted and loved Agatha enough to give the relic to Agatha before he died fighting Cadmus Pariah. We will do the same in his honour. Got me?"

Rebekah moved forward and looked at Agatha, then at Orphaeus.

"You've done well for yourself and you have a good conscience. Not the pathetic kind of conscience the Redemptors exhibit, but a good and true one. That's admirable. Agatha is safe around us; I give you my word as your Blood Mother."

A collective sigh of relief could be felt as the tension melted away. Orphaeus moved to one side and placed his arm around Agatha's shoulders. "So what is going on here?"

"We're trying to find the body of one Faust the Confessor. Know about him?" Mephistopheles asked.

"I got a fairly grotesque account of Faust's last days from Cadmus Pariah. Care to hear the story? It's a long one."

"We've got all night," said Rebekah. "And I'm tired of digging, if you must know. I'm starting to think we aren't supposed to find the body at all, if there is indeed a body."

"There's a body all right..." And Orphaeus began the tragic tale of Faust the Confessor and Cadmus Pariah. Agatha took notes furiously in between bouts of crying for this dreadfully sad Vampire who had the misfortune of grabbing the attention of the monster Cadmus.

CHAPTER 17
THE WELL OF MEMORIES

"Blend with the mob – their furious eyes, walk in their sleep, you can read 'em and weep. You can fear their disguise. Take it all to the crows at the end of the day, but the angels are here and they're holding your hand every step of the way" ~ Barry Andrews "Licking Honey from a Razor"

They were all asleep. After hours of hard discussion and bouts of bickering, the Vampires in the car with Dmitri had decided sleep might be the best recourse. They left Dmitri to drive in peace and, for that, he was eternally grateful. There was only so much of Thiyennen he could take before he leapt in the back seat and throttled the self-important, pious little git. Of course, it would mean a death sentence for him. Thiyennen was one of the Original Ten and more powerful than the other passengers in the car put together.

No, Dmitri didn't want to take that route. Instead he suggested everyone get some shut-eye while he drove into the deep Atlantic night. Alone with his thoughts, Dmitri tapped his well of memories and smiled as the face of Kelat came to him. He was always pleased when memories of Kelat drifted across his consciousness like a warm breeze in the English Spring. She was beautiful to him, pristine, and wonderful in every way. He could feel himself looking down at her, the genuine affection glowing in his face and exuding an emotion of unconditional love. There was also sadness. In the making of him, Kelat had instilled the need to seek out knowledge and philosophy, and this took him away from her side. They both agonized over this, but what was done was done. Dmitri was eternally dedicated to keeping in his vast mind the history of the people of Earth. He was often first to venture into new horizons here on Earth, and there was always something new to learn, something undiscovered and holy.

Kelat called him her Eternal Pioneer. He quested eternally for the answer as to why any of them were even here. He wanted mysteries solved, but he was never so thrilled as when he encountered a mystery that remained just that. Dmitri lived for the gathering of knowledge. It just broke his heart that this quest that drove his spirit often took him away from Kelat.

Kelat... His beautiful soul mate. They were not just lovers in Vampiric incarnation; they were eternal lovers, having traveled time and space through many incarnations, their souls seeking each other out like a parched man seeking water. It was an eternal decree that they should travel together. Dmitri touched his Well of Memories and watched as he and Kelat danced the reel of souls from one life to another, always in harmony with one another until the Apostate took Kelat hostage. Throughout an age, Kelat sought out the soul that would eventually become Dmitri. They suffered for having their dance interrupted by the curse of the Apostate. But it was a beautiful revelation when they finally found one another. Their hearts beat together and their spirits swirled like the triple helix of Kelat's Veiled Sanctuary.

Dmitri tapped the Well of Souls deeper to find a memory of him and Kelat before they'd found one another in this current incarnation.

There he was in a simple beige tunic roasting a brace of conies with some vegetables over a large fire. Beside him sat his Tarmian lover Lhihlhishian singing a song of the sea. He listened intently, envisioning the ocean and the sea spray, the call of the gulls. It was their wish to visit Meybhelahn, he and his wife. She was practicing the art of Singing the Sails.

It was a vision to behold, the Tarmian longships gliding flawlessly across the glass-like ocean, the Sail Singers standing on the masts, their arms entwined in rope, leaning forward over the waters. You had to be born with the ability to sing the sails. Lhihlhishian was one of those fortunate children and she longed for the sea with every fibre of her being. Alain, as he was known in this life, also wanted to sail the seas. He wanted to see the holy shores of Meybhelahn and learn the songs of that sacred place, for he was a musician and a singer of the Tarmian hymns of old.

Y'ma veth na pozhena mor
Ka'ya y'ma shredorlina sahr
U sa nori na emshi'shana
Dor'inna sor mora modra.

Across the sacred of seas
We utter the blessed tones
Hear me oh goddess of the deep waters
And I shall take repast in the blue beauty

This would be one of many songs sung by the Sail Singers as they began the journey to the western worlds. One last meal on the coast of Edai'gael'y and they would begin their journey. Dmitri listened to every song his lover sang and shivered with delight when his memories revealed the shining island many of this new age called Atlantis. Meybhelahn, his Avalon, beautiful and untouched by the trappings of the world. Here would he sing until it was time to journey into a new life. Life was never certain except that he knew he would always find his soul mate and, together, they would count the blessed memories between them and rejoice that they were once again together.

This rejoicing in the present life was always short-lived because Dmitri was compelled to journey the world, seeking out knowledge and the mysteries of Mother Earth. Of one thing he was certain, their reunion in New York would bring such gladness to his heart, Dmitri had to take a deep breath so the joy would have more room to inhabit his person. They had seen one another more this century than they had in the previous two centuries put together. After he left to chase the mysteries of the world in the fifteenth century, Dmitri and Kelat did not see one another again until the seventeenth century, when Dmitri visited France. They made love in the Canopy Ruins and communed as eternal souls forever bound to one another. No other joy could compare to the love he shared with Kelat.

He then moved on to another life, the one that always seemed to haunt him. He was being chased by villagers who called him a witch and would have his head on a pike. Kelat was there too. He couldn't remember their names. All he could remember was the killing blow on a high cliff where the smell of the ocean was one of such comfort as to make you weep. As he fell off the cliff, dying as he flew toward the water, he looked up and saw Kelat following him, her suicidal leap crushing him with sorrow, but the look in her eyes was one of unquestionable love. This life... If he could, he'd make the ending of this tale a much happier outcome. But it was always there...the cliff where Kelat proved to him that she would do anything for the love of her soul mate. She literally could not live without him, nor could he live without her. And that was the agony of the present, for they were separated so often and for so long.

"What are you thinking?" whispered Ishtar beside him.

"I was pulling moments from my Well of Memories. Every Vampire ends up with one, this deep, inexplicable liquid presence that allows us to relive our current past as well as past lives. Once you've been within the Hive for a while, you'll find your Well of Memories and will be able to explore it."

"Is it just your personal memories, or can you tap into the Hive memory?"

Dmitri cocked his head. "Believe it or not, I never thought about that. I see no reason why there wouldn't be a collective Well. I'm betting that anyone who tapped into the vastness of such a construct would surely go insane from beholding it all."

Dmitri then stopped, thinking.

"What is it?" Ishtar asked.

"I was just thinking...what if the Augury of Gideon is the Great Hive's Well of Memories. It might not be just prophecies or insights on the present, or what was Gideon's present at the time he inscribed the moment. Maybe Gideon went mad from tapping into the collective consciousness of the Great Hive. I don't think Kelat has even attempted something like that. I hope she never does."

"Maybe such a place as the Great Hive's Well of Memories is

reserved for the mad," offered Ishtar. "Maybe you have to be a little crazy to even comprehend its vastness. It might be like pondering yourself in the scheme and immensity of outer space; the further out you go, the less sane you feel as you realise just how tiny you are in the scheme of things."

"Perhaps you're right. When we get to New York, maybe we'll get an answer to that along with answers to many other mysteries. When Kelat becomes involved, you're sure to have an enlightening experience. I can't wait for you to meet her."

The night road seemed as endless the idea of the Great Hive's Well of Memories. They had just gotten on I-78, which would take about two hours to drive. Ishtar squeezed Dmitri's shoulder fondly and settled back in for more sleep. The soft even breathing of her and the others in the back seat comforted Dmitri in a way and he returned to his Well of Memories, summoning happier times.

CHAPTER 18
CADMUS' JOURNAL:
THE SCIENCE OF CONTROL

"Very little fruit is forbidden. Sometimes we wobble, sometimes we're strong. But you know evil is an exact science, being carefully correctly wrong.." ~ Shriekback "Nemesis"

Kelat is napping. Her incessant badgering about my emotions, or lack thereof, was driving me to distraction. Only around her do I feel like I'm losing control.

Control is everything. Without it misery is sure to follow. This is a truth I learned at a very early age, when Nissius began his litany of nightly abuses upon my young and nearly ageless body. If you are beaten mercilessly for crying because of some special torment, you learn to hold your breath, hold in everything you possibly can to avoid further punishment. You are taking on enough as it is; don't add to the agony of it.

There were some nights I would cry and take the beating because the beating would take away the pain of the other perverse acts Nissius had performed upon his apprentice. I took it as a lesson and allowed my body to release during the flogging, understanding how the flagellants might get the idea that their deeds brought them closer to their god. Ritual beating can create altered states of consciousness. I am almost certain that I saw the face of god on certain nights. That face was a leering, angry figure, hell-bent on the punishment of the living simply for having lived at all.

It has been centuries since I cried, but it has been almost as long since I was subject to the whims of Nissius Sanguinus. His abuses were all aimed toward the goal of perfect, emotionless control. He molded me well, very well indeed.

Kelat is so very different from Nissius. She seems a sad figure, but is also a vessel of such chaotic power, it's hard to believe that, when you look at her, you're looking at what is almost a Goddess made manifest. And, indeed, she has been mentioned in more than one holy book as a deity or a semi-divine being. The Hebrews in particular became obsessed with her early on. Some revere her as wise Goddess of the wisdom of the night; others view her as the night demon who steals away children and the sexual control of men.

Again, it's all about control. She is hated by many for her innate ability to make one lose control. Perhaps the Hebrews have twigged onto something when it comes to Kelat. Take away the owls and lions that repose beside her and all you have is a woeful figure lost in the desert of dreams.

I hate Kelat. I do not speak of the philosophical apex that mirrors hatred. I am talking about the actual emotion. Yes, I do feel that. It means that I have relinquished some of my control because only a neutral being can achieve perfect control, which is what I once had. Anger and hatred come to me easily, especially when I am in the presence of my mother. No matter what I do or say, she accepts me for all that I am and she loves me unconditionally. I know this because I tap into her psyche and see it there, swirling in magnificence, a bright and shining beacon calling to me to let go and fall under her sway.

I will not let her do it to me. She has taken away enough of my control.

When the time comes for me to achieve my apotheosis, she shall see her error. I will crucify her and drive spikes through her eyes so I will never have to look upon her silver-blue gaze of affection again. She will perish on a cross of her own making and her utterances of agony shall be as music to my ears.

I will crucify them all. When the relics are reunited and the final prophecies are revealed, then shall they know that their demise is nigh. I will hunt Kelat and her lapdogs down like the vermin they are and I will drive iron spikes into their bodies and raise their crosses in the deepest deserts of the Earth. There shall I behold them when the sun arises and takes away their sanity with the pain of fire and purification. My strength gained by walking the sun trials will allow me this luxury and will also allow me to see Kelat's prolonged pain since she, too, has walked the sun trial throughout her life. It only means that I can toy with her longer. I will immerse myself in the philosophical apex of joy when I tell her that her beloved Dmitri's head is resting on a pole beside her cross, his eyes upturned and blank as they stare at her with no hint of meaning. To listen to her weep from the knowing of this, but be blind to its reality, will gratify me and make all these times of misery in her presence worthwhile.

And when they are dead and the Vampire plague is but a memory to me, I will set myself above the world on a throne of bones and blood, and humanity will cry out with a great lamentation. I will punish them in every way conceivable for their weakness. Only the strongest amongst them will be allowed to remain in my presence and live, and they shall administer the torture I decree on their lesser man.

In Blood shall I bathe, my chalice forever full. The Blood Crown shall rest upon my brow and I shall be the only god of the Earth. This is what Gideon saw and this is what drove him mad. When the Augury is retrieved, the Truth of things shall be revealed and I shall afford myself the luxury of one more emotion; the feeling of utter triumph.

Until then, I must tap into my deepest reservoirs to find that silent void that is the seed of my control. I must practice the science of control and embrace what it seems I have always known. I am not that babe in the woods so sorely abused by his master. Not anymore. I am the master now and I will do everything it takes to maintain my control in the face of Kelat's chaos of emotion.

CHAPTER 19
THE WAITING AND THE HARE MOON

"I could come to you tonight, hold your hands and feel the world unravel. So tired of everything we know, see how the clichés flock like crows, pretty soon we're back to flint and gravel." ~ Shriekback "Bittersweet"

Kallum gazed in frustration at the Vampires assembled in the basement. No matter how much he infiltrated their dreams or gave them psychic proddings as to where his body was, none of them could seem to hear him or understand what he was trying to say to them.

Why do they not just dig me up? He asked Rosetta.

They don't know where you are. None of them know for certain and won't be able to find you at all.

Then what's the point in bringing them here?

The one who finds you has yet to arrive.

Ishtar, she's the one isn't she? He asked excitedly. *I knew there was something different in her.*

Yes. She'll be the one to find the buried jewel that you are. All you need is a little patience.

Don't the dead always have patience? I mean, what else can one have when one is a disembodied entity. My guess is that ghosts are the most patient creatures there are.

Rosetta laughed her bell-like angel laughter. *Indeed you are correct, but you are not a ghost, not by any stretch of the imagination. You are whole unto yourself, not a shade stuck between the worlds. Ishtar will be here soon, as will Kelat and Dmitri. When all are assembled, then shall you be found and some revelations shall be made.*

I just can't stand being like this for much longer. Either let me go home to my heaven or give me a body. I'd be happy with whatever choice God makes, just so long as it's soon. And what do you mean by calling me a buried jewel?

All shall be revealed in its time, young Kallum. All in good time.

Well, you could at least tell me a story while we wait. Kallum loved the stories that Rosetta shared with him. They spanned the gamut of religions and mythic poetry and they taught Kallum that not only his path was valid. He had come to realise that every path led to the same mountain, so he never balked at different religions in the stories Rosetta shared. He, in fact, thrived on such a thing, making him expand his horizons further and understand what he saw when he beheld the face of God, and why he beheld what he did.

Very well, I shall tell you a Tarmian story about our hare and rabbit brethren, Rosetta said merrily.

Daen Luma'Lieno Jonnsa
The Tale of the Hare Moon

Not very long after the great celebration of Mother Earth's boundless fertility, the animal and plant Goddess Artanis turned Her eyes to the deep heart of Etereh's woodlands wherein thrived the Fox nation, or the ti'kenda. They were a strong and healthy race, possessing the slyness and speed of the puma as well as the drive and vision of the wolf. The ti'kenda were perfect when it came to hunting, able to stalk and outrun any of their chosen prey, which could be any beast smaller than they, for the ti'kenda were not very discriminatory in their choice of food. Yet one animal that the ti'kenda refused to devour was the Ai'aafa.

The Ai'aafa was distasteful to the Fox. It was not a challenging hunt, nor was it friendly to the Fox's palate, weighing tough in the belly. It was small with tiny eyes, a blunt snout, and floppy ears that dangled uselessly. Moving in a shambling fashion, the ai'aafa was easily caught by members of the Fox nation, who took a special joy in slaughtering the ugly beast, leaving ai'aafa bodies strewn about uneaten and without honour.

The holocaust had continued until only one ai'aafa was there left, for it was that these beasts were not prone to procreation and keeping their nation alive. This lone ai'aafa it was that Artanis maiden of the Elderkin appeared before in the young evening of the Spring forests. She easily lifted him in Her arms before he could begin to amble away and She gazed upon him saying, "Little one, you are the last of your clan and you will not survive the ti'kenda's sport as you are now. And so I give you a new name and new hope for the new clan you shall lead."

"But how can this be, Mistress? I am but one now, and nothing but a slow and plodding thing."

"Nay," Artanis replied. "The ai'aafa are indeed no more. Henceforth you are Pnah'lienat, Father of the Runners."

And she drew the beast to Her until he dissolved into her bosom. That done, the Maiden of the Elderkin went seeking Krahl'ti'kenda, the king of the Sly Ones. She found the Fox King by the woodland streams, playing with his children. The Goddess sat down beside him, Her feathered tunic spread beneath her.

"Hello, Krahl'ti'kenda," She began. "I have been watching your sport, the ai'aafa hunt. Tell me Krahl, is their flesh that scrumptious?"

"Oh no, my Lady," the Fox King answered. "We kill ai'aafa because they are disdainful and distasteful to us. We are glad their kind is gone from Eterah."

"Are you now?" Artanis whispered as She touched Krahl lightly on the nose and the belly. The Fox King's stomach growled and grumbled, and his tongue grew wet with hunger. His children sniffed the air and ground for a food that was not forthcoming. Krahl'ti'kenda smelled this also and asked Artanis,

"What is this wonderful prey that we smell, my Lady?"

"Why Krahl'ti'kenda, that is ai'aafa! But it is an ai'aafa that your nation will crave like the fish crave water; an ai'aafa that will match your speed and your wits and will outnumber you ere you know it. This mysterious and alluring nation will be called Lienat, the Runners, and they are descended from the hated ai'aafa.

"You ti'kenda will want nothing but lienat, but rarely will you

111

catch one; rather you shall have to settle for a less appetizing meal more often than not. So happy hunting, O Fox Nation, for karma calls and your trials have commenced."

And, with that, Artanis left Krahl'ti'kenda, hungry and bewildered, and made Her way to Her mountain keep.

It was the first night of the Full Moon and time for the birth of a new race whom Artanis called lienat. Artanis lay upon Her downy couch, attended by great owl beings, and She went into labour, giving birth to the new-formed Pnah'lienat. He was sleek, with large eyes, powerful running legs, and a dainty nose. His features were marked and enhanced by large ears that stood erect, ready for any sound for miles around.

Following Pnah'lienat was the hare race, the lienat, all fully-grown with svelte bodies made for running. They dashed joyfully about the mountain halls, dancing and mating. Before Artanis was relieved of Her own labour, several female lienat gave birth to more lienat, this time babies.

Pnah'lienat came to the Goddess Artanis sometime after She had rested from her Labour, for She had summoned him, wanting to speak with him before the Hare Nation left to find their place throughout Eterah.

"Little father of the lienat, I wish to tell you of your nation's life on Eterah. Always shall you dwell upon the Earth but, know you this: the ti'kenda hunger mightily now for the lienat. And they shall strive to kill you, ignoring all other beasts if you are in their grasp. But the ti'kenda will succeed only when the lienat are not on guard. You are as wily as the Fox, and as swift. Use the gifts wisely and always be on the lookout, using your sharp eyes and ears, and the ti'kenda will have to settle for a less appetizing meal or go to bed with a hungry gut, unhappy and unfulfilled."

Artanis knelt and kissed the lieno king on the brow.

"Go you now to the plains and forests of Eterah. Dig mighty warrens and have great families. Bless Eterah as I bless you now by living and being happy.

So the lienat spread themselves across the face of Eterah, being as fertile as Mother Earth. Each year the Hare Nation would celebrate their genesis and give praise to Artanis Mnemen'lienat, Mother of the Runners, on the full moon after the Bealtainne. And it was henceforth called Luma'Lieno, the Hare Moon.

Kallum smiled widely. *Serves the fox right, eh Rosetta?*

Indeed, was her reply.

Tell me, Rosetta, are any of these stories, the Moon Myths of the Tarmi that you share with me true?

All myth possesses a mite of truth to it. You were fairly aware of that as a pre-Vampiric human and you certainly were more prone to believing such tales after you became a Vampire. Beforehand, you really didn't believe much in things such as Vampires. Rebekah and Mephistopheles educated you rather swiftly on that matter.

Ain't that the truth? I just wonder what the origin of these stories actually might have been. Was Artanis a real person, or was She an actual deity? Is she still around. Does anyone call out Her name in praise, or is She a long-dead Pagan Goddess that no one cares to know anymore?

As long as there are Tarmi on the Earth, Artanis' name and place among the gods is assured. Kelat is a priestess of Artanis so she will be heartened when she discovers you know some of the ancient tales. You, dear Kallum, are a vessel of mythic knowledge. When you beheld the Face of God, you were charged with keeping the old stories as faithfully as you do the books of the Bible. Every shred of myth is true because it sings to the heart of the listener. When you finally sing the song of Gideon, a certain holiness will possess you and, soon after, your job in this Earthly plain will be over. You can then come home.

Kallum's heart swelled at Rosetta's words. He wanted more than anything to go back to his heaven and dwell in perfect repose where no pain of his past could touch him or wake him from peaceful sleep. When you're in heaven, you have no nightmares, no flashbacks to the horror that took your life. Everything was simply...perfect. He would do what he needed to here, then surrender himself once more to his God in the hope that his heaven was still there waiting for him.

Rosetta? Kallum whispered as he hovered over the spot where his body lay.

Yes?

When I sing the song of Gideon, whatever that may be, will that bring a healing to these people who are drawn to my grave?

More than you can possibly imagine.

And will I be able to maintain my calm in the presence of Cadmus Pariah? I am afraid that my corporeal body will cringe in response to him and I may lose control.

I do not know, Kallum. The ways of the flesh can be a very different path than our bodiless forms. Whatever you do, remember that God loves and forgives all things. But I think you are stronger than you think. Remember, Cadmus lost his own control when you told him he had no power over you anymore. That still applies. Just believe in God and never doubt that I believe in you.

Kallum smiled, his spirit self shimmering in response to Rosetta's words. *I have the feeling this is gonna be a real gas. While I wait on Ishtar, I'll just keep poking around at the psychic peripheries of this motley bunch. So far, they've been great fun..*

CHAPTER 20
THE REUNION

"I will wait your return, I will watch from my window, I will sweep off the snow, I will trample your corn, Hold my arms out for ever, I can't leave you alone." ~ Shriekback "Hostage"

Two hours before Kelat's flight was to touch down at JFK International, Dmitri drove into New York.

"We must find a hotel before the sun rises," Thiyennen said. "Eve has no tolerance for the sun and I am still weak from my ordeal with Cadmus. I can't sustain long under the bitter rays of light."

"I've already got you a room booked at the Crosby Street Hotel. It's in SoHo where we've all been drawn, so I figured that'd be convenient. Yes?"

Thiyennen smiled at Dmitri. "Good thinking, son. I can see why my sister thinks so highly of you."

Dmitri returned the smile. Except for his bouts of zealotry, Thiyennen was actually a pleasant man. He was gentle, driven, and educated to the point of absurdity. Dmitri had the feeling that they could have endless conversations about philosophy and history, and never run out of anything to talk about. Despite their bickering over semantics, Thiyennen and Dmitri had come to like each other.

As the night became that ruddy dark that always heralded the coming sun, Dmitri pulled into a nearby parking garage and the Vampires all piled out of the car, got their luggage and hurried to the Crosby Street Hotel. They checked in; Dmitri, Eve, and Ishtar getting a nice suite, and Dmitri taking the smaller room for himself and Kelat. Once the Vampires were settled in their room and making ready for the coming sun by closing the drapes and putting the "Do Not Disturb" sign outside their door, Dmitri hailed a cab and went on to JFK to greet his soulmate.

Ishtar had asked Dmitri earlier how he knew what plane Kelat

115

would be on.

"I just know," he replied. "As soul mates, she and I share a link, a kind of bond that allows us to communicate on a certain level. It's mostly feelings instead of words. We know when we're far apart, or near to one another. I know she's coming in on the 6:45 flight from London. I know she's on a Virgin plane. A day ago, I didn't know so much because she was further away. All I knew was that we would come to be in New York within just a few hours' time. If you ever find your soul mate and he is a Vampire, you'll understand this bond."

Nibbling thoughtfully at her pinky finger, Ishtar said, "Maybe I already do. This connection I have to Kallum seems to be stronger than what the rest of you are feeling. It's like his presence is as natural and right as I feel when I'm about to fall asleep. There's a certain comfort and happiness in the knowing of him."

"You could be right. Once we get to where he might be, we'll see what happens. Whatever happens, it is sure to be a revelatory experience, especially with both Kelat and Thiyennen present. I'm more worried about their Beholding one another than I am Cadmus wreaking havoc on our little get-together."

He knew that Ishtar knew very little about what he was talking, but Dmitri was certain she'd learn soon enough. Ishtar was a quick study.

Dmitri got to JFK just minutes before the airplane taxied to its gate. He stood in the waiting area with about a hundred limo and taxi drivers, many of them carrying signs with the last name of the person they were supposed to pick up. Dmitri didn't need anything like that. He need only see Kelat's beautiful face to know she was there and with him once again. Baggage trailed along in a circle and people began to filter down to claim it as it revolved in a ballet of personal belongings. Dmitri watched intently as more people came down. Then he saw her...with Cadmus Pariah. Dmitri's heart leapt with both love and fear. His spirit didn't know whether to glow from having Kelat near him once again or compel him to charge the Pariah, pin him to the ground, and cut his throat. Of course, he wouldn't be successful. Cadmus Pariah was a hundred times stronger than Dmitri.

Kelat picked up the pace, leaving Cadmus behind. She walked up to Dmitri and they immediately placed their right hands on the other's cheek, touching foreheads as they communed in a way few mortals, or immortals for that matter, could comprehend. When Cadmus walked up, the soul mates separated and looked at him.

"The sun is rising. Do you think we could get our baggage and find refuge before this lovely journey becomes a sun trial. I am tired and I will not have my day begin with the discomfort of the sun."

"Charming as always, I see," Dmitri quipped.

They retrieved their bags and got a cab back to the hotel. Cadmus reserved a suite to himself a couple of floors above where the other Vampires were staying. Dmitri could only imagine the reaction his presence was going to garner from both Thiyennen and Eve. They were both convinced that Cadmus was the Devil himself and they could be right, but they were all here for a reason, so Dmitri simply accepted it and carried on. What else could he do? His primary concern was the safety of his soul mate, Kelat and that of his Blood child Ishtar. Everything else was secondary, but important nonetheless.

Once they were all settled in, Dmitri and Kelat sat in silence simply hugging one another. To feel her in his arms again was a blessing. Every time they came together, he hoped they'd never again be apart. Then the calling of the world would overtake Dmitri and he would have to go questing for the mysteries of the world. But, for now, they were together.

Slowly did he kiss her, feeling the warm reality of her lips against his. It was a gentle kiss, soft in its exploration of Kelat's tongue, lips, and the curve of her chin. She drew him more closely to her, wrapping her arms around his neck and mussing his hair with urgent hands. He could hear her heart beating and the Blood in her veins coursing furiously through her body. He wanted to taste her.

Picking Kelat up from the couch, Dmitri deposited her on the bed and crawled slowly up her frame to kiss her once again. As their kiss lingered on, Dmitri and Kelat removed one another's clothing so that their naked bodies could feel each other and sense the Blood that flowed through them.

Dmitri was already erect and ready for Kelat when she reached down and grabbed hold of him, guiding him into her. The warm presence of the two Vampires served only to excite them more as Dmitri moved inside Kelat, knowing every nuance of her secret self. When she took in a quick breath and lunged forward, so did Dmitri, and they found themselves in the sexual ecstasy of Ambrosciata. Sucking each other's blood with a fury that could crumble Roman ruins, the Vampires came together, their bodies writhing in the pure joy of their joining.

Slowly did they come down from their sexual high, and Dmitri wrapped his arms around Kelat as they lay together on the bed, drunk from the Blood.

"I love you," Dmitri said quietly.

"I love you, too."

"Tonight is going to be interesting."

"It always is when there's a relic to be had."

"It's the last one isn't it?"

Kelat nuzzled Dmitri's throat, licking the wound she'd made during their Ambrosciata. "Yes, which means that the story of us is coming to an end."

"What do you mean?"

"I brought the crown with me and Cadmus has the chalice. The relics are coming together. It has been rumoured that, once that happens, it will be an end to all Vampires. We may have come here to die."

"As long as I am by your side, I don't care if I die or not."

They hugged each other tightly and went to sleep, entwined in reunion.

CHAPTER 21
THE RESURRECTION

"Loud and proud and strong and wrong, gonna lift me up where I belong. Come grip the ladder with these cold hands, welcome baby to the month of sand." ~ Shriekback "Month of Sand"

Thiyennen did not sleep. He sat watching over Eve and Ishtar as they lay still as death in the sleep of the Vampire. He had tried to sleep at first, but the restless spirit that brought him here was close on the peripheries of his sleep urging him to come, come and find his body. Now that they were closer to the resting place of Faust, or Kallum McCreary as he was known in mortal form, the desire to seek him out was almost too much to bear.

The other two had heard the calling as well, but they did not seem to be phased by the proximity of their goal. Maybe it was because Kallum was Christian and therefore felt a closer affinity to Thiyennen. Whatever it was, the king Vampire was ready to be finished with this.

He paced the floor, read the literature left in their room about the hotel's many amenities, and thought the entire afternoon. When the sun began to set, the phone rang.

"Hello?"

"Thiyennen, it's Dmitri."

"Yes, Dmitri. Are you well?"

"Very well, thank you Thiyennen. I wanted to talk to you before we head over to Bleecker Street. Kelat is in town. She heard the calling as well and she wants to be present when we find Kallum's body. I know there's a risk of Beholding, but you both really need to be there when we find him. Are you amenable to wearing glasses that prevent peripheral vision and the two of you being placed to where neither can see the other? Kelat brought them in anticipation of the two of you being here."

Thiyennen thought in silence. Kelat, once his beloved sister, now his immortal adversary, the queen of the Great Hive, the very

119

core of the soul of Vampiredom. He wasn't sure if he could do what Dmitri was suggesting. In a way, it would be so much easier for the two of them to Behold one another and be done with this Vale of Tears.

No... He would not do it. There was still hope for redemption, Dmitri felt. From what he'd been told by this restless spirit, he mortated before dying, and he had been redeemed in the great all-seeing Eyes of God.

"Thiyennen?"

"Yes, yes, sorry Dmitri. What you suggest sounds like a logical plan. Bring over the glasses whenever you're ready to go. We'll take separate cars over, naturally."

"One more thing, Thiyennen."

"Yes?" Thiyennen prodded, his Blood running cold from what he knew Dmitri would say next.

"Cadmus Pariah is here as well. He was on the same plane as Kelat. He knows exactly which building we have to go to, so he'll be riding with Kelat and me. Are you going to be okay with this?"

"Cadmus..." Dmitri immediately found himself in a flashback to being crucified by his son. He rubbed the scar on his throat where the iron spike had been driven. "Oh my God."

"Thiyennen, are you with us?" Dmitri asked gently. "Remember, we've all been called for a purpose; we all need to be there for when Kallum is found."

"Yes, of course. I'm on board no matter what..."

"I'll be over with the glasses then. Please wake Ishtar and Eve and prepare Eve. She won't be happy to hear that Cadmus is here, not at all."

"I'll see you shortly then."

Thiyennen hung up the phone and roused Eve and Ishtar. When he told Eve that Cadmus was in town and would be accompanying them to Kallum's resting place, she broke down, weeping as though her heart would break. Both Ishtar and Thiyennen comforted her and cajoled her into accompanying them. She always knew that there was a good chance Cadmus

120

would be there, but the actual physical reality of it was still jolting to Eve's soul. Eve was still crying when Dmitri arrived with the glasses for Thiyennen.

Thiyennen took the glasses and inspected them. They were a lot like the wrap-arounds worn so much in the 1980s, but larger. The front of the glasses were cut out so vision wasn't hampered and the sides were painted a dark black acrylic. There was no way you could accidently see what was beside you with these glasses on. As long as you were careful of where you looked straight ahead, you'd be safe. In a way, Thiyennen felt a bit like a horse with blinders on, but it was necessary if he were to be in his sister's presence.

He looked over to find Dmitri talking to Eve.

"I promise I will do everything within my power to protect you from Cadmus. I may fail, but you need to know that everyone present will do the same as I. If it has to be a group effort to keep Cadmus from touching you, I promise you we will do it. You are precious to Kelat, being the last human to be touched by the spirit of what you call Atlantis. Nothing will happen to you as long as Kelat is around. Just stay near to us when we get to our destination and I assure you, all will be well."

"I hope so Dmitri, I really do. For too many years I've borne the burden of being Cadmus' bride and I am so weary of performing my duties as his garden of Blood. It has been a long time since he has visited me, I'm sure he's eager to get his hands on me again. I will have to feed sometime tonight. After I do, he will want me, and that scares me to the point of being paralysed right here. Please don't let it happen, Dmitri. Please don't let him near me."

"I promise I will do my best. As for feeding tonight, Thiyennen, could you feed Eve and Ishtar tonight so none of us will have to go out hunting. It will be a way to prevent Cadmus having any one of us to himself."

Thiyennen nodded. "Good thinking, Dmitri. I'm sorry we have not made acquaintance sooner, lad. You're smart and sensible, so much like your past incarnations. I see now why Kelat loves you so."

"Thank you, Thiyennen. That means a lot. I should be getting back to Kelat now. Cadmus will be riding with us. I've reserved two cars to take us where we need to go. Cadmus knows the exact street and building, so we won't have to depend upon the beacon we're all feeling. I imagine you didn't rest at all, did you, Thiyennen? The older and more powerful you are, the greater the beacon, according to Kelat, who remained up all day. Even I was bothered with it, but I still got a little sleep. Anyway, I'll call you when we're heading down. Wait a couple of minutes then come down yourself. This way we can protect you and Kelat from one another."

"Sounds perfect. We'll be ready."

A few minutes later, the phone rang. Ishtar answered. She nodded and said okay, then hung up the phone.

"It was Dmitri. Time to head on down. He said not to forget the glasses and suggested that you feed us on our way over to the apartment building."

When they got downstairs, Dmitri was waiting for them. There were no cars waiting for them. Thiyennen could see in the dusk two dark figures walking down the street.

"What happened to the drivers?" asked Thiyennen.

"We don't need them," Dmitri said. "Cadmus said that where we're going is only a half mile away. The building is on Bleecker Street. He's taking Kelat on to our destination and I'm staying behind to help you feed our ladies. Don't worry, Cadmus gave me directions and, even if I take a wrong turn, I think the beacon will help us find our way. No wonder it was unsettling to you and Kelat. We're practically on top of Kallum already."

They actually went back upstairs to Thiyennen's room to have the needed privacy to feed Ishtar and Eve. It didn't take long because the Blood was more filling than human blood would have been. Sated, Eve and Ishtar joined Thiyennen and Dmitri as they walked to their destination, veering onto Broadway from Prince

122

Street, then right on to Bleecker Street. Thiyennen put on his glasses and they entered the building, taking the stairs downward to the basement.

"Oh great, and the party just gets bigger and weirder!" exclaimed a beautiful Vampiress. "Meph can you believe this? I mean really? Really? I feel like we're taking part in a royal fete being held in some chamber in Hell. Who the hell are you people!?"

"This is Thiyennen – " Dmitri began..

"I know who he is, he's my dad," Rebekah quipped.

"Yours, too?" Ishtar asked in wonderment. She looked around at the assembled Vampires. Meph and the yet-to-be-identified Vampiress were in a two foot hole, holding a pick and a shovel. A red-haired Vampire was crouched, baring his fangs at a bald Vampire who stood with Kelat, who needed no introduction. Kelat simply *was* in all her glory. She wore the glasses that waylaid her peripheral vision and she stood in a manner that prevented her seeing Thiyennen when he arrived. There was a very frightened mortal standing with the crouched Vampire.

"Maybe it's best if we all just introduce ourselves before we actively begin seeking the body of Faust," Kelat said diplomatically. "My name is Kelat. I am the Hive Queen and one of the Original Ten."

She touched Cadmus' shoulder and Cadmus moved away from her touch, but complied with her wishes. "I am Cadmus, also called Pariah. I am the child of Kelat and Thiyennen and was once an agent of the Apostate. I killed the man whose body you seem so keen on digging up tonight."

"My name is Rebekah, the Dhampir child of Thiyennen. Mother Kelat brought me over centuries ago, essentially creating the beginning of the Hive of the Beast."

"I'm Mephistopheles, Rebekah's life mate and partner in crime. The two of us are the ones who performed Infusciata upon Kallum and transformed him into Faust. We are his Blood parents."

"I am Orphaeus Cygnus, Blood child of Rebekah and

Mephistopheles, and sworn enemy of Cadmus Pariah."

"I-uh...I am Agatha Crawford and I have no idea what I'm doing here."

"My name is Eve, the bride to Cadmus Pariah, and his sworn enemy."

"My name is Thiyennen Vathyella and I am the Hive King, I am also the father of the Hive of Redemption."

"I am Dmitri Oskarov, life mate to Kelat, and her sworn guardian."

"I am Ishtar, Dhampir child of Thiyennen, and Blood child of Dmitri," Ishtar said self-consciously. "And I know where the body of Kallum McCreary rests."

"Well it's about freakin' time somebody did," Rebekah said. "I'm starting to feel like a goddamned prairie dog. Come on over here, little sister, and point us in the right direction."

Ishtar stepped across the dirt floor, dodging the occasional piece of concrete Rebekah and Mephistopheles and cast off to one side. There were several digs already abandoned which mean not many places were left where the Vampires hadn't been digging.

"Here," Ishtar said, pointing at one of three sites yet to be excavated.

"You have got to be kidding me," Rebekah said. "Meph, did you not suggest that spot when we first got here?"

"I'm afraid I did, Bek."

"Well slap my ass and call me Susan. We've been going around in circles and – wait...how do you know for sure, little sister?"

"Because he just told me."

"Why everyone is so hell-bent on digging up the bones of a supposed Vampire martyr is beyond my comprehension," purred Cadmus to one side as he shielded Kelat from Thiyennen's vision. "It's like I told the Swan over there, I left his supposed incorruptible body behind a series of *geasa* so that it would eventually putrefy in the loneliness of this place. It was over thirty years ago, I don't see why everyone is on about this now."

"Of course you'd say that, Pariah," spat Orphaeus as he got the extra shovel and began digging along with Rebekah and Mephistopheles. "But he's the key to the Augury of Gideon and we can only hope that his body is perfect in repose, still, truly incorruptible. It distresses you that you may have had a hand in the creation of a Vampire saint."

"It distresses me that I find myself in the company of idiots and their apparent children. This is some kind of sick family reunion that I'm tempted to bring to an end by forcing Kelat to Behold Thiyennen."

"Don't even joke about that, Cadmus," Kelat said. "You know you're here for a deeply important purpose. Your role in retrieving the Vampire Relics has been a major one. We cannot do this without you, even though some here might wish we could."

"I do not joke."

"To hell you don't," Orphaeus said. You showed quite the sense of humour when we traveled to Rome.

"You lie."

"Enough!" Thiyennen roared, showing an extraordinary side of him, the spirit of command.

The room went silent and remained that way for several moments. It was Rebekah who broke the muted discomfort by asking,

"Should we continue digging then?"

"By all means," both Kelat and Thiyennen said.

"Don't use the pick, though," Ishtar said. He's not very deep. We don't want to harm him.

Four Vampires – Rebekah, Ishtar, Mephistopheles, and Orphaeus dug with shovels and plastic bowls found near the washer and dryer. They soon came upon the mortated and incorruptible body of Faust the Confessor. His eyes were closed, dusty lashes resting on his cheek in holy repose. Mephistopheles pulled him free from his decades-long grave and dusted him off as best as he could. Agatha found a spigot and brought a bowl of water over with a lost tee shirt near the washer. Ripping the tee shirt in half, she and Ishtar began to clean his skin, revealing a vibrant, albeit completely dead body.

"How does something like this happen?" Agatha asked

"He's obviously sainted," Orphaeus said, his Catholic inclinations coming out.

"Why doesn't he just wake up?" Rebekah said. "It's obvious that his spirit is hanging about and wanted us to dig him up. Just inhabit the body already."

"Something must trigger it," Kelat said.

"OW!" Exclaimed Ishtar, moving her finger to her lips. "Be careful Agatha, there's something sharp here in the dirt.

Agatha went exploring and found the offending item – a knife of great antiquity.

"That would be mine," Cadmus said walking toward Agatha. "I must have left it when I left this accursed place behind in 1977. Agatha back-pedaled frantically, staying as far away from Cadmus as she could.   She dropped the knife and Cadmus knelt, his eyes on Agatha. He lifted his eyebrows and blinked slowly. "What's the matter Agatha?   Afraid I shall do to you what I did to Paine Bryerson?   Just so you know, you're hardly worth the vague disinterest that I'm exhibiting to you right now. You've nothing to fear...yet. Relax."

"Does anyone have a Band-Aid or something?" Ishtar said.

"You won't need one," Dmitri said. "It will heal on its own in just a few moments."

"Wow really?" Ishtar said with delight, turning to meet Dmitri's gaze. A drop of her Blood fell onto the perfectly still face of Faust and it trailed into the corner of his mouth.

The Confessor's eyes flew open, two orbs of cerulean surprise and he croaked in two great lungs-full of air.   Everyone but Cadmus jumped feet away from the Confessor.   Then Rebekah quickly soaked the tee shirt with fresh water and ran over to him, squeezing water into his mouth.

"What happened, what happened," Ishtar said, looking at her already-healing finger. "What the fuck, I didn't do anything!"

126

"I think it was the Blood. You don't heal as quickly since you're still in your swaddling, so to speak," Dmitri said. "The Blood of the innocent quickened the heart of the saint."

"Wh-where am I?" that all-too-familiar voice said to no one in particular, but it already rankled Cadmus' nerves.

"You're in the basement of what was your old apartment building," Orphaeus said gently. "We thought you were dead."

The confessor crinkled his eyebrows. "I thought I was too. I vaguely remember...what happened? And...aren't you Rebekah?"

"You shred it, wheat!" Rebekah said, using the slang she knew Faust would understand. Then she said more gently, "welcome back, Faust."

"Not...Faust. Kallum. It was...the Blood."

All eyes turned to Ishtar. "I...I didn't do anything."

Rebekah continued where Agatha left off, cleaning Kallum's pottery-coloured face to reveal the living flesh beneath. He was truly alive, just like Cadmus, but in a different kind of way, being resurrected by the Blood. Where Cadmus was a living Vampire, Kallum was truly human, a Vampire who had mortated, but been resurrected into the Night Clans as a redeemed soul. It was too much to comprehend in a way. Rebekah just shook her head and continued to clean Kallum's face.

Mephistopheles brought a bucket of water over to Kallum, who dipped his hands in the cooling liquid and drank hungrily.

"Oh thank God, thank God! I was so thirsty!"

"But not for Blood?" Rebekah asked incredulously.

Kallum picked up the bucket and dumped the contents over his head, then shook his wavy hair free of the excess liquid, grinning like a guilty child who didn't care that he'd gotten caught. "No, Rebekah. I think I'm beyond that," he said, slowly coming into his own as a corporeal entity. "I think I know why I'm back. And I think I know why it is that Cadmus...Pariah, is it?...has this strange desire to scram at the moment. Why don't you come out of those shadows, ya pill, so I can punch you one good one?"

Cadmus emerged and was suddenly in Kallum's face. "I could

snap your neck in an instant. Care to have to heal from the damage I could do to your body *again* for the witness of all here? I have no qualms about doing it. Murdering you repeatedly could become my new hobby. That would make me happy as a clam."

Then, just as suddenly, Kallum changed the subject. "You nice people wouldn't happen to have any extra clothes on you, would you? It seems like ages since I was allowed to wear any...Isn't that right, Cadmus Pariah?"

"Do not worry about that," Kelat said. "Dmitri, can you take Ishtar and get Kallum some clothes while we decide what to do next?"

As Dmitri and Ishtar left, Kallum shyly wrapped the larger piece of tee shirt around his waist and sat up, looking at everyone. His eyes lingered on Rebekah and Mephistopheles.

"You can't believe how many nights I agonized over who you might have been and why you did what you did to me. Care to clear it up now? I have the feeling I won't be afforded the time to continue my studies and research, not that any of my books survived the apparent demolition of my old apartment. How else did I end up buried beneath this building when my body was left in the apartment, hidden by layers of *geasa*, courtesy of Cadmus Pariah, in all his infernal glory?"

"It's just what we do, Kallum," Mephistopheles said. "It wasn't our intention to mark you with what became your quest in immortality. A Vampire seeking God is much like a lion trying to become a vegetarian. It's not going to happen."

"Oh, but it did happen! I had to have the curse of what you made me tortured out of me, but it happened. Even now, I can feel the presence of my angel, Rosetta, lingering near to me. I saw the Face of God and I was brought into that state of grace, thanks to Cadmus' crude acts upon my person. But I'm back now, at least for a little while, and I still have questions. Why me, for instance?"

"Why not?" Rebekah said. "It was just something that we do. We turn creative people. Orphaeus here, he's your brother. He has his own opera house and theatre, and a family of creative

Vampires that perform and delight every night. And, some nights, they engage in the Bloodbath and dream of new ways to entertain and enchant their numerous fans and curious onlookers. You yourself came into the Blood with the special ability to draw people to you. It wasn't the Glamour, although you had a great deal of that, it was your natural ability to love and listen, and make both sinners and saints feel as though their own lives were worthy of themselves and whatever God they cried out to in the night. We saw in you a special something that we didn't want to see die. So we made you immortal. Simple as that, kiddo. Simple as that."

Kallum stared at Rebekah with those endless cerulean eyes and he smiled slowly. "Thank you for telling me," he whispered, his smile filled with Scottish charm. "And thank you for the years of dancing, singing, and acting. I would never have had the chance to fulfill my dreams in the way I did, had it not been for your blessing me with the Blood. I would never have become the Confessor of so many souls who needed peace. Thank you, Rebekah. Thank you, Mephistopheles."

"You're very welcome," Meph said, sounding a little choked up.

"Shall we sit and talk? Come, let's form a circle," Kelat suggested. "Thiyennen, if you don't mind sitting beside me, we can make this happen without our peripheral vision."

"I don't mind, sister." Thiyennen made his way to the hole in which they had found Kallum. He sat down next to Agatha. Then Cadmus guided Kelat, who kept her eyes closed, to the forming circle. She sat beside her brother and took his hand, squeezing it fondly. He returned the affection, much to her surprise. Cadmus sat down beside his mother and Orphaeus took his seat beside Cadmus, basically just to piss him off, which worked. Mephistopheles and Rebekah rested beside Orphaeus and they left room for Ishtar and Dmitri, upon their return.

Everyone introduced themselves to Kallum and told him that they had been drawn to this place by his disembodied spirit.

"I barely remember any of that. Once you're corporeal again, the spirit world seems so very far away. I think it's like when you're reincarnated, if that even actually happens – "

"It does," interrupted Kelat.

"Okay, it does. When the spirit returns in a new body, it's hard to remember anything prior to that happening. It might be some spiritual fail safe so the spirit doesn't suffer. That's the last thing God wants is for His children to ever suffer, even though suffering seems to be a common theme in the scheme of things. I know I certainly received my dose of suffering and then some."

Kallum gazed at Cadmus and a silence formed between them, lacing in amongst the undying azure gaze like a filigree of Celtic knot work.

About that time, Orphaeus and Ishtar returned with some clothes. A Joker tee-shirt that said 'Why so serious?' on it and a pair of blue jeans, along with some new Birkenstocks. "What no undies?" joked Kallum. "Guess I'll be going Commando then."

The Confessor stood and quickly donned the outfit. The Birks were a tad large, but functional. Kallum was happy. He sat down again and was joined to his left by Ishtar and Dmitri. Before he knew it, he took Ishtar's hand.

"So why are we all here?" Kallum asked.

"We were hoping you'd tell *us* that," Mephistopheles said.

"One thing you could tell us," Agatha ventured, feeling a bit self-conscious because she wasn't a Vampire. "Do you know what this is?"

Agatha reached into the breast pocket of her vest and drew out a dark red jewel, handing it carefully to Kallum.

The minute the jewel hit Kallum's hand, he knew...

"He handed it to me. He talked about genetics and the science of memory. He was forming a seed of remembrance for the ones he chose to carry on the legacy. It was tiny then, just a hint of a pebble then. It's so large now. Like a robin's egg, and so beautiful."

"What is it?" prodded Agatha, her Inner Reporter taking over once again.

130

"It is the Augury of Gideon. Everything he ever knew and saw rolled into this ruby of Blood. He had learned the art of programming cellular memory and anyone he voluntarily gave the Augury to could unlock its secrets and know everything he knew. He wasn't so mad as he was unstuck in time, knowing everything and unable to share it with anyone. He was everywhere and nowhere simultaneously. He worked religiously on this and was going to give it to me, but he saw what was going to happen to me, so he chose a Vampire named Paine to be his prophet. Where is Paine?"

"Paine is dead..." Agatha said. "Before he was killed...by Cadmus...he gave the jewel to me. I've had it for a few years now, never knowing how important it was."

"And now you've given it back to me. Since I was resurrected by the Blood, I should be able to decode the Augury, if that's what you all want. I'm getting slight visions now, but nothing tangible. I'm not certain how it's supposed to work."

"It's Blood," Kelat said. "Vampires drink it. Perhaps you are supposed to ingest the Augury for it to happen."

"That's not reuniting the Relics, though," Thiyennen said. "The one prophecy of Gideon that I do know is that everything will be revealed when all three relics are placed together in sacred space. I'd say this is not a sacred space and Kallum swallowing the Augury would probably only serve to give him serious indigestion."

Kelat squeezed her bag to her. She wondered if perhaps she should bring out the Blood Crown and demand that Cadmus produce the chalice, which she knew he carried on his person at all times. But this was not a holy place. This was an apartment building in the heart of SoHo in New York City. It then occurred to Kelat that the only holy place there might be that would even remotely work, other than her Veiled Sanctuary, was the Canopy Ruins.

"We need to go to France, outside Carcassonne," Kelat said carefully.

"What is there?" asked Thiyennen.

"The last hidden Tarmian refuge of worship." Kelat felt Thiyennen tense up. "I call it my Canopy Ruins for it is a great ring of trees that form a circle, which is cleft by a small pristine stream. It is open to all faiths and is perhaps the holiest place on Earth, save for my Veiled Sanctuary in Israel.

"Why could we not go to Israel?" Thiyennen asked. It would seem to me to be more amenable to those of us who follow the Bible.

"My Veiled Sanctuary holds my triple helix and is my Vampiric refuge. It's wholly dedicated to the Tarmian way and Tarmian magick by way of my Vampiric self. It would not be as open to different faiths as would the Canopy Ruins."

"Why could we not just go to a local church?"

"There are some here who would perish just by walking into a church. At least the holiness of the Canopy Ruins would not affect Vampires in such a way. Thiyennen, please. Do you not want to know how this ends? There's a possibility that we could all be healed of this curse. Are you not willing to do what it takes to learn what it was that Gideon saw?"

Thiyennen thought. There was a logic to Kelat's argument, but Thiyennen agonized over it. He felt like he was going backward. Just because he was of Tarmian descent didn't mean that his Christian inclination should be ignored.

"Would our convergence there be open to Christian presence?"

"Of course it would. If you remember, Thiyennen, the Tarmian way was open to people of all faiths. You didn't have to believe in Artanis to join in worship with the Tarmi."

"I'd love to go," piped up Kallum. "But I'm afraid I don't have a valid passport anymore, having been dead for the past – "he looked at Cadmus accusingly. "How long?"

"Thirty long years, you silly git. Couldn't your angel tell you that?"

"You can shut up about Rosetta."

"You dare speak to me like that. I'd as soon slit your throat right now as look at you. The only reason you're still alive right now is because of your importance in regard to the Augury of Gideon. As soon as your use is fulfilled, rest assured I'll take pleasure in killing you all over again."

"Don't worry, Kal," Rebekah said comfortingly. "Meph and I will get you one before the night is through. Meph you got your digital camera on you?"

"I do indeed," he said, pulling out a small camera. "Say fromage, Kallum. We're getting you a passport on the fly."

Kallum said cheese and his picture displayed a wet-haired youth with a goofy smile on his face.

"We'll be back before you can say 'shady dealings,'" said Rebekah, and she and Mephistopheles left the circle, which closed to form an even tighter klatch.

Kallum placed the Augury of Gideon on the ground in the middle of the circle. They all looked at the small jeweled circle, seemingly an uncut garnet or ruby, unimportant in its being, but possessed of so much treasure it was hard to comprehend. What scientists knew now about how cells can contain so much more than initially thought because of how the DNA is constructed. Genetic memory became a reality in certain scientific circles. That being the case, the Augury of Gideon, this small jewel of petrified Blood could be likened to a super computer, filled with so much data, it was nearly inconceivable.

"So it's all about this, then, is it?" Kallum asked.

"It would seem so," Kelat said. "And how do you feel about your role in the prophecies of Vampires?"

Kallum thought for a minute and his mind returned to that crippled Vampire he'd found on the street during the Great Depression. Vampires were really not that different than humans. They had the same emotions and fears, they cried, and they formed attachments to one another. Seeing the rapport Rebekah had with Mephistopheles made Kallum smile in spite of himself. Really the only aberration he could see among the Vampires assembled with him on this night was Cadmus Pariah.

"I'm fine with my role in the prophecies, but I'm afraid what might be revealed might not be exactly what any of you are expecting."

"Do you say this from a fore-knowledge or just a personal feeling?"

"Just a personal feeling. When I hold the Augury, I get flashes of things, but nothing is really concrete. It's all just an unintelligible mishmash. It's all balled up."

"And do you remember much from your time in the afterlife?"

"I knew everything when I woke up, but most all of it is gone now. Like I said, I think we're wired to forget so that we can learn all new things in each life. To me, and I could be wrong here, God is like a giant puzzle that exploded with the Big Bang. We're each a piece of that puzzle and we are strewn throughout the universe of his body accumulating information. When we've learned all we could, our piece is returned to the puzzle that's being assimilated and, once the puzzle is complete and we're all home, God will know who and what he is."

"You're a wise child," Kelat said, smiling at Kallum. "Very wise, indeed."

"I just studied a lot when I was Faust. My goal was to see the Face of God. I achieved my goal by way of blood and suffering, but at least I made it home." Kallum responded to Kelat slowly, never moving his eyes away from Cadmus' black hole gaze. "And I will make it home again after all of this."

"What exactly do you mean?" Agatha asked, picking up the Augury and placing it back in her pocket. As far as she was concerned, she was the relic's guardian until Kelat said so. It was the last thing Paine had given to her and she treasured it more than she realized until this convergence.

"I mean that, once the Augury is revealed and the prophecies are fulfilled, I will die."

"You say that so nonchalantly."

"I can since I've already died once that I remember. It really is no big deal, especially if you've got the guidance of a being from the otherworld. I was blessed in my tribulation. When I realized that I had been blessed and had become mortal again, I knew that Cadmus would kill me and release me from the torments he had been visiting on me for a month or more. I was ready to die; I embraced the idea of holy respite. And that is what was rewarded me as I crossed over.

"Cadmus how have you been, jelly bean?"

"That's an insulting term in your strange vernacular, isn't it?"

"'S'not for me to say. Really though, how've you been? You seem a little stressed."

"I have not been sleeping because *you* have haunted my dreams for the past few weeks. No amount of Blood relieved the stress I've been feeling over not sleeping. Unlike the Vampires, I *have* to sleep, and you have prevented it with your sing-a-long songs, unending babblings in Depression-speak, and basic idiocy ~ just anything to torment me."

"I don't remember any of that," said Kallum, not hiding his guilt.

Ishtar laughed. "You do remember that!"

Kallum nodded and giggled, leaning in toward Ishtar. "You bet I do, Doll!"

"Go ahead," growled Cadmus, a murderous look on his face as he stared down both Kallum and Ishtar. "Laugh all you want. Your laughter will be the cackling of the damned once you realise your fate from the Augury."

"Just stop it with the threats, okay Cadmus?" Orphaeus groused. "We're all trying to figure out what happened and why we were called here. It's obviously having to do with the Augury there in Aggie's pocket. And, Kallum, it's great to meet you. After having heard the story of your and Cadmus' last encounter, I can't tell you how glad I am to see you intact and happy to be alive."

"Orphaeus, is it? Yeah, I try to be happy no matter where I am or whom I'm with, or however that old saying goes. I just think that Cadmus might be a little surprised with the biting wit and wry humour I came back with. Thirty years is a long time to mull over how I might encounter you again, egg. Seems we'll be spending some time together while we work this whole Augury thing out, so we may as well try to enjoy ourselves. What say I taunt and make fun of you and you fume and throw empty threats my way?"

"This is not the Faust I encountered in the 70s," Cadmus said to Orphaeus. "Faust had an irresistible charm."

"I'm not Faust," Kallum said. "You killed Faust. I'm Kallum. Don't forget it. So tell me, who is this Joker fellow on my shirt? He looks nothing like Cesar Romero. Am I missing something?"

"We're back!" Mephistopheles exclaimed. "It's amazing the fine work you can get when you flash enough money on the streets. Kallum, consider yourself an official world traveler!"

Meph flashed what looked like the real thing. The hacker even made Kallum look a little better instead of like a wet pup on the Jersey shore.

"Nothing I love more than swift and excellent service. The New York Mob is so agreeable and effective at what they do, too," quipped Rebekah. "I should have gotten my passport renewed, now that I think about it."

"Oh thanks, guys!" Kallum said, looking at his new passport with relish. "So when are we off to France?"

CHAPTER 22
ISHTAR AND KALLUM

Rosy sees the dawn in through her calm lion's eyes -cuts a dashing figure in the gloom. The Tigris and Euphrates the Jordan and the Nile gush out from the corners of her room. So I say: 'blow me no more kisses, Scrape me no more bones. Talk to me of ecstasies of flesh and stone. Let's ask for absolution one more time: God's gardenias rain on me...'" ~ Shriekback "Gods Gardenias"

The Vampires had Cadmus take out his computer so they could book a flight together to Carcassonne International Airport. From there they could ride out of town into the country, where they would then hike into the forests where there stood hidden in pristine beauty the Canopy Ruins.

The first flight that could accommodate twelve first class seats that flew to France overnight was an Air France flight in two days time. This would give Kallum the chance to get more clothes and time to learn a little bit about what he called "this brave new world." He was particularly intrigued by the Internet and who else more qualified to show him around the 'Net than young Ishtar.

While the Vampires mentally circled one another over centuries of politics and religious paranoia, Ishtar, the young human turned Vampire and Kallum, the young Vampire turned human got along fabulously. It was magickal to behold and Kelat took the time to notice it and smile. They spent their time at a nearby Internet café, drinking coffees that were barely legal for their lethal combination of caffeine, and Ishtar would show Kallum the highlights of the Internet.

Kallum became particularly fond of You Tube and was intrigued by the whole 'Bukket Saga' involving that poor lolrus (wasn't that walrus?) who had lost his precious bucket. It was funny, but sad too. Ishtar showed Kallum her Facebook, which she'd changed to include her Vampire name as well.

"Won't your friends find you intolerable to be around?"

"Well, I never had many friends as it was but the ones I do have are golden and will stick by me no matter what."

"That's a sign of a good friend, that is! This Internet thing is just aces. Do you think I could start my own Facebook?"

"Sure, we could set you up one right now. Facebook is more for networking but, if you want to write in a journal, I'd suggest Blogspot, Wordpress, or Livejournal. I heard Kelat and Dmitri talking about Cadmus last night. Seems Cadmus has a Livejournal in which he writes, or tries to write, every single day. We could look him up, if you want to."

"That would be the berries, Ishtar!"

Ishtar leaned across him to type a few things into the computer and he could smell the clean linen of her blouse combining with the sweetness of her skin. Her coppery hair fell across his lap. Very carefully did he lift two fingers to feel the softness of her hair in his lap. It felt like rabbit fur it was so soft and Kallum smiled, his heart swelling.

"Ishtar."

"Mmhmm?"

"Thank you for finding me."

Ishtar looked up at Kallum, her face just an inch away from his, and she blushed. "Thanks for having faith in me. Not sure if you remember visiting me in my dreams, but I feel like you called the people you thought were strong enough for...for whatever this is going to be. Thank you for having faith in me. Not many people ever have."

Before they knew it, Kallum had leaned in and placed a gentle kiss on Ishtar's lips. "I have faith in you Sydney Ishtar McCurrie. We Scots ~ let's make a pact here and now that we'll stick together no matter what."

Ishtar smiled widely, the seed of love glowing in her eyes. "No matter what, we Scots will be our own tag-team."

Eventually, Ishtar found Cadmus' journal and they sat reading for hours, trying to psychologically pick the dark Vampire apart. They wondered to each other who this Mary Magdalene used to be and why she had had such a great effect upon Cadmus. And they were intrigued with Cadmus' fascination with emotion when it seemed clear to them that he could express and feel emotion relatively well.

"Perhaps that's where his Beautiful Pets come in?" ventured Kallum. "I'd heard tons of rumours when I was at the 54th that there was a Vampire that not only drank your Blood, but ate your soul as well. Maybe they were talking about him."

"Who else could they have been talking about?"

"Yeah, Cadmus pretty much is one of a kind. But seriously, his later entries were laced with an emotion of which he didn't even seem aware ~ a miasma of resentment, fear, anger, hatred, regret. It was all there in his writing if not in person. And he seemed more open to writing than expressing himself any other way. Hey...you thinkin' what I'm thinkin'?"

"I have no idea."

"I'm buying us matching laptops before we fly outta here. We can communicate on them when we can't for others being around. And we can snoop on Cadmus just to see where he's going. This last entry is disturbing to say the least. I think His Royal Spookiness needs a couple of chaperones."

"And how do you expect to pay for the computers?"

"Kallum McCreary bought stocks and bonds during the Great Depression. I'm sure they're worth a fair amount today." Ishtar smiled widely at Kallum.

The next day Ishtar was gifted with a brand new lap top, matched in every way to Kallum's. The other Vampires just glanced at this new turn of events with vague amusement. They hadn't seen puppy love like this in years, decades even. Kelat smiled to herself and squeezed Dmitri's hand.

"I don't want to interrupt her while she's having such a good time with Kallum right now, but I do want to talk to Ishtar while we're on the aeroplane. Let us make certain our seats are together. We can switch out later on, as the flight will be over 8 hours and we have a layover in London's Gatwick airport. In the meantime, I want you to speak with Kallum. I want every shred of information he knows and most of what he doesn't think he knows. With the three Relics in such close proximity, given the importance of his role in this as well as the undeniable importance of Cadmus, I want to make sure I am at least vaguely aware of all the risks into which we might be walking. I don't want to do this blind except for the peripheral protectors I must wear in the presence of my brother."

CHAPTER 23
THE WAY OF THE DARKBLOOD

"Stand elated at the burning –all our murders look the same, we are the thought and the display, the explanation and the side-effect." ~ Shriekback *"Despite Dense Weed"*

Their ride to the airport was uneventful. Those who could not tolerate the sun dashed easily from the front of their hotel straight into a dark-tinted limousine. It took two limos to get them to the airport. The first limo held Kelat, Dmitri, Cadmus, Kallum, and Ishtar. The other carried Rebekah, Mephistopheles, Thiyennen, Orphaeus, Eve, and Agatha.

The sun was down by the time they got to JFK and loaded out of the limousines. The drivers helped unload the luggage and smiled widely at the large tips they were given by Kallum. They gave their names and strongly suggested that the Vampires ask for them by name, should they ever need limo service again.

The group headed for their gate, stopping briefly for Kallum and Agatha to get some food. The Vampires needn't feed yet but, when they got to Carcassonne, blood would definitely need to flow.

It didn't take long before First Class boarding was announced. The Vampires took up about half of First Class as they loaded themselves and their luggage onto the plane. There was one obnoxious human, a male of about 25, who didn't seem to appreciate so many people in First Class.

"This is the first time I've flown where the place looks like coach. I wanted a seat to myself so I could do my work. How am I supposed to do my work with so many people around me? I'm a broker trying to do my job. Do you know how hard it is, especially these days, to be a broker? If I don't get things exactly right, people could lose their jobs, their homes, their livelihoods!"

"Sir, I'm sure the trip will be quiet and without incident," the flight attendant began.

"Can you promise me that? Are you a fucking psychic? Oh,

never mind. I'll do my best to do my work on this joke of a plane, but let me assure you the management of Air France will be hearing from Scott Parsons. You won't do this to anyone else, I can tell you that."

Scott Parsons sat down heavily on his aisle seat and turned to the person next to him.

"Excuse me, do you have a problem?" he asked, his entire being immersed in rudeness.

"Me?" Cadmus said smoothly. "I have no problem whatsoever, other than being a little hungry. That shall pass soon, I'm fairly certain."

Scott secured his carry on snugly underneath the seat in front of him and buckled in, trying to ignore the all-encompassing gaze of Cadmus Pariah. He wasn't at all certain he would be waiting until Carcassonne to feed. It would just be a matter of taking his soul to keep him silent, then bleeding him into the chalice. Once the flight leveled out and the flight attendants came by to offer up drinks, Cadmus would be alone with this obnoxious, rude individual. He could almost taste the utter delight of the man's dismay at being trapped like a moth in a jar within Cadmus well of souls.

As for where everyone else was seated, Kelat sat beside Ishtar and Dmitri sat beside Kallum. Then there was Orphaeus and the mortal Agatha, Rebekah and her life mate Mephistopheles, and Thiyennen and Eve sat together further back and at an angle to prevent any chance of Beholding. Kelat and Ishtar were at the front and right across from Cadmus and his new friend Scott. Kelat gave Cadmus a look as though to say, *Don't do it, Cadmus. It could cause trouble for us. Please comply with my wishes. Do..not..do it.*

Cadmus looked back blankly, his eyes half lidded, his brow lifted in a noble slope. He would do as he pleased and he felt it would please him beyond comprehension to swallow this rude man's soul and turn his blood into the ambrosia of Vampire blood to drink from his precious chalice. No look from Kelat would stop

142

him from taking this man's soul and blood, especially after the way he dared talk to Cadmus. He deserved to die. The world would be a better place without him, not that Cadmus was out to make the world a happier one for anyone.

The plane taxied and took off without incident. Once it leveled out, the flight attendants came through offering drinks.

"Yeah, get me a Scotch on the rocks, and make it a decent Scotch," said Scott Parsons. "I don't want that horse piss you usually pawn off on people. I'll know the difference."

"You don't seem old enough to know the difference between a good Scotch and a bad one," Cadmus said, egging the man on.

"Was I talking to you? Listen, I just know. How I know is really none of your fucking business."

Cadmus said nothing else, but a faint smile spread across his face. What was this? Was he actually feeling amusement? He believed he was. It wasn't a philosophical apex, not at all. Cadmus was actually amused. Now he knew he'd have a great deal of fun torturing this soul once it was trapped inside his well of souls. The flight attendants came back through with drinks for those who wanted one, then settled down to wait for anyone who may page them.

Scott drank his Scotch in two quick gulps, not the way you drink it at all.

"You're supposed to sip Scotch," Cadmus crooned. "Someone of your great experience should know that."

"Listen," Scott said, turning to Cadmus. "Did I not already tell you to mi-i-ind...your...bus..."

Cadmus drew Scott out of his body and into his own as he linked Scott's stare with the event horizon that was his gaze. He saw Kelat's wide eyes in the peripheries of his vision and raised one hand to block the stare. Even at this distance, there was a chance that he could link up with Kelat's gaze as well, and steal her soul. Why he blocked that opportunity, he did not know. It would have been a perfect opportunity to destroy the Vampire hierarchy right then and there. But something told him not to do that, his

143

business was with Scott Parsons and Scott alone.

Already he could hear Scott screaming impotently inside him, yelling for help, pleading for someone to tell him where he was. It heartened Cadmus to no end. Cadmus then took out his Dragon claw knife and punctured Scott in his jugular vein. He slowly stroked the man's penis through his clothes to make the blood flow faster into the chalice. Soon the man was dead, his erection of no use to himself or anyone else, much like the man himself, Cadmus surmised.

A flight attendant came by and asked if either of them needed anything. Cadmus said, "I believe your problem child here is sleeping and I have my own drink here, thank you very much."

The flight attendant stuttered, "We-well, if there's anything, *anything* you ne-eed, just p-press the buzzer. My name is Jillian."

Jillian smiled widely and sauntered back down the aisle. Cadmus smiled after her, again a genuine smile. He could feel it in his eyes. What was happening to him? Maybe it was because he was so glad to be rid of his flying partner. That had to be it. He quickly licked the wound on Scott's neck, getting rid of any sign of foul play. Scott screamed when he saw his dead body through Cadmus' eyes.

Kelat couldn't believe he'd actually done it and gotten away with it. Cadmus was the smoothest Vampire she'd ever seen when it came to killing. They were all hungry, the Vampires on this flight, but they were maintaining their hunger for when they could feed in a safer environment so that no one would be exposed to the human population as a true supernatural Vampire. That would certainly mean doom for them all. But Cadmus, he even showed Jillian his goblet of Blood and she saw it as wine, never noticing that the man beside Cadmus was no longer breathing and had a puncture wound on his throat.

Cadmus was magick made manifest in this way, and Kelat was fairly astounded by his abilities. When he raised a hand to her, she wasn't sure of why until her soul settled in on itself. Then she realized...Cadmus was protecting her from being drawn into his eternal gaze and being trapped within the labyrinth of his soul. Cadmus protecting? Those words did not seem to ever be used in the same sentence, but that was what he was doing. And his smile at Jillian, it reached his eyes. He had experienced mirth whether he knew it or not. Kelat's heart beat a little faster. Prophecy and promise swirled around her like a Sufi dancer and she was almost caught up in the furious joy of it when Ishtar spoke.

"Grandmother?"

"Yes, child."

"I never got a chance to tell you what an honour it is to meet you."

Kelat smiled at the young woman and stroked her long copper hair. "It's a great honour to meet you too. There are very few humans who live with Tarmian blood in their veins. You, being Dhampir by Thiyennen, carry our ancient blood by half. This makes you very special to me indeed, especially since you came into the Vampire fold as one of the Darkblood."

"Thank you, Grandmother. I will try to live up to your expectations of me."

"That, child, is why I wanted you to sit by me. Not very often do I get to instruct a freshly-made Vampire in the ways of their clan. If you would do me the honour of having patience with me what being a Darkblood is, it would hearten me greatly."

"Of course! I want to learn. I want to be the best I can be."

"Very well, then."

KELAT SPEAKS

The Darkblood Hive is perhaps the largest hive within the Great Hive. I'm sure that Dmitri has already told you of the five different sub-hives that comprise the Great Hive, so I won't repeat him. I want to speak of the Darkbloods and what it means to be a Darkblood Vampire.

We are the classical Vampires that most humans refer to today when they speak of Vampires in general. We live primarily by the night, eschewing the sun and all it has to offer the living. Our time is the night, although there are exceptions, like Dmitri, who can walk in the daylight without perishing beneath the rays. I, too, can walk under the sunlight, but it has taken me years to build up a kind of immunity and I can still die, of that, there is no doubt.

Darkbloods are primarily sexual Vampires. We bring our prey to the brink of orgasm before we bite and, as we bite, we bring the orgasm over, letting the blood pump itself into us from the excitement of the body's rapture. Although we do not need to kill all the time, kill we must at least once a week. This is when we engage in sexual intercourse with our prey. The act of the *la petite mort* brings about the actual death and we take a piece of that person's spirit into us before the soul moves on to whatever afterlife awaits him or her.

I can tell that you've yet to feed in this way because Dmitri has been taking care of your Vampiric needs. Once you get to France, you must kill or you will die, no matter how much Dmitri feeds you.

Darkbloods harbour the history of Vampirism. We teach one another by rote what transpired on the night of the Apostate's curse and we tell of how the sub-hives were formed. We are the librarians of our kind. The known prophecies and utterances of Gideon the Mad are of great importance to us, for it seemed as though his visions held a certain truth. Most believe that Gideon was simply a madman. The Darkbloods consider him to be a shaman of great import.

Now that we have the Augury of Gideon, it is my intent to unravel the entire relic and complete the Darkblood Library. All shall be revealed come that blessed night.

Those of the Darkblood Clan embrace our Vampire nature and do not seek out absolution for what we believe is a natural aberration that was meant to happen to us. Yes, we are the product of a curse, but who's to say that the curse was not supposed to occur? No one. So we live our lives in accordance with our nature and take our food in the manner in which it was intended. We do not rip into our prey or bathe in blood like the Beasts, nor do we beat and cut ourselves and cry out for forgiveness like the Redemptors. We are not handicapped, subsisting on the stale and decomposing blood of fresh corpses like those of the Tribe of the Tomb. We are the heart of the Great Hive. When someone mentions a Vampire, they are most often referring to one of us.

You can read human literature about Vampires and most of the time, you will be reading about the Darkblood Clan. Humans desire to be with us and to become us. They are fascinated with the idea of Vampirism and often envision the whole of Vampire Hive as being just like the Darkblood. Of course some humans focus on the more violent Vampires and are drawn to the Hive of the Beast, but they often do not consider them Vampires; rather, they are focused on the idea of werewolves, for that is where the idea of lycanthropes comes, from the Hive of the Beast.

Most often you will encounter Darkbloods living in opulence and appreciating the bounty of art, literature, and music that humanity has to offer. Many times we will have humans as companions to serve and protect us. We protect them from other Vampires, allow them to live in opulence with us, and feed from them, for that is what they want more often than not. Of course, they also want to be turned and, after some time has passed, many Darkblood will turn their human protectors. It is a mutual arrangement of convenience and trust.

Darkbloods live all over the globe, in every facet of human life. We are as connected to humanity as humanity is connected to the animal world, for food, pets, the advantage of certain arrangements like the hunter and his dogs. I don't mean to downgrade humanity at all but, compared to Vampires, they are truly helpless and unaware of the supernatural world that surrounds them and affects their lives on a daily basis. If they knew what dangers lurk around every corner they take, they would come clamouring on the front lawns of Darkbloods begging for some arrangement of protection. That's just the way it is and why we must never ever reveal ourselves completely to the human.

As a Darkblood, you need only kill once a week. The rest of the time, if you feed, you must hide the fact that you've done so. Licking the bite wound will make it disappear and leave the human with an incredible sexual dream which he or she will cherish for the rest of their life. As a Vampire, you will always carry a certain hunger with you. It's never totally sated and thus is our curse. We are constantly seeking a way to curb the hunger, but what you must understand is that the Vampire is hunger made manifest, so there is no way to fully get around or cure what is our burden to bear. Darkbloods handle the curse of the hunger the best way we know how. We touch humanity only when needs be and we hide our presence with an incredible finesse. Dmitri will teach you these tools, but know that they're already encoded in your Blood. As a Darkblood, you know these things to be true and you will follow them and carry them on into the next generation of Vampires, should you decide to turn someone.

Darkbloods can be killed, but fewer Darkbloods are killed because of our code of ethics. We don't leave humans with marks, we only kill when we have to, and we associate with humans on a level they can understand and appreciate. We are never suspected of the Dark Ways and are often enlisted to be leaders of our respective communities. I know of an instance where city council meetings were scheduled at night because the Mayor was a Darkblood and couldn't tolerate the sun. He, of course, told them some lie like he suffered from porphyria or something like that, but the Mayor was a beloved town leader and the humans did what needed to be done in order to keep him as Mayor.

When you see Vampires in the movies, you're seeing the Darkblood Hive 90% of the time. We are the quintessential Vampire and, as such, we must be very careful and behave in a manner that will protect us as we walk among humans. Being Gothic is one way to do this. Having a sunny disposition despite being allergic to the sun will win people over. Withdrawing completely is also an option, but we Darkbloods tend to crave the company of one another and of humanity. You must find your way in this manner, but you will be helped by Dmitri and myself.

Another thing that is of utmost importance is your persona. After a certain time, you must relinquish the life you are living and create a new persona for yourself. Since you do not age, the humans around you will eventually notice that and will out you as a Vampire. That is one reason why Vampires are given new names upon transformation. To the world of Sydney McCurrie, Sydney has disappeared. The authorities will look for her and put her on the missing person's lists of the FBI. Only Ishtar survives. You must move from Asheville now and create your own life and your own persona. Only after decades have passed can you use your original name, like Dmitri is doing now.

That is the sorrow we all must endure, the sacrifice of a good home and people we have come to know and love, but who now eye us with suspicion as they are reaching their twilight years and we are still as young and vibrant as the day we walked into our present life. It may be too much for you to bear. You may end up living in solitude, collecting memories and the shades of memories, like I do. But I hope you do not take that route. I believe that you will live a long and happy life with people who will accept you up to a point. Be mindful and work on becoming wise, for a wise Vampire is a Vampire that endures.

"So do you think you can do this?" Kelat asked Ishtar.

Ishtar nodded slowly, taking in everything Kelat had said to her. "Yes. Yes, I believe that I can."

"It will mean leaving Thiyennen if he doesn't want to leave Asheville. I know you've been helping Eve take care of him, but there is no doubt that you cannot go back to Asheville. There is also the problem of Thiyennen and Eve being Redemptors and you being Darkblood. We can live in close proximity for a while, but these two Clans will eventually always come to actively disagree with one another. I want you to part company with your father on good terms. Will you be able to do that?"

"Yes...But where will I go?"

"I want you to come to Jerusalem with me for a while so that I can mentor you. This is something I wanted to do with Rebekah, who is your Dhampir sister, but she would not tolerate it, being a Beast...the first Beast. She had her own path to tread and her own Hive to form. She and Mephistopheles are the much-needed chaos in what is almost always the perfectly-ordered world of the Vampire. They are the clowns and the wolves, the Joker in a deck of cards. You cannot predict what a Beast might do next and that is their wisdom and how they endure."

"So after we solve this Augury of Gideon mystery, I'll go to Jerusalem with you to the Veiled Sanctuary?"

"If you so desire, yes."

"Can Kallum come too? For some reason, I've grown very attached to him."

"I'm not certain what Kallum is exactly, but I do know he is not a Vampire, not anymore. He was Darkblood when he was a Vampire, so I believe he'll understand the wisdoms I'll be sharing with you. He may even glean some wisdom himself, since he was left to fend for himself by Rebekah and Mephistopheles. And perhaps he can shed light on some wisdom even I do not know. Everything is in flux right now. Who knows what paths we will tread after the Augury of Gideon is unraveled?"

"Thank you, Grandmother Kelat. Thank you for telling me all of this and for being so understanding. Already, I can tell that you're a treasure and I will learn great things from you."

"I just hope I'm a good teacher for you and that you find comfort in the magicks of the Veiled Sanctuary."

CHAPTER 24
CADMUS' JOURNAL: THE SMILE

"Coming out the other end, a sentimental point of view. We can contemplate each other but the other is no fool. We are in this anyway, breathing in what you breathe out. Couldn't think of nothing better, only got what we don't need." ~ Shriekback "A Kind of Fascination

Cadmus put away his chalice and pulled out his laptop. There was something he wanted to write about in his journal. Pulling up Live Journal, he began to type.

> Just a few moments ago, I smiled not for the first time, but for the second time in a mere span of a few minutes. The smiles weren't expressions of philosophical apices that I pulled out of my well of souls so that I performed in accordance to the social situation. No no, they were genuine smiles. One was at this wholly unpleasant man whom I just finished eating. The other was at the flight attendant who asked if either myself or my rude traveling partner needed anything.
>
> I do not know what is happening to me. Never before have I felt amusement before. I've felt the shade of amusement as a memory of one of my beautiful pets, but I've never achieved it on my own. That rude man, Scott, amused me because I knew I was going to end his unpleasantness and trap him within my well of souls where he could suffer in eternity a hell he never realized existed.
>
> The thought of his suffering in such a way brought a genuine smile to my face. You should have seen the flight attendant when I smiled at her. She literally

melted right there at her station on the aeroplane. If I smile like this at everyone, would my Glamour be even stronger? How would a smile affect another Vampire? Will my hunting be made even easier because I have the ability to truly smile now? Will laughter come next? Yes, I have laughed in the past, but it was only an act. Eve knew it. My laugh scares her into petrifaction. I wonder what a real laugh what do to her. Would it kill her with fright or ease her fear of me? Not that I want her to not be afraid of me. Her fear fulfills me on a level that I have difficulty expressing. No, I won't be trying to laugh in order to ease Eve's mind and I certainly won't be attempting it in front of Kelat, who has an unhealthy interest in my emotions, or lack thereof.

Already, I believe she saw me smile at the flight attendant. If I am right, she will be pestering me no end the first chance she gets. I will tell her the truth that the smile came forth unprodded and I am unaware of why I suddenly possessed the ability or if I believe I can do it again. If she pushes me too far, I will once again push my boundaries and see if I can overcome her with Compulsion. Our little Compulsion wars are one of the few things about being around Kelat I can say I relatively enjoy, or imagine that I enjoy, should I know what that means or how it feels. Maybe I'll try to smile at her and see what sort of response I get out of her.

Hm, it looks like the kiddies are pulling out their computers. As they say in poor television sitcoms, there goes the neighbourhood. Had I the knowledge to do so and the inclination, I would hack into Faust's, oh I mean *Kallum's* computer and make it the miserable mess its owner once was beneath my deft and devious knife.

Cadmus closed the lid to his laptop and looked around the first class section of the airplane. Besides two living mortals and the dead one who appeared to be sleeping, the rest of the first class passengers were Vampires or mortal friends of Vampires. Cadmus wasn't sure what to call Kallum. He seemed to be totally mortal, but he was revived with Vampire Blood. That would need to be explored further if given half the chance. Could he endure the pleasures of the flesh that once they'd shared in the 70s and heal from such an ordeal? Mortal pain always seemed so much more intense than Vampire pain. If Cadmus could find himself a mortal that could heal like a Vampire, there would be no end to the unholy wonderment in which a person could engage.

Cadmus closed his eyes and pretended the others weren't there. For now, since he'd been satiated on the transfigured blood of Scott Parsons, he would sleep like a wee babe in the woods, just like he was in the long-lost days in Gaul when all was happiness and the newness of life before the coming of Nissius.

CHAPTER 25
FLYING INTO THE SUN

"Can anyone fly this 'plane? Does anyone know the time? Has anyone seen the cameras? Why do places look the same? Can anyone speak Chinese? Does anyone know the way? Where did I leave my passport? Can someone help me please? We're looking like refugees." ~ Shriekback "Midnight Maps"

There was a great deal of turbulence going into the flight. Agatha tensed up with the take-off and was increasingly tense throughout the turbulent early flight. Orphaeus comforted her as best as he could, which helped some.

"Why don't you pull out your reporter's pad and take some notes while I tell you more about us Vampires?"

"That's the best suggestion I've had all day."

"So ask away. My life is an open book."

"You mentioned once that Vampires don't have to sleep? Why is that and why do you choose to do so anyway?

"Vampires need not answer to the trappings of mortal behaviour," Orphaeus explained. "Many call us undead or the walking dead, but that's not necessarily the case, excluding the Tribe of the Tomb respectfully. We don't have to eat or sleep, but almost all of us choose to do so anyway. Eating and drinking is more for fitting in amongst mortals. People tend to eye you warily if they never see you eat and drink, especially at a party.

"Sleeping is a more personal choice. We sleep because, just like you, we get bored. There is also the theory, especially when applied to younger Vampires, that we're trying to cling to our mortal selves in spite of our undeniable immortality. The third, and probably most important reason we sleep, is because we dream.

"A Vampire's dreams are filled with utter delight, most of the time. We dwell in a sacred symmetry with the realms of Morpheus and, as a result, our dreams are where we can live any life we wish,

154

be it under the sun or swimming in the teeming ocean tides. We dream lucidly and are active parts of the dreams we dream. It's like opening a whole other astral world to us where we can control our own actions and interact with people, beings, even the living plants. To be a Vampire is to dream the reality of dreaming. I think only the aboriginal people of Australia could possibly fathom what I'm trying to say here. Suffice to say; most any shaman would describe a Vampire's dream as astral travel."

"I heard Dmitri mention earlier the term 'thrall.' What exactly is that?"

"Something not often done. I believe he's only done it twice and you're looking at the product of his efforts when you look at Rebekah and Ishtar. Thralling is the act of giving a human just enough Blood to bind him or her to you. I'm sure you've read *Dracula,* neh? Well, Renfield in that book was a thrall. The act of thralling entails the impregnation of the woman and the castration of the man. Why, I don't know, unless it lowers the humans' inclination to breed during the time they're being used by the Vampire. I think it's a bit extreme, but I'm not one to thrall a person. The thralling also leaves the person believing that, someday, they will become a Vampire as well. More often than not, they are abandoned by their master without any hope of fully transitioning over. It eventually drives them mad, which is exactly what happened to Ishtar's mortal mother. I've heard through the grapevine that Rebekah's mother Reah fell on a sword to end the unbearable longing. So much suffering...and for what?" Orphaeus eyed the back of Thiyennen's head."

Feeling a need to change the subject, Aggie asked, "I've noticed all the Vampires eating and drinking, but not Cadmus. Why?"

"Well, like I said, we can do whatever mortals do as far as our digestive systems. We don't glean much nourishment from it all, the blood we drink being nourishment enough. But Cadmus is a different animal. Even though he is alive by our standards, he can neither tolerate human drink or food. The only nourishment he gets is from the Blood of Vampires or the transfigured Blood of his chalice. It truly is as if his body is reanimated based on the myths and legends of human Europe. He must also sleep, like any mortal. I believe that this may be a kind of a curse for him, because he feels inadequate around his immortal peers. Oh, and that's another point about Cadmus; he ages when he doesn't get to feed. When he was brought out into the world, he looked no more than 15. But he didn't have the chalice then, so all his meals depended on what kind of hunter he was and how strong the Vampire he felled had been. By the time he took hold of the chalice, Cadmus appeared to be 30 or so. This was centuries in the making, though. Cadmus is connected to the fate of the chalice, just as he is the Blood Crown now that he's worn it. Perhaps the Augury of Gideon will shed some light as to what fate that might be when the relics are brought together in Kelat's secret circle sanctuary."

Orphaeus smiled and waited for the next question.

Right in front of them sat Eve and Thiyennen. They whispered quietly together, their heads almost touching.

"I am unsure about your plan, Thiyennen. Surely there had to be a better way than entrapping this monster and torturing him to death. I get the feeling that he is indeed more powerful than you and Kelat now and that even attempting to capture him would result in your death."

"It has to happen. He needs to see the error of his ways. He needs to feel the pain of Inquisition just as he inflicted it on me. It is the only way to cleanse him and perhaps heal his spirit before it's too late to reconcile him with God. Just as we enter holy places to purge our bodies of the sin we carry, so too will Cadmus Pariah know the agony of the banshee and cry out for God's mercy."

"What if the other Vampires balk your plan?"

"That's why we're keeping it secret, dear Eve. What we plan on doing is no one's business but our own."

Kallum had gotten out his new laptop and turned it on. It had a beautiful black sheen on the outside and the light grey keys glowed in the light of the computer screen.

"So you're going to talk with Ishtar on that thing during our trip to France, eh?"

"That's the plan, Stan."

"You know you could just switch seats with Kelat."

"Where's the fun in that? Besides, I think Kelat wanted to get to know Ishtar a little bit. Or am I wrong?"

"You're right. I just think it's odd that you want to communicate like this when you're already in such close proximity."

"Well, we're wanting to discuss this," and Kallum turn the computer around to show a blog called **Philosophical Apices**. "It's Cadmus' online journal. Now is that not enough to want to drag out your computer and discuss the madness with someone? Besides, I want to see if I'm mentioned at all. Surely the man has thought about me and what he did. Do you think he feels guilty?"

"I think he feels very little right now, but Kelat says his feelings will eventually come to the forefront and that it will be a monumental day when that happens. I tend to agree with her, but I don't know why. Why Cadmus seems to be so important in this quest to reunite the relics is beyond me. And you. You're the one who called us to what would have been your final resting spot, but your restless spirit wouldn't allow it. We all came for you and the moment you were brought up out of the ground, Agatha revealed the Augury of Gideon. You're the only one who can unravel it, but do you know how?"

"It has to do with being in sacred space and bringing all three relics together. As for details of what needs to be done, I'm as clueless as anyone. I have faith that the hand of God will move us all accordingly. I certainly know that God brought Cadmus to me, to purge me of my sins and bring to me an island of solace inside what was the agony Cadmus inflicted upon me. By the time Cadmus was ripping into my broken body, I had already left it and felt nothing. It was as though I had overcome the horror of the physical and been brought to the holy sanctity of the spiritual. I

157

did not want to come back here but, again, the hand of God moves us all to where we need to be."

"You have a profound way about you, Kallum. I like that and I like you."

"I like you too Dmitri. Your happiness will soon be eternal and I will smile from far away for you."

That last sentence sounded like prophecy to Dmitri and he tucked it away in his mind so that he'd never forget the winsome words of Kallum McCreary.

"Ah," Kallum said. "There she is. Now we're in business."

Kallum hunched over the computer in an almost slouch and began tapping furiously with his index fingers.

Mephistopheles leaned back in his seat and pretended to be asleep.

"You're a bad actor, Meph. If you're going to sleep, then just sleep,but don't pretend, it's ridiculous.

"I'm trying to avoid being bothered by flight attendants. In coach, you have to beg for attention, but in first class, they stumble all over each other to meet your every need. My need is to be left alone.

"Well then, set up a *geasa* or something, for Bob's sake. Don't pretend to sleep. The snoring is absurd and it's irritating the hell out of me. Besides, I want to talk to you."

"About what?"

"Well, don't you think it's a little strange that three of our children are on this quest with us? The most powerful of the Beasts, besides me, and the Dhampir child we kidnapped and made our own so many centuries ago? And now she and her sister are travelling with us to do what? I don't know, do you? And what about Kallum? What the hell is he? He was revived by Vampire Blood, but he's a human. He was once a Vampire for decades, but now he's mortated back to humanity. We never even thought that this was possible, but he's evidence that it is. What do we have to do become mortal again? Allow some psychopath like Cadmus to

158

rip us to shreds as soon as we healed until we saw the error of our ways? I'm not up for any of that. Are you?"

Mephistopheles thought in silence, and then turned his head to Rebekah. "I think that the Relics will bring to bear everything we've ever done and said in this long life of ours. The joining of the Relics will have us make a choice about our immortality and what it is we want out of life. I do not believe that Kallum or especially Cadmus will have a role in the decision we make when that time comes."

"You have such a way with words Meph."

Rebekah kissed him leisurely on the lips and then settled back with him. If they were going to pretend to sleep, they may as well do it together. Eventually, both of them were asleep and the flight attendants left them alone in their slumber.

What do you think of his journal? Asked Ishtar of Kallum.

I think it's the most honest thing I've read in a while. The man certainly doesn't hold back in his blog, that's for sure and true.

It bothers me that he hates so much. How can a person come to that, to hating everyone around him?

The things I saw when he was torturing me and my spirit would lift out of my body were visions of torment much like what he was inflicting on me.

I don't see how you survived it for as long as you did.

It was my angel, Rosetta, who kept me company in those dark days. Had it not been for her, I would have died a madman and probably ended up haunting that apartment building, unable to move on to the light.

And you did move on, yes?

Oh yes. I was called to come on this quest with you and, then, I get to go back.

What do you mean? I'm sorry, Ishtar. But as soon as I fulfill my destiny with all of you here, I will die again. Don't worry though. When you pass on, I'll be there to guide you to the light.

Perhaps we'll share a paradise.

Orphaeus loved talking with Agatha, even though he knew everything he told her would end up in a book somewhere. Not that anyone would believe it.

"Tell me more about these Unfortunates, the members of the Tribe of the Tomb."

"Oh wow...not much to tell with them. They are the origin of the frightful *Nosferatu*, all spindly fingers and funky teeth. They shamble throughout life as though in a waking dream. Unable to properly feed themselves, they subsist on the blood of animals, particularly rats, and the rotting blood of the dead. Used to, they would hang out in cemeteries and feed off newly buried bodies. When people started removing all the blood and embalming the dead, the Tomb huggers began to haunt funeral homes so they could get the blood before it was discarded by the mortician.

"As I said before, no one knows why these Vampires are the way they are. It's not like someone decided to turn the mentally or physically challenged one day. The turning does it to them. A friend of mine in the Hive of the Beast turned a history professor with whom she was smitten. The minute the Vampiric spirit entered into his body, he became wholly unaware of who or what he was. He shuffled off into the night and she never saw him again. She was heartbroken and wondered if her ability to turn humans into vampires was somehow faulty. A few years later she turned someone she hated, hoping he would come into the curse of the Tribe of the Tomb. But no, he became a Beast. He now feeds almost nightly in and around Miami."

"So there's no rhyme or reason as to what hive you end up in if you're turned into a Vampire."

"No."

"That's frightening. I've thought about asking to be turned, but now I'm too afraid I'd become one of the Tribe of the Tomb."

"It's a risk one definitely takes. All you have to do is roll the dice and roll with the result."

"I think I'll stay human for now, thank you very much."

The two laughed quietly.

"I wonder what they're laughing about," Kelat said quietly, looking back at Orphaeus and Agatha.

"Whatever it is, it sure looks like they're having a good time," Ishtar observed as she typed on her new computer.

"I wonder if Agatha will ever want to be turned. Her experience with us has been pretty much ongoing for years, yet she seems perfectly happy to remain human. I think I would be too, were I her."

"I hated being human," Ishtar said. "I always knew that I was different and the kids in school reflected my own social hesitance by making fun of me and shunning me in every way they could. Children can be so cruel..."

"I am sorry, Ishtar. Sorry that you were born Dhampir and had to endure such cruelties and injustices. I'm just glad you have no sense of vengeance."

"Oh, but I do. There's just no point in exacting it anymore. I've grown beyond my self-conscious, miserable self to a pristine moment in time. This is my moment and every moment that follows will be mine and I will celebrate it."

"You have definitely come into a strong sense of wisdom at a very early age."

Ishtar smiled and typed some more.

"It's Kallum's influence I think. From the moment I saw him, I loved him. It makes no sense at all, but it exists nonetheless. We have some sort of bond and a destiny to fulfill. I think we'll both do our best to make sure it happens.

Ishtar typed some more then closed the lid of the computer.

"Grandmother, have you ever thought of a way out of your curse, this Vampiric existence of yours?"

"It is what compelled me to make the chalice."

"I want to someday see this chalice."

161

"Oh you will. When we reach the forests outside Carcassonne and come into the sanctity of the Canopy Ruins, you will see the chalice."

"Do you think I'll get to drink from it? Kallum says he intends to drink from the sacred chalice when the time comes, but he won't say anything more about it. What does it do?"

"It fortifies and strengthens the Vampire drinker and enslaves and makes into an addict the human drinker. It's a relic I sometimes wish I'd never made. Somehow, I magickally bound the entire Great Hive to the chalice. With the chalice, you can call all the hives to you and kill them if you wish. If the chalice is ever destroyed, so too will the entire Vampire race die with it. Since it is in the possession of Cadmus Pariah, I worry that he will grow weary of this Vale of Tears and destroy us all one day. The only thing that stays his hand is his dependence on my Blood that's entrapped therein. If he cannot find a Vampire from which to feed, he can always drain a human into the cup and let the blood be transfigured into my Vampire Blood since the Blood is the only thing he can ingest."

When Kallum closed the lid of his computer and put it away, Dmitri looked at him sidewise.

"Finished chatting then?"

"For now. It's a long plane ride. I may just surf the web if I get bored."

"Did you read up on Cadmus' journal?"

"Oh yes. You should read it sometime. If ever there was a thing that could turn into a beast filled with spite, it's Cadmus' journal."

"I'll have to give it a read sometime. I'm not too big on computers and the Internet. I just never seemed to get the hang of it."

"You just need to dive in and see where your fingers take you. It's hard at first, and I guess the older you are, the more difficult it is, but you eventually get it. If Cadmus can do it, so can you."

"Hm...maybe I'll give it a whirl someday."

"Well, you're more than welcome to use this computer to get a head start."

"I might take you up on it."

They sat silently together for a little while. Kallum leaned his seat back a little and closed his impossibly blue eyes and Dmitri continued to read his book, *Philosophy of Religion: An Anthology.* Dmitri never stopped trying to learn, trying to expand his mind, but he was also a little set in his ways. A Kindle was not a book to him. He had to feel the weight of the paper in his hands, and turn each page with a sacred grace. Even though he engaged in telepathy with Kelat, he was still keen on discussions that engaged the mouth and the spoken word. He liked to talk to people face to face. Even the phone irritated him. Dmitri wanted physical interaction, not the technological facsimile thereof. Sometimes he felt that all the technology that brought people together actually was tearing them apart. More and more people sat by themselves at home chatting on the computer rather than going out with friends and possibly watching a movie or even playing games, like Monopoly or Scrabble. From what Dmitri saw of this new age of the computer, he would definitely contend that humanity had never been lonelier than they were right now. And what was so sad was, they didn't even know it.

After a time, Dmitri glanced over at Kallum. He was sound asleep, his breath even and heavy with the weight of slumber. Dmitri wondered exactly what Kallum was. He had definitely been dead, no doubt, and incredibly untouched by the finger of death. His body had been perfect in its long repose in that building on Bleecker Street. Not only had he survived the rage of Cadmus' knives upon his flesh, he had also survived the demolition of his apartment building and the building of another, where we found him buried beneath the basement. He was truly incorruptible. Dmitri made the sign of the cross on his breast.

But what was he now? He had been revived with Vampire Blood. Would that not make him a Vampire? He was certainly mortal when they dug him up. Dmitri felt no draw to him that Vampires experience with one another. No, he had been mortal, mortated from Vampire to human once more before he had been murdered by Cadmus. Dmitri wondered if a drop of human blood would have revived him. He doubted it. Would his awakening after taking Vampire Blood make him a thrall? Dmitri saw no sign of that either. He didn't seem to want to comply with every wish Ishtar had. He did have a strange bond with Ishtar though. When Dmitri saw them together, even though they'd known each other only for a couple of days, he could tell the two youngsters truly loved one another. But how would an arrangement between the two of them work? Would Kallum be willing to become a Vampire once more to be with Ishtar? Dmitri would think not. Kallum was an entity unto himself and his path was that of a mission that needed fulfilling. He was afraid that Kallum wasn't planning on staying amongst them for very long.

This mission had Dmitri curious. When the three relics were brought out in sacred space, what exactly would happen? Would Kallum become this super being? Or would Cadmus finally be rendered helpless so the Vampires could kill him? Dmitri wondered if any of them had the moxie to do such a thing. Rebekah and Mephistopheles most definitely would do it. Their whole existence was based upon the murder and desecration of individuals, being the first of the Beasts. Maybe that's why they're here. Then again, they could just be here because Kallum wanted his parents present. They all were, after all, drawn to Kallum's resting body by his restless spirit. There were so many possibilities and unanswered questions.

Dmitri looked over to Kelat, who seemed to be resting herself. What a beautiful being she was. He never grew tired of gazing upon her Elfin beauty and cherishing ever moment he had to do so. Time had been kind to them lately. Ever since the advent of Cadmus rise to power, Kelat and Dmitri had been together more often than not. They were always working toward some way to take the chalice from the dark priest and assure Kelat's official dominion over the Great Hive. Right now, she was the figurative great mother of the Hive, but the chalice is what guided the Hive mind. Should Cadmus decide to use it to that end, it would surely result in a Vampire war and much death would occur. Kelat assured Dmitri that Cadmus would not do such a thing. To Cadmus, the chalice was merely a way to transfigure human blood to Vampire Blood. It was an object of subsistence to him, nothing more. If the three Relics had to come together to unravel the prophecies of the Augury of Gideon, would Cadmus even be willing to put up the Chalice long enough for the magick to happen? Dmitri felt that he would most likely balk at such an action and none of the Vampires were strong enough to take the Relic away from him, at least he thought not.

Dmitri sighed. So many unanswered questions and problems that seemed unsolvable... How could he rest with all this weighing down on his shoulders? It was not possible. He looked over at Kelat again. There she rest in holy perfection, her sloped brow framed with that wild brown hair that had caught his attention way back in the fourteenth century when he was a furrier and she was a nightmare to men who feared their very nature because they were told to do so or risk the probability of going to Hell. Dmitri had shed those fears and succumbed to the Witch. If he had it to do all over again, Dmitri wouldn't change a thing.

Dmitri looked around at all the passengers. It seemed that everyone had quietened down. He moved his seat back to its resting position and closed his eyes. Soon he was dreaming, his soul mate singing the sails and him near the mast where she stood, watching the whales swim with the ship, returning her song with their own harmonic wonderment. If this were heaven, then surely would he live there in happiness forever.

CHAPTER 26
THE CANOPY RUINS

"Is there a fire in the sky? Is there a moon up there? Is anything alive now? This darkness is what I hear. This is a breathless silence, A moment out of time. I see your face in the shadows The tell-tale signs are in your eyes: ~ Shriekback "This Big Hush""

The plane landed without incident at the Carcassonne International Airport. The sun was just coming up over the horizon as the Vampires collected their luggage and were driven to Citea Barbacane where they found refuge from the flaming orb. Everyone slept except for Kelat. She looked over at her lover, deep in repose, and her heart expanded within her breast. Kelat never looked at Dmitri without the pang of love taking her over completely. She crawled into bed with him and lay there thinking about what would happen when they reached the Canopy Ruins and how she had brought Dmitri over in that sacred place about six hundred years ago.

Would this be the end for them all, the unraveling of the genetic code that Gideon has woven inside the Blood jewel. How long had the Vampires thought the Augury of Gideon was a written tome? In a way they were right, it was just written in the collective consciousness of Gideon's people. Kelat thought about her triple helix that was almost perpetually moving in flux with her mood in the Veiled Sanctuary. The triple helix represented the whole of Tarmian existence. Within that helix, Kelat could meditate and remember the blessedness of her people and how they once walked in harmony with the humans of this world. That is why she chose the Canopy Ruins instead of the Veiled Sanctuary for this ritual that was to be had. The Canopy Ruins were more conducive to both human and Tarmi. And, since the Augury of Gideon was created for Vampires of both tribes, it felt right to go to the Ruins instead.

Kelat thought back to when she transformed Dmitri and how beautiful he had been on that night that he awoke into the Blood.

166

She knew he could never be by her side forever, but she also knew that he would love her unconditionally in this cursed life, just as he had all previous lives. And, if the Augury of Gideon means their deaths, Kelat was certain that she and Dmitri would meet along the way in some future life and their soul bond would sing its special song to them and they would live that life together in some capacity. That was the way it was for soul mates. They always knew and they always found one another so that their journey in this life would carry a special meaning known only to them.

"Stop pondering and sleep a little," Dmitri whispered to Kelat.

"I know that I need to, if only to regenerate."

"Come, let me hold you."

Kelat turned over and let Dmitri cradle her in his arms.

"Dmitri, do you ever regret my transforming you?"

"I told you then, Motya, I did not regret it. I was sad to lose my family and way of life in a way, but you set me on a path that I had always longed to tread. I was the walking dead when you found me and you gave me life. You gave me my life back. You let me be who I had always wanted to be. And after all these centuries, despite the sorrow and the horror I have seen in my journeys, I regret nothing except I'm not with you nearly as long as I want to be."

A single tear fell from Kelat's porcelain face. Dmitri moved in and licked the tear from her face and then kissed her. The passion of the kiss told Kelat all she needed to know. The two Vampires made love on the small bed, drinking one another's Blood as they moved to a rhythm only they could hear. And, when Kelat came, she moaned in absolute joy against Dmitri's throat, which made him release inside her as he drank her Blood. His grunting against her aroused Kelat again and she tensed against her lover, taking joy in his presence and his love. Slowly they released from one another, sated in every way a Vampire can be, their spirits still on fire from the intensity of it all.

"Do you think you can sleep now?" Dmitri whispered as he nuzzled her throat.

"I think so," said Kelat. "I can always sleep in the sacred presence of my soul mate, for I know that within his arms, all is well and life is safe and blessed."

They slept in silence as the sun bore down upon the French countryside.

Come sunset, the Vampires met in the lobby. Kelat bade those who needed to feed to go and do what they must do, then return to Citea Barbacane in two hours so they could go together into the forest.

Cadmus was the first to leave. He strode the busy streets of Carcassonne, looking for a Vampire to satiate his needs. It didn't take long. Standing outside a nightclub was a young female Vampire, freshly fed and enticingly plump from all the blood she had drunk.

Walking slowly up to her, Cadmus said in French, "Good eve and how are you on this fine evening?"

The Vampire looked at Cadmus and her eyes widened with desire. "I'm wonderful, thank you. Have you fed tonight?"

"Oh no, I'm still looking for the right candidate."

"Are you interested in the Ambrosciata or are you on the hunt for human blood."

"I think I have found my prey for the night," Cadmus said, moving in on the young Vampire. "What's your name, pray tell?"

"I am Anouk, child of Sabastien, child of Braecca."

"Well, Anouk, child of Sabastien, child of Breacca, I am Cadmus, the child of hell incarnate."

And, with that, he began the slow soul sucking from her eyes to his all-absorbing eyes, and he could feel her frightened spirit deep within his breast. When the deed was done and all that stood there was a vessel of Blood, Cadmus drank his fill and let the empty body fall to the ground outside the night club. Let the authorities try to figure that one out, if they could. Cadmus touched the new soul and she screamed with horror. Anouk was going to be fun for a while as she realized she was trapped inside

168

Cadmus' well of souls for as long as he lived. And Cadmus was going to live forever.

Cadmus returned to the hotel exactly two hours later. He could have been back within the hour, but he wanted everyone to wait, and he could never deny a grand entrance, which is what he made. Everyone turned their eyes to him as he entered the lobby.

"Shall we go then?" he asked flippantly.

Kelat slung a backpack on her back and stood up. "Let's not waste any time then. Off we go."

They got taxis out of town and into the countryside where they began their hike. They walked in the forest for what seemed like ages. A mist covered the forest floor not allowing them to see exactly where their footing was. Agatha and Kallum had particular problems with this because they didn't possess the keen eye sight that the Vampires had. Ishtar helped Kallum and Orphaeus was always by Aggie's side, helping her along.

Soon they came to a ring of giant trees, some oak, some yew. The trees were so close together, they had to squeeze to get through into the area beyond. Inside the ring of trees were a few long-felled standing stones and a small creek with split the circle in two. The ground was covered by a soft moss and ferns. You could feel the ancient sanctity of the place.

Agatha found herself crying.

"What's wrong Aggie?" Orphaeus asked, concerned.

"I don't know. I think I'm weeping for all that we've lost thanks to the Apostate. This place would not be a ruin and people would come here often to feel the magick of the planet and all that she encompasses. I'm just ashamed and sad that we humans followed the lies of the Apostate and turned places like this into something less than it should have been. I weep because Kelat still has to keep it secret in order to keep it safe. It's so sad. So very sad."

Orphaeus hugged Agatha. "It's okay, Aggie. Everything is gonna be okay."

Eve moved Thiyennen off to one side so he would be unable to see Kelat when she turned around to greet them all to the Canopy Ruins. She had her glasses on so that her peripheral vision wouldn't allow her to see her brother.

"Welcome to the Canopy Ruins. Here, very long ago, Tarmi and humans joined in harmony to celebrate the ways of Mother Earth. The trees here are ancient and can tell stories of the old days and ancient ways. They whisper the songs lost so very long ago. Trees remember and weep for moments lost. They are the secret keepers and guardians of the sacred. Here they form a circle and, high above, the oak and yew comingle to create a giant canopy. This is a haven long forgotten by humanity and barely saved from destruction by the Apostate and his warrior priests. Few of the sacred standing stones survived their desecration, but some did survive, enough for us to be able to form a proper circle within the ruins. Please join hands. Kelat took Dmitri's hand and, to her right, she took Cadmus'. Cadmus seemed to be trembling.

Are you able to do this? She asked him telepathically.

Of course I am. I am just not one for group ritual.

You'll be okay.

Out loud, Kelat said, "Bless this sacred place, O guardians of the otherworlds and of this world. Keep us safe within the Canopy and show us the way of the ancients. So mote it be."

It was a simple call for blessing, something that wouldn't offend Thiyennen's sense of responsibility to his Christian faith. When Kelat sat down, everyone else did as well. From her backpack, Kelat pulled out the Blood Crown and set it before her.

"Cadmus, can you produce the chalice for us? It's needed for this ritual so that we can discover why we were called and why we are here."

Cadmus reached into his priestly robes and pulled out the chalice, which he set in the circlet of thorns.

"Aggie, if you would, give me the Augury of Gideon."

Agatha pulled out the ruby and gave it one last squeeze before handing it to Kelat, who placed it on the ground inside the circlet of the Blood Crown at the base of the chalice. Everyone was holding their breath to see what happened, but nothing happened.

"Maybe you should put the Augury inside the chalice while it's inside the crown," suggested Kallum.

"Do no such thing," commanded Cadmus. Only blood goes into the chalice.

"But, Cadmus," said Kelat quietly, picking up the Augury. "This *is* Blood."

And before Cadmus could protest further, she dropped the Augury inside the chalice. It made a clinking noise as it hit the bottom. Watching, Kelat saw the Augury melt and mingle with her own blood and the chalice was filled with Blood."

"Who dares to drink it?" Kelat said. "I cannot, for this is my own Blood."

"I will drink it. It is my chalice."

"No, you're the keeper of this Relic, but it does not belong to you, Cadmus Pariah. And if you try to take the Chalice, I will fight you with all the power I possess. I'm sure the others here will help me."

"Who do you think should drink it, then?" Ishtar asked.

"The one to whom was given the Augury, at least for some brief period of time. This Blood belongs to Kallum McCreary, if he dares to drink it."

"But...I'm not a Vampire anymore."

"Nor are you truly human, but a spirit in human form whose Vampiric self touched and handled the Augury of Gideon. Only two Vampires touched the Augury and could speak of the prophecy held therein: Paine Bryerson and Faust the Confessor. Both are dead, but the spirit of Faust lives. It is you, Kallum. Here, take the chalice and drink the Augury. Let us see what destiny holds for us."

Kelat carefully passed the goblet to Dmitri, who passed it on to Ishtar. Ishtar held the cup for a moment, and then gave it to Kallum.

"This won't hurt him, will it Kelat?"

"No child. He's fulfilling his purpose here."

Kallum held the chalice in both hands. "The last time I drank from this, I was weak from the blood hunger and was being tortured by Cadmus Pariah," he said quietly. "I came to love and hate the chalice because I knew with every swallow of blood I took, the faster I would heal and the more Cadmus would tear into me. Why, Cadmus? Why did you torture me like you did?"

Cadmus ducked his head and lifted his eyebrows as he stared at Kallum. "Because I found the very thought of you unbearable. And...I still *do*."

Cadmus moved to take the chalice and Kelat looked at him with fury and said, "Paedi'arawn!"

Instantly was Cadmus immobile within the circle of Vampires and mortals. He could barely move his eyes to Kelat and his lips to whisper vengefully, "Release me, Mother Kelat."

Kelat psychically held Cadmus who stood before Kallum, murder in his eyes. "You've drunk from my chalice before. Remember to always leave a few drops. Stop short of drinking in entirety or I swear, Kallum McCreary, I will rend you asunder with my bare hands."

Kallum looked at Cadmus blankly. "Don't you remember what I told you the day you came and murdered me? You have no power over me. You never did and, now, you never will."

Cadmus tried to lunge for Kallum again and found that Kelat had placed upon him a *geasa* that prevented him from moving. Watching with no small amount of horror in his breast, Cadmus beheld Kallum drink the Blood from the chalice, draining it until it was utterly empty.

"No! No! What have you done?" Cadmus screamed this, woe and outrage filling his voice. And then he fell silently to the ground, consciousness leaving his body.

All eyes turned to Kallum, who stood and handed Kelat the empty chalice.

"Heed me, people of the Blood, for I am the Augury of Gideon," said Kallum. "Gideon was not mad. He was a shaman and a seeker. He knew that once the chalice of Kelat was finally drained, the keeper of the cup would become mortal and possess within him the blood that would break the curse. All the prophecies that surround him have already come to pass. His reign of terror, now over, he can live to heal those who wish to return to the light. His death will mean the end of Vampirism completely so, choose wisely the path you wish to take, for vengeance is a cycle."

CHAPTER 27
DREADFUL ABSOLUTION

"There's no rest in the galaxy, no escape in the life to come – people gasp in my atmosphere, I'm on a turning wheel and I swear I feel like a planet, I ache with the sun, I feel like a planet and I wander the night till this terrible year is done." ~ Shriekback "(feels like) a Planet"

All eyes turned to the unconscious Cadmus. Orphaeus even stood and walked over to him. Pulling him onto his back, he examined the sleeping man. He was humanoid. There was no bluish pallor to him anymore. The natural Glamour that he gave off even in sleep was muted. Orphaeus looked up to Kelat and shrugged, his eyes wide. Lying at his knees was a Tarmian male with no mark of the Vampiric upon him any longer.

"What do we do?" Rebekah asked fearfully. "What do we do with him?"

"Won't he be drained to death by Vampires looking for mortation?" asked Dmitri.

"What if he refuses to give the blood?" pointed out Eve. "Won't our taking it be tantamount to rape? Not that I much care. I will be first in line to drink his blood and see if what the Augury says is true. He's raped me repeatedly over the years, it's only natural that he gets the same treatment."

"Remember what the Augury warned of, Eve," Kelat said gravely. "Vengeance is a cycle."

"I don't care!" shouted Eve. "He's a monster, that one. A monster, a murderer, and a rapist! He should be punished for his crimes. He should be tortured and murdered just like he did Kallum here."

Kallum lifted a finger in askance to say something. Eyes turned to him. "You can't really kill him. He's the saviour of the Vampire race. Only in his suffering and sorrow will the Vampires find the road to salvation."

As he said this, the Blood Crown moved up and through the air to finally rest once more upon Cadmus' brow. As it did so, the crown melted into his flesh and disappeared, but Cadmus now seemed wholly angelic. Where the Crown was a curse to Vampires when worn by the Apostate, now it would be seen as a mark of salvation for all who sought it. As soon as the Crown sank into his skin, Cadmus awoke and sat up.

"What has happened to me?" Cadmus scrambled across the ground and grabbed up the chalice to behold its emptiness. "No no no."

He continued his mantra of desperation. "No no no please no no...what will I do if I can't hunt?"

Kelat walked over to Cadmus and placed an arm around him. "Son, you don't need to hunt any longer."

"Wha-what do you mean?"

"When Kallum drained the chalice, you mortated and you now wear the crown of the last magus."

"Wha-aat? I don't feel the crown on my head."

"It's inside you now, but it's evident to anyone who sees you. You are Vampiredom's saviour.'

"This can't be! It can't be! Mother, help me. Help me please!" Kelat just shook her head and hugged Cadmus tightly.

"There's nothing I can do," she whispered. "It's the prophecy fulfilled. All those dreadful prophecies we knew of that pointed in your direction were only part of the story. Now that Kallum has drunk the Augury of Gideon combined with my Blood, I have the whole story now. The terrible presence of the Pariah was necessary for the Redeemer to be born. Out of darkness and dread deeds will he come, the one who shall end Vampires worldwide. It's you, Cadmus. All we need do is place a few drops of your blood in the chalice and the deed will be done. You can live out your life as a free Tarma now. You can be alive and feel and do everything everyone else can do now. No longer are you subject to the dark magicks of the Apostate. May we take a few drops of your blood Cadmus, so the healing can begin?"

"Why would I want to heal any of you? Hm? Tell me why?

Give me one reason. I hold you all in disdain, petty little bloodsuckers, always gazing at your navels because you are Vampires! I hate you all! My mission was to destroy the Vampire clans."

"And you will complete this mission if you just give us a few drops of your blood. Watch what happens. Swiftly did Kelat open a wound in Cadmus' hand and the blood spilled into her chalice, the one that had inspired wars and caused so much sorrow over the years. Eve, come."

Eve approached the two and sat down, hatred mingling with fear as she came so near to the Pariah.

"Eve, cut yourself and let the Blood spill into the chalice."

Eve did as Kelat instructed and they waited about ten minutes before Kelat said, "Now drink, but leave some in the Chalice."

Eve turned up the chalice and drank the contents, leaving just a little bit inside. Her Latino features, so enhanced by her Vampiric nature, softened and settled into her newly mortated self. Everyone around her gasped at the transformation. She smiled beatifically and then looked down at the broken Cadmus.

"No longer am I your Garden of Blood, Pariah. You may have taken away my chance to see the Holy Isle by tainting me with your presence and forcing me to kill in order to live, but I have nothing more for you than a kind of hostile pity.

Cadmus wrapped his arms around his legs and lowered his head onto his knees. "Very well, do whatever you want. You have my blood and you'll do as you please anyway."

"If a few drops of his blood is all we needed," Thiyennen said. "Let us kill the monstrosity and be done with it."

"No," Kelat commanded. "No one will harm my son. He has suffered untold miseries in his life and I will have no one adding to it. Do you understand me?"

"You have no regency where I'm concerned, sister. And you weren't crucified and tortured by this monster you call a son. Let those of us who've experienced unspeakable agony at his hands show him the error of his ways."

"I cannot be tortured, Mother," Cadmus said woefully. "I am a mortal who remembers every moment of my suffering to the point I want to perish. Every memory is as fresh as the day it happened and I don't know what to do about it. And what is this?"

Cadmus reached up to his eyes and then stretched out his trembling hand.

"Those," said Kelat quietly. "Those, my son, are tears. You are weeping for all that you were and for all that you are and can be, I am hoping. Don't try to stop them. Let them fall and take healing from their shedding. It's a mortal thing you do, and one you've been denied for way too many years. But now you have time to explore these new emotions and to finally live a life instead of eking out an existence of hatred and instinct."

"I do not want this, Mother. Give me back my powers. Turn me into a Vampire."

"Son, you were never a true Vampire to begin with, you were always alive. Your Blood was that of the living scourge that held us all hostage as barely alive beings who craved the blood of mortals. As such, you had to drink Vampire Blood to survive. Now that the chalice contains your blood, it has become an object of healing and redemption. Through your blood, the Vampires, any who wish to do so, will be redeemed of their curse, healed and made mortal once more."

"But what am I to do if all the Vampires are healed and my chalice can no longer make Vampire Blood for my subsistence? I shall surely starve."

"Cadmus, you are mortal. No longer are you subject to that dreadful curse."

Before he could reply, Thiyennen was on him, binding him with layered *geasa* to the point Cadmus could not breathe. He could barely hear, the bonds were so tight and thick in the air around him, but he could hear.

"Thiyennen, release him!" Kelat commanded.

"His is the path to absolution. I will take the chalice and the former chalice master home. There forgiveness and the blessing of

177

God shall be had for all Vampires."

A scuffle was heard and Thiyennen was uttering words so ancient, they prompted Cadmus to cry harder than he already was. How far they had all fallen from the grace and beauty of the way of the Tarmi. Cadmus ached with the realisation of it and how he himself had worked to twist the Old Ways in his own insignificant way. Suddenly, Cadmus was pulled to his feet and pushed forward. He was leaving the Canopy Ruins, being prodded by either Thiyennen or Eve, he knew. They were the only two who might want him to meet whatever fate they had in store for him.

"What are you doing to me? Where are we going?"

"Shut up," said Eve behind him. "Just shut up, you evil creature."

"Let me go. I am of no use to you now that you have the chalice. Just let me go off and die in peace."

"You who've given no peace to anyone who's ever had the misfortune of being in your presence will receive no peace from us. Your path to salvation shall be one of suffering as we take your blood and absolve all Vampires. You shall behold their transformations and speak the tongue of agony as we bleed you just as you milked the unfortunate captives at your West Country home."

It was Thiyennen who had spoken.

Out of the Canopy Ruins, they walked the secret paths of the forest until once more they were on the road to Carcassonne. The night was still young. A taxi soon picked them up and they were off to the airport where they booked a flight to Charlotte, North Carolina. Asheville was too small of an airport. Before he knew it, they were on an airplane, heading west into the endless night. No one sat beside Cadmus, who sat rigidly, pained by the *geasa* that held him tightly. Thiyennen wouldn't even loosen them enough for Cadmus to accept a glass of water from the flight attendant.

The flight was long and Cadmus was alone with his thoughts. He remembered back to his early childhood when he had been a young mortal child, playing in the sun and nuzzling the teats of his

Dragon matrice. Those had been truly happy times for him, despite his beastly treatment of the Dragon mother. He was young and stupid. He didn't realise what he was doing, he was simply following the aberrant instinct that had been encoded in his genetic make-up.

Genetic make-up brought him back to the Augury of Gideon. Surely that wasn't all there was to the Augury of Gideon? Everything happened so fast and everyone was so keen on finding out if Cadmus' mortal blood was the cure for Vampirism, they didn't prod Kallum any further. There had to be more. Just drinking Cadmus' blood with abandon couldn't be the final and only prophecy Gideon the Mad had to offer in his jewel of Blood?

Now that Kallum had drunk it, they needed to prod him further for more information. How the Vampires were made could easily be in his memories now. How to mortate them certainly was in there, but what if there were repercussions? Had anyone paid attention to Eve? Was she truly mortated, or just a Vampire of a different sort?

Cadmus was one to study all details of any certain action. He jokingly suggested to his victims that it was the Virgo in him, not that he was much of a believer in astrology. There was something too simple about Gideon's prophecy and the use of the chalice to mortate willing Vampires. And now that Thiyennen was in possession of the chalice, only God knew what was going to transpire. There was something...not right about it.

Behind him, he could hear Thiyennen and Eve.

"How are you?"

"I've never felt better, my liege. Will you be taking the blood as well?"

"Not for a while. When we get to Asheville, we will secure the monster, then bring in the Vampires of Asheville and redeem them of their sins."

"What if they don't want to become mortal?"

"They will have no choice. I am their king and they will do as I say. If we have to shackle them with *geasa* to make them come to the place I have prepared, then so be it. This curse will end with the blood of the monster as he is bound to my construct for his own absolution."

What did he mean "bound to a construct?" Cadmus thought about what was said and let his mind wander the great pools of his endless memory. He came across the Spanish Inquisition, that time in history when the Apostate was at his very strongest and laid his will upon the brow of the people so that the *auto da fé* was a daily celebrated occurrence. All that blood and madness built upon the memory of a dead magus whose magicks had been destined to forever bind the Tarmi and humans in grace and wonder. It had never failed to amuse Cadmus when he was a part of the Inquisition, how something so wonderful could be used to produce something so vile as the Inquisition. Humans were stupid, petty little things on whom Tarmi should never have wasted their time. If the Tarmi hadn't tried to teach humans the way of Mother Earth, the Apostate would never have had the power to twist the wisdom into such horrible things as Vampires. He would never have had the knowledge to create Cadmus Pariah. ...and Cadmus would not be suffering now.

The tears came again. Were they tears of regret? Fright? Sorrow? He did not know. He was lost to the onslaught of emotions that clamoured around him wanting acknowledgment, wanting to be felt, to be known. Cadmus wanted his mother. He needed his mother.

For two hours they had all been unconscious from the *geasa* Thiyennen had uttered. Two hours of not knowing what had happened. The Vampires and their mortal comrades left the Canopy Ruins to return to Carcassonne and regroup.

Suddenly, however, Kelat began looking up into the air as they all trod across the secret forest floor. Then she stopped and clasped a shaking hand upon Dmitri's strong shoulder.

"What is it, Kelat?"

"Cadmus needs me. He's flying, flying westward, and he needs me. He needs his mother."

"So we fly westward, love. What else can we do?"

Kelat nodded. Then she spoke aloud where everyone could hear her. "I'm flying west to find my son and rescue him from whatever horror Thiyennen has in store for him. You may come with me and Dmitri, or you may choose a different path, the choice is yours.

"We're in," said Rebekah immediately.

"So am I," Ishtar said. "Maybe I can talk Father out of whatever he's going to do."

"I'm with Ishtar," Kallum said.

"You can't get rid of us that easily, right Agatha?" Orphaeus said.

"I go where the story goes," she said.

Rebekah looked at Mephistopheles and he looked back. They shrugged their shoulders simultaneously.

"Seems we have nothing better to do. Let's go!"

CHAPTER 28
THE PROPHET

"Haunted: voices in dreams. Ghosts in whispers speak through the halls of silence. Ancient as the stars on darkened pools echo the sky above. Implacable as energy, as regular as breath, from now we hear the Sirens sing their songs of love and death. Though aching in the crush of years, through all of this I drink your tears. In one kiss we are absolved, Dissolve, Dissolve." ~ Illuminati *"Dissolve"*

Following the lead of Ishtar, the group of Vampires booked a flight to Charlotte for the next evening and they all returned to the hotel in Carcassonne to get some rest. Kelat, however, was restless and uneasy. Nothing Dmitri did could make her calm down. He knew she had a special bond with Cadmus and he had heard about some of the horrors he'd endured as a child and young adult. He understood her fears that Thiyennen was about to take a route that would mean damnation for him and untold misery for Cadmus.

"Cadmus has done dreadful things in his life, things he need not have done, but did anyway. Why? Because that is what he was taught. At every turn, Cadmus was shown only the way of dread. He was sorely abused and taught that life was something to hold in disdain. His treatment of the Vampires was a taught reaction along with his genetic need to drink Vampire Blood. I am not making excuses for him because he has gone beyond his call of duty more than once and he has enjoyed the suffering he's exacted on both Vampire and Human. But what Thiyennen has in store for him, I fear it shall thoroughly break his soul or make him even more dangerous than he is. Perhaps it will be a little bit of both. Nevertheless, he's close to being uncontrollable by even the strongest of us, and Thiyennen is stronger than I in binding other Vampires. If Thiyennen begins to torture Cadmus, I fear not even his bonds will hold the Pariah."

"Well, you know we will all do the best we can to help you release Cadmus and try to rein him in a little. Thiyennen seemed to have all this planned, did you not notice?"

"He could not have known what would happen with the chalice and the blood, but I do believe he had hoped for a chance to capture Cadmus at his weakest point. I believe he has had something dreadful planned for a very long time. Thiyennen has not been the same since Cadmus crucified him,. I fear that his mind is not where it needs to be. Perhaps his fate is foretold in the Augury of Gideon. I need to speak with Kallum at length about this, so I will be sitting with him on the trip to Charlotte. The Augury of Gideon is full of encoded information. We need only to tap into it to know what our purpose is to be. Kallum needs to learn to sing the song of the encoded information. I will help him along."

When they boarded the plane early the next evening, Kelat sat with Kallum.

"So tell me, Kallum, how do you feel after drinking the blood of our prophet?"

"I don't necessarily feel any different. Maybe a little queasy, since I'm not a Vampire anymore, but also I feel a strength akin to what a Vampire feels after feeding. I remember that feeling all too well," he said smiling. "Not that I want to go that route again. I have my angel waiting on me as soon as I fulfill my duties here."

"What exactly are your duties here, Kallum?"

"To sing the song of prophecy to the Vampire race and to bring to them the redeemer of all Vampirekind. I thought I had already done all that when Cadmus bore the Blood Crown and his blood mortated Eve, but there must be something more."

"Do you know all the prophecies of Gideon now? Can you tap into them?"

"Honestly, I haven't tried. Getting near to them in my psyche gives me the heebie-jeebies, if you know what I mean."

"Can you try to do so for me?"

"Anything for you, Kelat. Anything at all."

Kallum closed his eyes and his voice became that of Gideon's. "I'm encoding this into the Blood, for there's no other way it can be protected. I tried paper, but paper burns. I've tried oration, but what I want to say never comes out right. They call me mad for my babblings, but that is how it comes to me. It is the Shaman way to speak of things to come in a way that can garnish a thousand different interpretations, but I don't want to be the mad shaman for the rest of my life. So I encode."

KALLUM SPEAKS FOR GIDEON

I have seen much in my visions. Some, but not all visions will come to fruition, for they all depend on the ebb and flow of the players in the game. I have seen my sister-wife and brother bound together, back to back, so that they could see the things that I have seen. The only way they will be able to see everything is to Behold one another, and that will be the end of all things for the Upyr. No. No, that will not happen. Not in the way it is perhaps thought to happen. They will mortate, both of them. And they will Behold one another as mortals.

Thiyennen I see walking a path of darkness, engaging in matters only the Apostate would find pleasing. It is up to Kelat to rescue him from this darkness and only as a mortal shall she be able to do so. Let her drink of the chalice and feel the soft breeze of summer on her face.

The accursed one, known as Pariah, he will succumb to the Will of the ancients and find there repose and reconciliation. Only then can he move on, and move on he must. His blood will be held sacred and shall be stored in the clay pots of the Tarmi on the shelves of the Sanctuary. All things holy eventually go to Jerusalem. This is the path the Pariah will take. For his emotions will overwhelm him and his need for love will overcome him, and he will cry for all that he has done and all that he has lost, thanks to the Apostate. His mother shall appear as a Goddess to him. Only then, shall lamentation be transformed into a kind of comfort. Bless the outcast, for his is the path of redemption for any Upyr who wishes to take it. The chalice is the way to salvation, the blood is absolution.

The bloodied saint shall show the way and speak with the voice of the shaman. Once his journey ends with the final prophecies uttered, then shall he return to the bliss that he earned by the knife of the Pariah. They must come together and sing the song that shall set the people free. The way to salvation is through the voices of mortals.

Kallum opened his eyes and looked at Kelat.

"It seems we're on the right path then, going to get Cadmus, or whatever we end up doing once we get to Asheville."

"Indeed, it does seem that way."

"Cadmus did terrible things to me, Kelat. My first instinct when I saw him was to attack him and try to do as much damage as I could. If he enacted only a fraction of what he did to me on Thiyennen or Eve, then I'm afraid that he may be dead by the time we get to Asheville."

"No, son," Kelat whispered. "Cadmus is stronger than that, even in his mortal state. He will endure until we get there. He will sing this song with you in the hope of sweet release. Then we shall see what happens. Keep your visions safe and secret until we speak again. For now, rest Kallum. You truly deserve it.

Kelat waited for Kallum to begin breathing the slow heavy breaths of someone asleep before she moved to an empty seat in front of Dmitri, who was sitting with Ishtar. Ishtar was asleep, thankfully. Kelat didn't want her to hear that Kallum could very well die after this because she knew the girl had fallen in love at first sight with the Confessor. They shared a bond tighter than just a physical attraction. She had found him buried in the dust of the SoHo basement. It was her Blood that had revived him. They shared a true connection there and one that might need to be broken so Kallum could move on, for it was apparent to Kelat that he was unhappy to be back amongst the living. He had seen the Face of God and found his own paradise. To be back here had to be jolting to his spirit.

"Dmitri, it is foretold that I will drink of the chalice and become mortal again. Thiyennen was driven mad by what Cadmus did to him. His magicks are going down the same path as the Apostate's I fear. Eve had mentioned to me in private that Thiyennen had prepared a place for Cadmus, should the chance to capture him ever came available. I'm afraid that it is not much different from an Inquisitor's dungeon, but Thiyennen is not looking for an answer or the salvation of his victim. All he wants is revenge for what Cadmus did to him. We must stop him and the only way I can do it is to be mortal so the Beholding won't kill us all. I don't know if I can return to my Vampiric self afterward. This separation between us may be the final blow to our already tentative relationship. What is it that you think of this, my friend and my lover? Can you stay with me in my mortal state? Can it even work? Would you be willing to become mortal to remain with me?"

Dmitri leaned forward and cradled Kelat's kewpie doll face in his rough hands. "There are some days I feel I've learned all I could about the world and then I see your face and know that mystery is still alive and flourishing. Whatever path you take, I shall take it with you and we'll see where it takes us together."

Tears welled up in Kelat's eyes and she offered Dmitri a smile before he kissed her lovingly. She returned to her seat beside Kallum and rested her eyes, feeling the mortal beauty of Kallum wrap around her like swaddling. She would be mortal again. It was foretold. All she had ever worked for, all the magicks she had made to attempt to remove the Vampire curse rested in the chalice. The chalice and her son were the keys to salvation, but not if Thiyennen killed him before they could make it to wherever the King Upyr had taken the newly mortated Cadmus. They must find Thiyennen and Eve. They must stop a tragedy from happening. Kelat's skin crawled whenever she thought of what Thiyennen may be doing to Cadmus. She could barely tolerate the horror of her own imagination.

"He's safe for now," murmured Kallum.

"How do you know?"

"'The son of the ancients will go there and he will behold the fires on the mountaintop, the sign of the Witch, before returning to his people, those who are not his people at all. Together with his deepest enemy in harmony will he utter the final prophecy and give himself over to the gods and ancients.'"

"What does that mean?" Kelat asked.

"I don't know, but I do know that the passage means he's safe for now and he will escape the clutches of your brother. Tell me, Kelat, how could things have gone so wrong between the two of you?" Kallum asked, his role as Confessor kicking into high gear.

She found herself telling him of how they left Thessalonika and came upon the Welas tribe, and how a group of them went out into the wilds to hold a ritual when the minions of the Aspostate and the Apostate himself were suddenly amongst them. She spoke of how the transformation and partial beholding of his sister in her true state, drove Thiyennen into a religious fervour, a type of madness from which it seemed he could not be cured. All he ever focused on was the punishment for the crimes he must commit, but never on a solution as to what made him commit those crimes.

"And so we are here, on the precipice of fate, and it all boils down to Cadmus, the one who would redeem the entire Vampire race. You were the key to that redemption, you know. You, and your utterance of the prophecies of Gideon the Mad."

"He wasn't so very mad, was he?"

"Not by any stretch of the imagination," Kelat said, smiling. "Now, can you touch upon the well of prophecy that lay still and waiting within your spirit and share with me some more?"

"I will certainly try, for you Queen Kelat," and he closed his eyes.

KALLUM SPEAKS FOR GIDEON

I have seen the lights of the Witches in the mountains. From afar, I see them and long to be with them, but I cannot. Only on the clearest of crisp Autumn nights, can you see them and take heart that not all things of the future world can be so easily dismissed or explained. Such is the way with the Vampire. Do we sanctify ourselves and turn away from centuries of dark magick or do we remain to give the human world a place of dread enchantment? Everyone must make the choice for themselves.

Know this, however: if the Original Ten all choose to return to their Tarmian selves, a choice must they make ~ to live in exile for the extended years a Tarmian lives, or to return home to Meybhelahn to join their brethren who await with open arms. This is what will happen should the Ten choose mortality.

The vessel, the dark priest, he who is outcast will be brought down and humiliated by father and daughter, priest and consort. Suffering will be his destiny until the song can be sung. Only the earthbound angel and the indwelling demon can effectively utter this song. And once it is sung, the choice of each darkling can be made in his or her heart. No blood need be drunk, no suffering be had. The heart will guide each person, the song touching their souls all over the world. Some will perish, others continue on as the night accursed. Some will seek out their mortal selves and live a life of joy until they die of old age.

But the song, the song, I can hear it now in my head. This song must be sung and, when the time is right, when the time comes, so shall it ring out for the world to hear.

"Do you know what the song is?" Kelat asked Kallum.

"I have absolutely no idea, but I'm betting I'll know all the words, if there are words, by the time we reach Cadmus."

"So the closer you are to him, the more the prophecies will show themselves," Kelat said reflectively.

"Now you're on the trolley!" said Kallum without explaining what he meant.

Behind Kelat a voice piped up. "He means you've got it right." It was Rebekah, sitting with an amused Mephistopheles. "Kallum is a lot better now than when we first met him. He was a walking museum of 1920s slang. Since we try to learn the language of the age, in order to fit in, we never had a problem talking to him. The few interactions we had with him before bursting into his apartment and turning him, you'd think we were speaking anything but English. He's a good egg, though, that Kallum McCreary."

"Made one hell of a Vampire, despite his charitable acts," pointed out Mephistopheles.

"Well, you win some, you lose some. I'm still not sure on whether or not we won a damned thing in the escapade. What's your verdict Meph?"

"The jury is still out, but I must admit, I'm having fun."

"We always have fun, eh?"

And the two of them laughed. Kelat looked at Kallum, who was smiling wryly at the exchange between the two Vampires.

"I never knew you two stalked me."

"And you'll never know who we pretended to be before we transformed you either. It's no fun that way. Now, you'll be walking memory lane trying to figure out which stranger was who and how strange were any of the strangers you encountered right before you were transformed," Mephistopheles laughed. "You may as well not even try, it'll make your brain leave skid marks in that skull of yours."

"Listen to him, Kallum, piped up Orphaeus. "When they said they'd talked to me a few times after curtain, when I was an opera singer, it drove me up one wall and down the other trying to figure out who they'd been. To this day, it makes my head hurt, just thinking about it."

Rebekah and Mephistopheles giggled with delight.

Kelat listened to all this banter and her heart swelled with love for all these crazy characters she found herself surrounded by. She looked back at Orphaeus, who was seated with super-aware reporter Agatha Crawford and the women's eyes met. In the waves of laughter that roiled through first class, the Queen of the Vampires shared that sweet moment with a "mere mortal" because of an ancient ball of petrified Blood. What were the chances of that ever happening? The slimness of such a happening made the connection that much more precious to them both.

CHAPTER 29
THE STRICKEN BIRD IN WINTER

"I'm a stricken bird in winter, I'm blind and raw with a molten core like a planet...I ache with the sun." ~ Shriekback "(feels like) A Planet

Cadmus opened his vast shark eyes to the rising sun and he instinctively tried to jump back from it, but could not. Around his throat was an iron collar on a short chain that was clamped to a strong half circle of iron embedded in concrete. He tried to pinch the iron in half, which would have been incredibly easy to do if he still had his powers, but it was impossible now. Following the thought through to its logical conclusion, Cadmus should no longer be intolerant to the sun. Cadmus looked down and saw that he had on no clothes. This must be a relatively private place for him to be outside, naked and chained, without some nosy neighbour calling the police.

He crouched, watching the great burning orb top the trees. There was no pain. He was safe to walk in daylight for as long as he had left to live. Cadmus remembered now. His chalice betraying him with the taint of Gideon's mad blood being dropped into its contents. After all these years of nurturing the chalice and keeping it pure so that, when his time rose, he would forever be afforded the luxury of satiation. Now all of that was gone and, replacing it were these mad emotions. Cadmus felt that he may go mad from them, how they clamoured and bickered for his full attention.

Still uneasy with the rising sun, Cadmus looked about what seemed to be a courtyard of sorts. Just within his reach, Cadmus found his satchel. Inside was a set of clothes and his computer. Quickly Cadmus pulled on the jeans and an old Bauhaus tee shirt, which had been cut in such a way as to allow him to wear the shirt without having to be unchained. He got his computer and opened it up. It had full power. While he waited to see what was going to befall him, he decided to write and try to ignore the ever-increasing sun.

191

The trip back to the States was without incident. I'm not exactly sure where I am but, since it was Thiyennen who took me, I'd say I'm back in Asheville. The air smells like mountain air and the way the sun dances in tiny spotlights on the ground because of all the trees, I'd make a pretty safe wager if I were to bet I were in Asheville.

I have lost all my powers. They took the chalice away from me and tainted it with a madman's blood. The minute that happened the hold the chalice had on all Vampiredom was broken and I was mortated, if that can even apply to me. I was never a full Vampire to begin with, so I am not certain what I am now. The mark of the Tarmi is still on my brow, as is the stain of humanity on my heart. I haven't tried dragonfire, but I believe I still have that ability. I'm still what I was born into except my Vampiric nature which came fully to me during my puberty. I am not sure how to handle myself and this new body.

I'm imprisoned in a courtyard somewhere in Asheville, North Carolina, which is the King Vampyr's stronghold. He and my former bride inviolate, Eve, have brought me here to exact a kind of punishment on me, for all the supposed dreadful deeds I visited upon them and so many others. If they're looking for an apology, they are looking in the wrong direction. I don't care how they prolong my suffering, I will refuse to apologise for what is, by inheritance, my very nature. Should I apologise that I took pleasure in my deeds? Perhaps. Will I?

No.

If I am anything, I am an unapologetic creature and I refuse to change today for an extra day's worth of living, especially if that living is one of torment and humiliation. I've been chained in the past. The chaining is the least of my worries, if history repeats itself, and it always does because history is comprised of stupid people with no will or intention to ever learn from their mistakes.

Thiyennen is quite mad, I believe. And I know Eve has always teetered on that fine line between sanity and madness, thanks to my taking her all those years ago. No one will be able to talk them out of whatever it is they're going to do with me. And I am helpless, save for the dragonfire. I might could break this chain with the dragonfire for that matter. I am going to try.

Cadmus closed the laptop and took a deep breath, looking at the chain that bound him as though it were something tasty to eat. In a long spitting exhalation, the dragonfire flew from Cadmus' lips and broke the chain in two. He was free. Cadmus grabbed his computer and satchel and ran off into the early morning light. Thiyennen, Eve, and their congregation would be in pursuit by this evening and he didn't want to be caught by that lot if he could avoid it.

By all indication, Cadmus was in the ritzy part of town. Biltmore was home to America's largest castle as well as most of the doctors, lawyers, and successful business men. Cadmus couldn't very well find help in getting this iron collar from around his throat here. He had no money, so he walked. It took time, but he soon found himself in West Asheville. He walked into a shop that featured exotic items and sex toys, along with thrift clothing. Walking up to the clerk, Cadmus said,

"I was wondering if you or anyone here could help me get this chain from around my neck. My lover lost the key, see, and I just can't go to work like this, if you know what I mean."

He attempted Glamour upon the clerk, but it didn't seem to work. She was nevertheless charmed by his natural human beauty. Checking out the chain, she said,

"I could pick the lock. I've picked a lot of them in my day, just don't tell anyone."

"My lips are sealed and my heart is grateful!"

The clerk pulled a bobby pin from her thick black hair and bent it in an almost "W" form. She then set to work on the collar. Cadmus was stone still as he listened to the clerk fiddle with the lock and hum to herself. There was suddenly a soft snap and the collar fell away from Cadmus throat.

"Oh thank you so much!" Cadmus said, feeling genuinely happy and grateful. The emotions sent him reeling and he lost his balance, grabbing hold of the counter so that he would not fall. I have no money to pay you, though. What can I do to recompense your kindness?"

"Well, this collar is kinda cool. Mind if I keep it?"

"By all means! Thank you so very much!"

"Any time, dude. Hey, you want a shirt that's not all cut up? We sell thrift, but I don't think it'd be a big deal if I gave you a shirt."

"That would be outstanding of you."

The thin clerk rummaged through the clothes at the back of the shop and came back with a Magnificat shirt."

"Here you go. You know, you sorta look like that Cadmus Pariah dude from Magnificat."

"I get that a lot," Cadmus said uneasily

"I wonder whatever happened to that band. They were pretty good."

"Maybe they ran out of blood and had to go their separate ways to find it."

The clerk laughed at that. Handing Cadmus the tee shirt, she said,

"I hope you don't mind my saying so, but I always found Cadmus to be very sexy and good looking. You look exactly like him, so I have to ask. Are you Cadmus Pariah?"

After Cadmus popped the tee shirt over his head and pulled it down over his thin frame, Cadmus leaned in to the clerk, his lips only an inch away from her ear.

"In what seemed like an age ago, I used to sing for a band called Magnificat. I drank the blood of thousands. But that was an age ago. Now, I am nobody for you to be worried with. Then I was Cadmus, the king of everything he purveyed. Today I am Pariah, outcast and hunted by the angry mob. If anyone asks you if you saw me, tell them no. For my sake, tell them you've seen no one in your shop that fits the description of Cadmus Pariah."

The clerk pulled back and kissed Cadmus on the lips. The sensation was wholly pleasing to Cadmus and he felt the pleasure move down his spine and into his groin. This had never happened to him before. He kissed back, wanting more of this unusually pleasant sensation.

Soon they were in the back room of the shop, shed of their clothes and moving together in rhythm to the exotic music being played on the shop's speakers. Cadmus could not stop kissing the clerk, whose name was Jill. He wrapped his arms around Jill's neck and kissed her time and time again. With each deep kiss, his urge to penetrate her grew more frantic. He lay her down on a bed of thrift store clothes and opened her legs. Kissing her thighs slowly, he finally reached her musky wetness and pressed his lips upon her clitoris, licking it slowly with his cleft dragon tongue. When Jill lifted her hips in pre-orgasm, Cadmus stopped licking her and moved up to press himself inside her.

They no longer moved to the rhythm of the store's music. They had their own rhythm, slow at first, then faster and faster as both built up to orgasm. Jill came first, screaming her lover's name. Then Cadmus came and he was silent, feeling the waves wash over him. This was a cramp that felt wonderful. He spilled copious amounts of seed inside Jill. So much that it began pouring out between her legs and soaking his testicles. He did not care, though. He was feeling joy, true joy. Not a philosophical apex. This was magickal.

Cadmus leaned down and kissed Jill on her nipples, then her throat, each cheek, and then slowly and sensually on her lips.

"You are wondrous," he said in that accent that could melt any woman's heart. "Thank you for freeing me, in more ways than one."

Cadmus stood and pulled on his clothes, smiling at the irony of wearing a Magnificat shirt, and he left Jill in afterglow, into a world he was beginning to see very differently now that he could feel emotions. Perhaps the world and its inhabitants weren't so bad after all.

He found a café that provided free WiFi and sweet-talked the waitress there into a double latte. Now that he was mortal, he could try real food. Today, he wanted coffee. The waitress came back with his coffee and pressed her finger to her lips. Cadmus genuinely smiled at her and opened his laptop to get online.

> I had sex with the woman who removed the chain from my neck. It was unintended and spontaneous...and the most wonderful sensation I've ever had. I have had sex before; so much sex a person could not fit all my so-called escapades in one volume. But it was always to put the person at ease so I could make them a Pet or kill them outright. With the Vampires, Ambrosciata was always part of my method of killing. Perhaps that was the Darkblood in me.
>
> But this time it was different. I felt a fondness for this clerk named Jill. She was friendly toward me and seemed so incredibly genuine. She did not swoon at realizing I was once the leader of Magnificat. She took me for who I was and who I

am now. She asked no questions about the iron collar. Jill was simply Jill and, because of that, I felt a profound closeness to her. I didn't just have sex with her. No. We...we made...love. Although I didn't feel love, I did feel a deep fondness for this hippie clerk. She treated me well and I left her fully sated and satisfied.

I would not mind seeing Jill again, if the fates allow. I feel a great affection for her.

I'm in West Asheville now, reading a flyer about all the great places to visit. There's one place called the Gnomon Garden that sounds very interesting. It says that the Gnomon is by nature a dark place, featuring red and black plants, and flowers of unusual shape.   There are also metal work sculptures abounding. If I weren't on the run, I would go to this place and soak up the atmosphere. It sounds like it is charged with energy, and that is something I could truly use at this point.

My encounter with Jill was astounding and I drew a great deal of energy from her, but I also gave her energy. It wasn't a feeding, it was an exchange. Come to think of it, I'm writing as though I am still a Vampire, and perhaps I am. I'm craving energy and I'm utilizing energy to get what I need. Perhaps I am a psychic Vampire. I've heard of them. They are not part of the Hive, being wholly human, but still engaging in the pulling of energy from their fellows. Perhaps I am one of them now, for however long I've got. Thiyennen's minions will find me eventually; I just hope Mother Kelat reaches me before Thiyennen does.

Hope? Did I just write that I hope for something?
Do I actually hope?

Cadmus took a sip of his latte. It was incredible. He'd never tasted coffee before and this was something miraculous. He wanted more of it. He gulped down the coffee, ignoring how boiling hot it was splashing down his throat. He was enamoured of the latte. He asked his nice waitress for another and she winked at him as she went off to get him another free coffee. Cadmus continued his writing.

> I believe that the chalice's contents, the Blood of Gideon mixing with the Blood of Kelat, are responsible for what I am enduring now. Even though the emotions are what I had always striven for, I am distressed that I no longer am in possession of the chalice and am wondering if I will starve for Blood now that I am dispossessed of all my Vampiric qualities.

> I'm drinking coffee and it is filling me up. This is a good thing. Next I must try to eat something. Perhaps I can finagle a scone from the kind waitress.

> Ah, mission accomplished. I am eating a blueberry scone and drinking my second coffee, all of it free. Perhaps my Glamour isn't gone after all. Or maybe it's just in my nature to charm people. I know that there are humans like that. Maybe it's the way of the psychic Vampire to be able to draw humans to them. How else could one pull the psychic energy from them?

> I must find shelter before night falls. Thiyennen's agents will be out in force as soon as the sun goes

down. They will want to bring me back to that place, whatever it was. Something tells me that I was better off chained outside than to be inside that structure. I have been tortured in my life. When I was but a youngling, being forged in the fires of the Apostate, I was put to the rack. They also hung me by my wrists and whipped me like a common cur. I was imprisoned in the Iron Maiden and flailed whilst imprisoned in the stocks. There are so many ways to torture someone. Each one cleanses the soul, makes a person a living *tabula rasa* upon which the one in power may write a new person into being. I have been there. The person I am today is because of the cruel punishments I endured then. I do not want to feel that horror again. My only hope – and, yes, I said hope – is that Kelat finds me before Thiyennen does.

I don't know what I am feeling about being a mortal Tarma now. I don't know how much of the Apostate's humanity resides inside me. I am not even certain of what I feel now that I can feel. Terror? Unease? Displacement? I know that the thought of Thiyennen capturing me does fill me with a sense of horror.

I was beyond unkind to him when I held him in my Asheville home. The crucifixion of a Vampire is considered the worst form of punishment, for the Vampire remains alive, but perpetually feels the death of a Vampire. And, as long as the Vampire is on the cross, that torment is there every single minute of every single day.

Will Thiyennen crucify me? I am not certain that he would want to do that since it would probably kill me now that I'm truly mortal. I'm sure he's found or invented certain structures to ensure my suffering.

Yes, I am scared he will find me first. I'm scared of the pain I will endure. I'm scared that he will kill me. I want to live, even in this diminished state. I want to carry on and explore the magicks I know to see if I can return to my former self. There's got to be some way, and that way depends upon my reclamation of the chalice.

If I could somehow steal the chalice away from Thiyennen, then I could experiment with the sacred cup and become what I was before this weakened state. Although I am enamoured of my newfound emotions, I would prefer to be my old self. No one dared cross me. I could tap into my philosophical apices if I needed to exhibit some emotional response, and I was actually tapping into true emotions with Kelat's help, so my former state is preferable to this. Even though I'm a Tarma with a little human, I feel so small and weak in comparison to the demigod I was before. I am no longer Cadmus Pariah. I am simply Cadmus. And it is distressing.

Cadmus read what he had written and pressed the "post entry" button.

"Can I get you anything else?" the waitress asked, her voice laced with a soft filigree of Southern accent.

"No, poppet," Cadmus purred. "You've been very kind to me. I do so appreciate it."

"No problem. As long as the owner doesn't know we're good, you and I. And don't worry about leaving me a tip. I've been where you are before, so keep whatever money you have, sweetie."

"Thank you."

Cadmus watched the waitress walk away and it occurred to him that, had he been in his previous state of superiority, he would have dismissed this woman completely. She wouldn't even have been good enough to feed the chalice. Cadmus felt a new emotion now. It began as simple gratitude, but then slithered into a moment of shame. Cadmus was ashamed at how he had treated people just like that waitress over the years. He had behaved horribly toward people and manipulated them with his Glamour. His was a history of shameful behaviour and he felt the weight of memories crushing his shoulders and back.

Eating the last of his scone and downing the remaining coffee, Cadmus trekked onward to the heart of Asheville, the downtown refuge for the hippies, the homeless, the freaks and the weirdoes. There he would find a place to hide until Kelat came. And he knew she was coming. It wasn't a psychic awareness. It was...faith. Cadmus had faith that Kelat would come and rescue him.

The prophecy of Gideon was that Cadmus and Kallum would sing the final song that would redeem the Vampire race. That meant that Kelat would have to come to Asheville and bring Kallum with her. She had to come and stop Thiyennen before he had the chance to kill Cadmus.

Cadmus felt a jolt of fear at the thought of Thiyennen and he hated that. Fear was not something Cadmus had felt since the early days with Nissius. Immediately Cadmus shut those memories down. He couldn't deal with that yet. If he were to live this life as a mortal Tarma, he would eventually have to tackle the memories of his childhood, but today was not that day.

CHAPTER 30
RETURN TO ASHEVILLE

"Nothing is for free the story goes. You hear it and believe, now don't you grieve or look behind. He's saying why, why do we do this? This is the very thing that's preying on his mind" ~ Shriekback *"Everything that Rises Must Converge"*

The airplane took off from JFK after an uncomfortably long layover. While they waited, Kelat reserved four rooms at the Grove Park Inn on Kallum's computer.

"We could have just stayed at my place," argued Dmitri.

"Your place is too small for all of us. Besides, I want everyone to have some peace as the morning dawns over the Smoky Mountains to greet the Augury of Gideon.

"You mean..."

"Yes. Kallum has embodied the essence of who Gideon was as well as absorbed all the prophecies he saw. So much confusion over such simple revelations..." Kelat mused. "We are so close to redemption. Not just you and I, but all of Vampiredom. We must find Cadmus tonight. I'm sure he's at a loss, being transformed as he has been. I ache for him. I ache with him."

"You can feel him, then, even if he's wholly mortal now?"

"He is Tarmi as am I. We are always linked together. Just as I know that Thiyennen has set out minions to try to find Cadmus, who has escaped whatever the Redemptor King has in store for him. I know exactly where my son is."

"Where?"

"Right now, he's on Lexington Avenue, mingling with the locals and tourists, and waiting for me. It's just a matter of who gets to him first; me or Thiyennen's agents.

"And what are we to do with him, when we do capture him? Drain him of his Blood and bring ourselves to his cannibalistic level? I think I'd prefer to remain a Vampire, thank you."

"Kallum said under no such circumstance will Blood have to

flow. All we need is for Kallum and Cadmus to sing the song that's encoded in both of them. Kallum's melody is one of holiness, the essence of the great shaman Gideon. Cadmus' counter-melody is, if I'm not mistaken, the song of healing we Tarmi always used to sing. It will be a beautiful thing and it will unravel the Great Hive. We will choose then what we want to be. I imagine the Tribe of the Tomb will become mortal by default and their healing can begin. There's just so much in my head that I want to relay to you but, the more I try to tell you, the more I sound like Gideon the Mad instead of Gideon the Mage."

"You need to sleep, to recharge. Come, I will hold you until you sleep, then I will hold you in your dreams."

"What the hell are we doing here, Meph? I mean, I've been confused ever since we got that beacon from Faust...or Kallum... whoever the hell he is. I'm about to throw my hands up and bolt. What do you think?"

Meph lay back on his first class seat and studied Rebekah in quiet repose. Then he spoke.

"I believe, Bek, that we'll know why we're needed once we bring Kallum and Cadmus back together. There's gonna be a rumble in order to retrieve the Pariah and who better to get into a fight but we beasts? As long as we have each other's back, you and I will be okay."

"I know. It's just all this rigmarole in between happenings, Meph. I'm a woman of action."

"Oh baby, don't I know that," Mephistopheles growled appreciatively as Rebekah straddled him, much to the dismay of the flight attendants.

"We should get Cadmus and re-turn him, make him one of us for real and true."

"Wouldn't that be hilarious?"

"A scream, Meph," Rebekah nipped at her lover's throat. "A real scream."

Agatha sat in agitation beside Orphaeus, who had his eyes closed. She was wondering exactly what had transpired back in France. Why had they all been frozen, unable to move even a mite, while Thiyennen and Eve left taking the chalice and the freshly mortated Cadmus with them. The *geasa,* as the Vampire was calling the bonds that held them, did its job for at least an hour while the King Vampyr and his cohort made their escape. She could tell that Kelat was increasingly concerned for the health and well-being of Cadmus. Agatha knew that Cadmus was Kelat's only son, but she couldn't understand Kelat's dedication to him. He had tried to kill her on more than one occasion. He had threatened her with death. He'd threatened and killed her loved ones. What must the beast do before Kelat draws a line and says enough is enough, already?

But Agatha wasn't a mother. She'd never had the inclination to breed, instead focusing all her attention on her journalistic career. After all these years, she never thought she'd still be at that joke of a newsrag, *The International Herald*, but it had afforded her a chance at a much larger story, even though she was going to have to have it published as fiction in order to protect those Vampires who'd been so good as to protect her.

Agatha looked through her copious stack of notes, insights, and interviews. She also had some photographs, which she wouldn't publish, that would help her visualize the ebb and flow of the narrative. She was very excited to get home and start her book but, for now, it was back to Asheville where Agatha had lost her best friend.

She thought of Paine often and wondered where his immortal soul finally found peace. It was then that she mustered up enough courage to approach Kallum. She stood up and squeezed past Orphaeus, who only grunted a tad, then repositioned himself. The seat across from Kallum's was empty, so Agatha took it and whispered his name.

He opened those impossibly blue eyes of his and smiled merrily at Agatha. "Hey there. You're the reporter, yes? Agatha? It's nice to meet you. I'm sorry we haven't had much of a chance to talk, what with everyone running around like chickens with their heads chopped off. What's going on?"

"It's nice to finally meet you, too," Agatha said. "I've been told a great deal about you and I saw your dead body dug up and revived by Vampire Blood. I felt your spiritual pull to that building in SoHo, so I know there is life after death. I was just curious... Is there really a Hell and do all Vampires go to Hell when they're killed?"

"This is about Paine Bryerson, isn't it?" Paine asked quietly. Agatha nodded, giant tears welling in her blue eyes.

"We all must account for the things we did when we were alive, but I don't believe God has a place of eternal punishment. We all have our special heaven and, if you feel you need to atone for sins committed whilst alive, the punishment pretty much matches the crime. Then the cleansed soul is given paradise. At least that's how I understand it. Your Paine was a good man, a decent Vampire who did not kill lightly and worked toward the betterment of his race. I daresay, he loved you very much and would have gone to great lengths to protect you."

"He did, he did," Agatha said, the tears flowing now. "I just miss him so much. This idea of becoming mortal again would have been something Paine would have done anything to achieve. It just breaks my heart that he wasn't around to see this happen."

Kallum took Agatha's hand. "Don't worry for your friend. He's immersed in his own bliss and will come to guide you to yours when the time comes. Trust me on this."

Agatha smiled at Kallum and squeezed his hand in thanks. She went back to her seat further back in first class and eked by Orphaeus again to look out into the night sky as the airplane shot through the atmosphere, carrying them all to Asheville.

Orphaeus was deep within his dreaming and was not stirred by Agatha's coming and going. He was standing on a vast plain and in the distance was a tall and spiraling tower. To his left was the setting sun and to his right was an impossibly large moon rising over the horizon. At the top of the obsidian tower was a crystal beacon and he felt he must reach the top of that tower in order to finish his quest, whatever that quest may be.

The plain between him and the tower was grassy and leaves of grass blew gently in the Summer wind as the sun set to his West. He began to walk slowly toward the tower when he realized he was not alone.

Beside him walked Cadmus, his long black priestly robes blowing in the wind making him look like the figure of a crow about to land. He cocked his head a little and looked at Orphaeus, smiling.

"Why do you go to where you know you cannot ever reach?"

"What do you mean?"

"This place is reserved for those who chose to die. Yours is a different path altogether. You cannot possibly reach the tower and touch the light within as you currently are. I will hold that light in my hands long before you ever dream of taking a different route. So why do you walk this plain and ache for a place you willingly eschew?"

"You mean immortality, don't you?"

"We're all immortal, Orphaeus Cygnus. It's just a matter of which immortality you choose; the kind that binds you to the physical realm and compels you to take life or the kind where you live out your life as a physically mortal being only to move on to touch that light in yon tower. Which will you choose, Orphaeus Cygnus? Whatever you do choose, know that I'll be here before you, but I'll be here as your friend."

"You? A friend?"

"Stranger things have happened, Swan. Life and Death so often change the rules and make the players take different routes, routes they would never have imagined taking. You and I formed a bond on our journey to Rome. Before I might not be able to do so, I want to thank you for saving my life when I donned the Blood Crown for the first time. Thank you for taking me back to Kelat. Thank you for your kindness, in spite of what I'd done to you in the past. You are a good soul. Never doubt you'll reach the top of the tower when you're finally ready to walk this lonely road. And, when you do walk this plain of death unfettered by the trappings of life, don't be surprised if I walk it with you, your dreadful spectre in the night.

Orphaeus opened his eyes and felt a tear slide down his cheek. What was this that he would dream such a dream? Cadmus was always plaguing him in his dreams, taunting and terrorizing him in some form or fashion. Orphaeus had gotten used to that. But this was different. It was a kind of goodbye as well as a word of warning. He'd heard the prophecy of mortation, that the choice could be made in your heart and no blood would be needed. But he enjoyed being a Vampire, and he had a family of Vampires back home who he doubted would want to become mortal after all these years of decadent delights.

Orphaeus reached down and absently rattled his bag of finger bones. He had been raised a Catholic and he doubted that he would be allowed entry into Heaven after all the bloodbaths he had taken over the years. If he chose mortation, it would take a lifetime to absolve himself of all the sins he'd committed over the long Vampiric years. He was no Redemptor. He felt he needn't apologise for anything. Despite his inclination to rip asunder his prey, he always made sure they were blissfully unaware of their own death. He was a decent enough fellow, he reckoned, but not by the standards of any religion that he knew existed on Earth. Even the Tarmian religion could not tolerate the things that he had done.

No...that tower would have to wait, possibly forever. He would not walk the windy plains with Cadmus of all people.

Cadmus surprised him though, by thanking him. And, even more surprising was Cadmus showing emotion. Smiling and having a genuine look of fondness upon his face. It was like the end of the world had come for Orphaeus to behold such an incredible phenomenon.

He looked over at Agatha who was staring at the icy clouds over which their airplane skimmed.

"Are you okay?" he asked.

"I suppose so. I was speaking with Kallum. He's an exceptional young man."

"He's older than you think."

"Yes, yes, I know. But to me, he's still a young man. I wonder what will happen to him when he and Cadmus come together again. Will it be the end of all of you?"

"No, I don't think so. I believe we'll be called to make a choice and to abide by that choice."

"What are you going to do, Orphaeus?"

"I'm staying as I am," Orphaeus said gently. "My family needs me and I'm not yet ready to tread the path of mortation. I have too much fun just as I am. Just call me a natural sinner and love me the way I am, 'cos that's how it's gotta be for me.

Agatha smiled.

"I sorta figured that would be your answer," she said. "I'm curious about this song. Do you really think it's a song?"

"The way Gideon's prophecies are, it could very well be a song, or just an utterance made by both Kallum and Cadmus. I don't really know for sure. Gideon's prophecies have always been so convoluted, but the ones Kallum have given have been pretty lucid. It's like Gideon poured all of his sanity into the blood jewel and let the madness of his visions take over his physical self. So, when he tried to prophesize, all we got were strange riddles and nonsensical rhymes. The insights he's giving through Kallum are much clearer, and Kallum has become the Vampires' shaman, despite being mortal himself. He's sainted, incorruptible, touched by God himself; yet, here he is uttering prophesies that affect possibly the greatest atrocities known to history. I'm amused by the irony of it."

"I can tell."

Dmitri and Ishtar both slept lightly and some heavy turbulence woke them both. Ishtar rubbed her eyes and ran her fingers through her long copper hair. She looked over at Dmitri, whose pale countenance was nothing short of beautiful. His long dark lashes sat at half-mast as his eyes were barely open, but open nonetheless. His mouth was set and calm beneath his whiskers. He turned his head and looked at her.

"Did the turbulence wake you too, then?"

"Yes, but I wasn't sleeping very well anyway. How much longer before we reach Asheville?"

"At least another hour, maybe more, I'm thinking."

"When we get there... Dmitri, when we get there, are we going to die?"

"No... I believe we will be called to make that choice, though. I do not believe that Vampires will start dropping like flies. I do think that we'll have the chance to become human once more and live out our days as human, aging and dying as we were originally supposed to do."

"What are you going to do?"

"I'd like to say I'll make the choice Kelat makes, but I really don't know."

Dmitri wanted to remain at Kelat's side, but the call to learn more about the ancient Earth and to walk in history in the making was so very strong. He was addicted to the world and all its trappings. If Kelat chose mortation, she would most likely seek a way to go to Meybhelahn. Dmitri wasn't even certain he would be allowed to go there if he decided to become mortal again. And then he'd be alone, with a hole scooped out of his heart for having lost his soul mate, and he would die alone, not knowing the gentle touch of his beloved Kelat'menan. What sort of choice was it? He was torn in two. It would just be so much easier if Kelat chose to remain the Hive Queen and they could walk in harmony with each other until his questing spirit took him away. But that wasn't fair to Kelat. He knew she suffered for his soul to be with her when he was away and she also longed for the sacred Tarmian veils to part for her to walk again in blessedness. It was a difficult situation at best and he didn't see how their decisions would not bring tears one way or another.

"I don't think it's fair to have to make a choice now. I've just begun to learn what I am and tread the path of the Vampire. Now I'm being given a choice that seems to be etched in stone. What if I make the wrong choice? Will I die if I make the wrong choice?"

"We all eventually die, even Vampires."

"I thought we were immortal."

"We are, but we aren't perfect. If you stood on a train track long enough, a train would come and pulverize you. A Vampire can't withstand such an injury without dying. And, believe it or not, there are still Vampire hunters out there. They'd be more than happy to drive a stake through your heart if they could find your resting place during the day. There are many ways a Vampire can die, and all of them are exceedingly unpleasant, Inochka. And I am one to believe that fate will eventually catch up with us all, each and every one."

"What are you going to do, Dmitri? What will your choice be?"

"I honestly do not know. When the time comes, I guess I'll be standing at Kelat's side, ready to journey with her, whatever road she may take. Either choice may bring us great unhappiness or bliss untold. We won't know 'til we get there, Inochka. And you? What choice will you make?"

"Like you, I'm torn. I have a special bond with Kallum. I dreamt him so many times and I know that I love him, despite the fact that we've hardly been together for any length of time. I do love him. But I know, too, that once he sings this song or whatever he's supposed to do, he will die. He wants to die, to return to his angel Rosetta, and the bliss he left behind. Where will that leave me? Should I return to my mortal self, part human, part Vampire, unable to fit into any social circles because of my Dhampir nature? And there's so much I can learn as a Vampire. I don't know...I just don't know what to do."

"It would seem that you and I are in the same boat, then. When that boat docks, I suppose we'll either stay put and wait for the tide or jump to the land with a fervour. I wish I could ease your discomfort, but your dilemma is one that only you can solve. Do what you feel is right in your heart, is all I can offer. The heart never lies to you."

And with that statement, Dmitri made his decision for when the time came. He could rest easy for the rest of the flight. It's funny how helping someone else with their problems often opens the door to your own problems as well. Dmitri smiled and scratched his beard. He knew what he was going to do. His heart was finally at rest.

Kelat sat with Kallum in silence, although both of them were awake. She held the young mortal's hand, squeezing in comfort on occasion. Kelat felt very protective of Kallum, as though she would kill anyone who dared even threaten the young man. She couldn't understand it until sleep took her to the state of dreaming.

> She was amongst her tribes mates singing the ancient songs of the Tarmi, dancing in the flames of their great bonfire, leaping through it as though it were nothing at all. For the Tarmi, it was not. Kelat made no leaps through the balefire, but she saw her beloved Daddwyd there and he leapt through without a problem, even though he was human and the balefire was huge, made for the Tarmi who often grew one or two feet taller than the tallest human. She sat with her child Andharwhyn and sang to her. He looked up at her, his giant blue eyes staring in love and wonderment, his eyebrows almost reaching the top of his forehead as he listened to the songs and tried to emulate the ululations of Tarmian language. He was only two, but already he was speaking both Tarmian and the ancient Welasian tongue.

211

"Andharwhyn, do you want to jump the balefire with me?" Kelat asked. "I can carry you through and then we will have such luck, you cannot even imagine the blessedness of it."

"Yes mother, carry me through."

So Kelat took her child and easily jumped through to the other side where Daddwyd was waiting. They gathered their family together at the base of a standing stone and continued singing in celebration. And every time Andharwhyn looked up at Kelat in her deep memory, she saw the mark of Kallum on his face.

Kelat opened her all-seeing Tarmian eyes and turned to face Kallum.

"Do you have the gift of deep memory, child?" she asked him, urgently hoping for the impossible.

"What do you mean?"

"Do you remember any of your past lives."

Kallum grinned that sidewise grin of his, his merry eyes dancing along Kelat's face. "I was wondering when you'd remember me."

With that, Kelat grasped hold of Kallum and pulled him to her, hugging tightly and crying. "My Andharwhyn, my Andharwhyn, so sorely have I missed thee."

Kallum hugged back lightly, a little bemused by Kelat's reaction to his statement.

When Kelat sat back, she apologized for her outburst. "You must know that the dreadful thing I did, I did out of instinctual necessity. We had not yet retrieved our senses and were as animals in the night, feeding on whatever came to us. I am so sorry I took your life. My son, my son..." Kelat wept bitterly. "I never wanted to hurt you. I would perish if something were to happen to you."

"Remember, though, Kelat," comforted Kallum. "I'm not your son in this life. You've got no reason to come to my defense. Besides, soon I'll be gone. You can make the choice to join me or choose to remain here when the song is sung. As for what happened aeons ago, do not worry. My soul has long forgiven you that moment of feral instinct. As your son, I always loved and trusted you. Because of the Apostate, you could never have raised me and I would have been outcast from the tribe because of I was your son. What you did was for the best. Never forget that and never forget that I love you, Mother Kelat."

Again Kelat drew Kallum to her in a tight embrace. "Remember this, young Kallum. I will always love you and I hope we find one another again in the Dance of Ages."

"I don't doubt it, Mother. Not at all. We all choose our own bliss. I believe yours will carry you to a place of great beauty with the souls you've loved the best throughout time."

"Perhaps you are right. What is this song, Kallum?"

"I don't know what it is, but it's something that both Cadmus and I have to sing, or utter. It will herald all Vampires and give them the choice to carry on in their accursed lives or to become mortal and live out their life as a human or Tarma. But the Vampires will never be the same. The time has come for Vampirism to end. Those who choose Vampirism will live incredibly long lives, but they will have the mark of mortality upon them. This is Cadmus' gift to the Upyr. There will be an end to the curse. They will not be able to turn anyone else and, over time, they will age and die. How will this happen? It has to do with the chalice. Cadmus will know what to do. Right now, he is struggling with his own mortality, realizing that the Night is no longer his. But he is, by his very nature, a great priest of the Craft. His destiny is to guide the lost to the light in the tower of heaven. Trust in him, Kelat. He will do what he must to make sure his destiny is realized. You must prepare yourself to say goodbye to him, depending on your own choice and depending on his. When we get to Asheville, everything will change. You're a strong woman, Kelat. What will transpire will test your strength because the most important things to you are the people that you love. You love deeply and eternally. There is nothing stronger than the love of the Tarmi. Let that love guide you and the ones who must choose along with you."

Rebekah looked up the aisle with interest when she saw Kelat suddenly embrace Kallum.

"What do you think just happened there, Meph?"

"Maybe it's Christmas and we missed it. Maybe he went to Jared. Hell if I know...or care for that matter. Stop being such a busy bee, you."

"Well, I can't help it, you know? We could very well be on the verge of a Vampire apocalypse and all you want to do is calmly sit there and let it all happen."

"Well, it's gonna happen no matter what I do, so I may as well be comfortable when the Terrifying Squeegee of God slides us all off into oblivion."

Rebekah chortled with laughter. "You are so not right, Meph."

"And that's why you love me. As for what's going on up there, in all seriousness, I have no idea, but I think that if affection is involved, then it must be a positive thing. Kallum was always a special soul. That's why you and I chose him all those years ago. He's certainly shaken up the Vampire world, hasn't he? We chose wisely I think.

"And look at Orphaeus: a beast being the protector of a mortal. Most beasts would have already torn her apart and eaten her heart while it was still Beating, but not Orphaeus. We chose wisely there, too. I don't think we have anything to worry about when it comes to our Blood children. We set them loose on the world and, most of the time, they've done us proud."

"You're absolutely right, Mephistopheles, my friend and lover. Whatever may happen in Asheville, at least you and I can say that we have chosen wisely."

"Indeed," breathed Mephistopheles.

An hour later the airplane touched down at Asheville airport and the Vampires and their mortal friends were driven to the Grove Park Inn just as the sun began to peek over the mountainous horizon. Four rooms had been reserved by Kelat on Ishtar's new computer. They all retired before the sun had a chance to rise Dmitri and Kelat, Orphaeus and Aggie, Rebekah and Mephistopheles, and a very nervous and self-conscious Ishtar and Kallum all made for their respective rooms.

"We could switch around if you wish," Dmitri said merrily.

"No! Uh – I mean no, that's fine. I'm sure we'll manage" they quickly said together.

Kelat smiled and led Dmitri off to their room that overlooked the majestic Smoky Mountains.

CHAPTER 31
THE CONSTRUCT

"We hold the Life in one hand as the one who bakes the bread, (the erection at the hanging and the tearing off of heads)"~ Shriekback "Despite Dense Weed"

Dusk came too soon for Cadmus' taste. He knew the hunt for him would begin in earnest. Even though Eve could now tolerate the sun, being mortated and human once again, Cadmus knew she wouldn't leave Thiyennen's side for fear that Cadmus would come and kill him in his weakened daylight state. Now that the sun was no longer an issue, the two would be actively seeking him out, calling on other Redemptors in Asheville to find the mortal Pariah and bring him before the King.

Cadmus was hoping that Kelat and her band of ne'er-do-wells would find him first. Though he no longer had the keen Vampire senses on which to depend, he did know that Kelat had finally made it into town. His Tarmian senses felt her very near, but they weren't strong enough to pinpoint her.

Finding a way into the old abandoned Woolworth's on Haywood Street, Cadmus made his way to the basement level of the department store. A few wire hangers lay strewn about on the floor, along with tissue paper used to box a freshly-purchased piece of clothing. It wasn't the best of refuges, being dusty, dingy, and dark, but it would have to do until Cadmus could meet back up with Kelat.

He sat in a corner, alone in his thoughts. He was sleepy and hungry, but he was too caught up in the adrenal rush to succumb to either of those trappings of the mortal coil. He hugged his knees, rocking back and forth on the balls of his sandaled feet.

He wondered what Thiyennen would do with the chalice now that it was in his possession. Cadmus' reckoning was that Thiyennen would keep the chalice and have a line of Redemptors from his door stretching halfway across the country eager to be mortated so that they could sufficiently atone for their numerous

216

sins as Vampires. A few drops of Cadmus' Blood was now trapped inside the chalice. It would transform any Vampire Blood into mortal bloodwhichthe drinker could then imbibe and become mortated. Just like Eve.

Cadmus' thoughts drifted around the image of Eve, his beautiful Garden of Blood. She had been the first to try the chalice, so eager was she to be rid of Cadmus' taint. It was a little ironic that Cadmus' blood was what transformed her back into a human. He figured it really didn't matter to her, just as long as she was free from Cadmus and the nighttime visits that terrorized her, not to mention her compulsion to drink the blood of children so that the Blood she gave Cadmus was the most pure there ever was. Eve certainly had her reasons for wanting to become human and atone for her sins. Of any Vampire, Eve had her reasons to choose a mortal life.

And Cadmus had no need of her anymore, with him being mortal now as well. Something told him that he would die before getting the chance to be transformed back into the realm of Vampirism. He didn't think it would even matter anyway. Once Kallum caught up with him, the supposed song they were to sing would alter Vampirism irrevocably. Cadmus could not go back. That path was blocked, bent like a prism to where Cadmus would never find his way.

Cadmus put his fingers up to his mouth, nibbling at his cuticles. His fangs were gone and his mouth felt funny as a result, even though he rarely displayed them. The flood of emotions threatened to crash through and leave him helpless on the floor. After all the centuries through which Cadmus traveled emotionless, a killing machine with the force of all that was futile shining blackly from his all-absorbing eyes, the mortal Cadmus was now at a loss for what to do with himself. He was tired, yet super aware of everything. He remained perched on the balls of his feet like a bird and then realized this was how the Tarmi often stood and walked, with their heels in the air. His Tarmian self was coming to the fore and that was what made his emotions all too alive for Cadmus to handle.

"No, no, no..." he chanted as he rocked harder. "No, no, no, no, no, go away, I do not want you. Give me back my philosophical apices, these emotions are too much. No, no, no, no."

It was then he heard footsteps on the stairs coming down.

"There he is," Eve said. "Take him."

Two large Redemptors fell on Cadmus before he could attempt to fight them off. He was so weary and hungry, he wouldn't have been able to anyway.

"Did you really think you could hide from us?" Eve asked. "Even though we're both mortal, you and I, I can still sense you, like a stench on the open air. You can never hide from me."

She slapped Cadmus hard across the face. "Look at me when I talk to you, you animal! I'm taking you back to Thiyennen, who has a special surprise for you. Bring him," she said to the two Redemptors. "We've got to get a taxi to Biltmore."

Cadmus slept a little on the ride out to Biltmore. Exhaustion took him over with the rhythm of the car's engine. When they drew near to Thiyennen's secondary home in Biltmore, the Redemptors took Cadmus whilst Eve paid the fare.

Thiyennen's second home in Biltmore was cloaked with *geasa* and contained every form of torture a person could imagine. He had been collecting these items ever since he had been tortured and raped by Cadmus. This had become his hobby, turning himself into a Grand Inquisitor. The torture devices weren't to be used on Cadmus, though. No, there was a special place for Cadmus; the item Thiyennen had named the Construct.

It was five wooden wheels bound together with rope and tar. At the top and bottom of the Construct were thick leather constraints affixed to rope that ran to the back of the Construct. The rope was connected to what looked like the steering wheel on a pirate ship. The more you turned this wheel, the further apart the constraints became, thus stretching out the body of whomever was bound to the Construct outward and away. The wheel in the back possessed niches so the pressure could continue until the user of the Construct either freed the prisoner or decided to increase the pressure another notch.

As soon as Cadmus was brought into the house of horrors, he was stripped of his clothing and placed upon the construct. As payment for their good deeds, Vasily bade both Redemptors drink from Cadmus. Cadmus hissed in pain as the Redemptors took their turns on his body, biting his throat and taking in one long draught before standing back and feeling their transformation from Vampire to human complete itself before their very eyes.

"Do you see now?" Thiyennen asked softly from the muted shadows of this place of pain. "Do you see what my Construct is for now? At first it was only to cause you a fraction of the pain you caused me when you did this."

Thiyennen came out of the shadows and violently pulled down his turtleneck to display the raw scar on his throat.

"But now it has an even greater purpose, more so than this accursed chalice. The chalice lost all its power when your blood was poured into it. It truly is a useless relic now that Kallum drank the Augury of Gideon and the Blood Crown buried itself into your mortal scalp. Tell me, Cadmus, do you feel the crown of thorns on your head. I can see it as I'm sure any Vampire could. After I drink from you, I wonder if the phenomenon will still be visible. Let's see..."

And Thiyennen moved to Cadmus and bit into his femoral artery, taking a long draught of blood from his son's thigh. He fell back and seized. Eve screamed and ran to Thiyennen, attempting to hold him to the floor until it was over. Soon it was and, when Thiyennen opened his eyes, his eyes were that of a Tarma once again, but a Tarma who was still badly damaged psychologically.

"God be praised...the curse is gone. Eve, go tell the others and have them spread the word. Our way to salvation rests upon the Construct."

Thiyennen stood and walked behind the Construct and, without hesitation, turned the wheel two notches. Cadmus' scream was that of a damned soul. He would have writhed in pain, but there was no way to do so, his body was so taut. He could feel every

219

joint begging for release and the very discs of his spine threaten to separate. And that was only two notches. What would happen when Thiyennen decided to turn the Construct's wheel another notch or two? Cadmus wasn't sure he would survive it.

Thiyennen continued. "The mighty Cadmus Pariah, how you've come down in the world. What once was great is now a vessel of pain stretched across my sense of purity and vengeance. I will never go so low as to call you my son. You are the mutated afterbirth of my nighttime issue. That is all you ever were and all you shall ever be. Kelat might call you son, but I call you a demon sent straight from Hell."

Cadmus raised his head and looked Thiyennen in the eye. "You've never tasted Hell, O King." And with that, he spit dragon fire right into Thiyennen's face. Thiyennen didn't even get a chance to scream before his head was eaten completely away by the acidic dragon fire. Cadmus remembered the day in the desert when that almost happened to him, and how his biological mother Kelat had nursed him back to health in spite of his vow to destroy her. Now he wished she would find him and save him again. Then Cadmus laughed, truly laughed. When all is said and the day is done, the only thing a person wants when it boils right down to it is his mother. Cadmus couldn't believe what he was thinking and feeling, and he soon found himself in hysterics, laughing and crying all at once, succumbing to the tsunami of emotions that he'd long abandoned in a field of unmentionable abuses. There he was, naked and strapped to a wheel-shaped rack, staring down at his headless father while the dragon fire continued to sputter and spit around the corpse's shoulders, and all he wanted was his mother. Cadmus' sense of absurdity had reached a breaking point and he screamed with the emotions that it unleashed. The scream ended with his merry laughter filling the torture chamber.

CHAPTER 32
MYSTERIES OF THE AUGURY,
ISHTAR AND KALLUM

"I had a dream I walked the desert. I saw a virgin and a lion."
Shriekback "Invisible Rays"

The Vampires were on the last leg of their journey, landing at the Asheville airport right before dawn. Two cars waited for them and they were driven swiftly to the majestic Grove Park Inn, where they checked in and settled in for a day of rest before searching the poetic mountain night for Cadmus Pariah.

Kelat had paired Kallum and Ishtar to share a room. It was the only logical placement for all the people that were involved in this mission. They were escorted to their room by a very polite bell hop. Kallum shyly placed his satchel in the corner of the expansive suite and sat down in the chair at the desk. He studied the rich stationery that was displayed proudly on the desk. He noticed that one of the amenities was free Wi-Fi, so Kallum pulled his computer out of his satchel and was online in mere moments.

"What are you checking for?" Ishtar asked.

"I'm checking Cadmus' online journal to see if there are clues as to where he may be. It looks like he was in West Asheville not so very long ago. He might still be there, perhaps haunting the Gnomon Garden he mentioned in his blog. He seems both enamoured and horrified by his sudden transformation into a true mortal. Cadmus could very well be on the verge of a holy madness found in prophets and priests. He certainly is connected to the Augury of Gideon by way of the chalice and the Blood Crown that rests on his head, its invisible barbs digging into the skin of his scalp, always there as a reminder of who he is and what he must do."

Ishtar stared at Kallum. She truly did not understand a word the man had said, but she was tired and dreadfully hungry. The sun prevented her from going to hunt and blood was the only thing on her mind at the moment. Cadmus be damned. She didn't care about Cadmus and his newfound responsibility within the Great Hive's destiny. All she wanted was blood.

Kallum looked up at Ishtar and noticed the look on her face. It was pinched with a hunger that would keep her awake all day and hinder her ability to function when the blessed dark came 'round again. He knew that expression. He'd had it many times in his past, when he was Faust just learning the way of the Vampire.

"You need to feed," Kallum said simply. It wasn't a question, but a direct statement of fact.

"Yes..." Ishtar replied, her eyes glassy from the hunger.

"You can feed from me, if you wish. I am a mortal after all and I'm healthy, young, and strong. Check out the muscle." Kallum playfully flexed his right arm to counteract the discomfort of their situation. "Seriously, Ishtar, you can take my blood. . Just don't kill me. I still have a job to do."

He pulled Ishtar to the bed, pulling back the comforter to reveal white satin sheets and pillows that resembled the clouds of heaven. He got on the bed on his knees and pulled Ishtar to him. Murmuring to her, Kallum said, "You brought me back from the dead. The least I can do is to offer my life blood to you, lovely Ishtar."

And with that, Ishtar kissed Kallum fully on the lips, savouring the anise seed taste of him and listening to the blood flow through his veins, welcoming Ishtar's deep bite. Oh indeed it came quickly, for Ishtar was famished, almost starving, being a young Vampire and needing more blood as a result. She had not fed the way she needed to because of this quest they'd been on. Kallum was determined to catch her up tonight. He leaned into her bite, never flinching, but embracing Ishtar as she drank from him. Her hands mussed his sandy hair and pulled his head to the left, moving fully against him, sucking the lifeblood out of him with abandon. Within moments, she had taken at least two pints and Kallum had to pull away, he was getting weak from the feeding.

But Ishtar wanted more than just the blood. She moved in on

Kallum again, unbuttoning his shirt to reveal the sandy hair that covered his chest. Moving down, she unbuttoned his pants and reached into the front of them to find his highly responsive penis. She rubbed him up and down, pulling on him, encouraging him to grow longer and thicker as she removed her own clothes with his enthusiastic help. Soon he was ready and willing, and Ishtar mounted Kallum, her knees clasping to his hips as she moved like a slow and determined leopard, keeping pace with the rhythm of the blood that coursed through her now, fortifying everything she did. She had dreamed of this time with Kallum. She had loved him from the moment he appeared in her dreams. And now she was making love to him after he freely gave her the blood she so desperately needed.

Faster she moved now and she bent over Kallum to suck and lick his nipples as he explored the weight of her young breasts. Then their lips met one another and the tenderness of their kiss brought Kallum to orgasm. He bucked against Ishtar in the throes of physical ecstasy, then came to rest, still hard enough for Ishtar to continue her motion. Soon, soon...she was almost there. Yes. Yesss... The walls of her vagina rhythmically squeezed Kallum pulling in every drop he had to give. Soon it came to an end and Ishtar collapsed beside her mortal lover.

"I love you," he said to Ishtar. "If I could, I would give you more blood now, but you might kill me...although I'd die a happy man. Why don't you call room service and have them bring copious amounts of orange juice. I have the feeling I will need to boost my strength in the coming days...or hours. Whichever comes first."

Ishtar laughed. "You have such a way of saying things without ever saying anything. Are you intentionally like this or does it just come naturally?"

"Well, it's a little bit of both," Kallum said, playing with Ishtar's ginger locks. "It all depends on when we find Cadmus, see. If it's tonight, then I won't have much time to refuel, so to speak. If it takes us longer, then I don't see why we couldn't do this every morning before going to sleep."

Ishtar smiled at Kallum and kissed him tenderly on the lips. "I love you too. From the moment I saw you in my dreams, I knew that I loved you."

The lovers fell asleep cradled in one another's arms, giving their spirits over to the realm of Morpheus for a few hours of bliss.

Kallum didn't sleep as well as Ishtar. He was weak from her feeding and his dreams turned dark as the Augury boiled forth to show him visions in his sleep. He saw the Lion of Judea standing in front of the sun, which created a great halo around its head. At its feet lay the broken body of a tainted lamb and a scarab resting upon its dusky wool. Then he saw Thiyennen, a pale shade of an entity walk out of the vision to reach out to Kallum, who recoiled from the King Vampyr's touch. The vision was grey and shades of grey, fading in and out like an old movie being played on a projector. "Killed me..." Thiyennen said his voice muted and silent for all its earnest. "Killed me...bound to the wheel, his own dark satellite. Redeem us. I am lost to redemption. Lost and cold."

Kallum then saw the mountain with the ghost lights dancing along the crest like giant fireflies. The Witch's mountain, far and away from Asheville. He would know the route, he would remember the name of the mountain upon waking. The fires of Brown Mountain. Where the ghost lights danced is where they would end it all.

Constantly the visions came rolling forward with snippets of prophecy or promise, he didn't know which. And a melody began to play in his mind. Over and over again, this simple melodic phrase, like filigree and spider silk weaving the visions together in a song that would not be silenced. The song must be sung and the lights will dance for Gideon the Mad. The lights that build. The lights of redemption...indeed shall they dance.

Soon Kallum was stirred awake by the odd visions and the melody in his head. He went downstairs to dining and ordered himself a whopping big breakfast with plenty of orange juice.

Alarmed at how the waiter looked at him, he caught his reflection in the coffee pot on the table. He looked a mess, wan and barely able to sit up straight. His hair was askew and standing on end on the left side of his head. Kallum ran his fingers through his hair to try to get it to behave, but it was hopeless. He turned his attention to the gigantic breakfast he'd ordered. Eating every bite on his plate and drinking an entire carafe of orange juice, Kallum then relaxed in culinary afterglow with a strong cup of coffee in front of him.

Surprisingly, he was joined by Kelat.

"Good morning," she said smoothly, reaching out to stroke his face in a motherly fashion. "You could not sleep, I see."

"No. Ishtar and I finally admitted to carrying a torch for one another, and one thing led to another, and I figured I should come down here and try to regain my strength before she bumps me off by accident, you see."

Kelat smiled at his verbal acrobatics, weaving the modern with the antiquated. But she was up and in the sun for a purpose, not to discuss Kallum's unusual love life. "You had visions of Thiyennen, did you not? Dark visions?"

"Yes. Yes I did."

"My brother is dead. He died overnight, a victim of Cadmus, who is also near death. Do you think you can find him before it is too late?"

"That won't be a problem. I can do it now, if you wish, but I figure everyone will want to be involved, so it'll have to wait 'til tonight. Right?"

"Yes, unfortunately. His spirit wavers on the peripheries of my own. He is a mortal being forced to endure what would easily break a Vampire. How he's surviving it, I do not know. Kallum," Kelat said as she took his right hand in both of hers. "He is my son. And, based on what you've told me, it's imperative that he survive whatever trial has been set before him. Find him for me so I can take him home."

"Of course I will, Grandmother," Kallum said, smiling sidewise, his indigo eyes flashing with determination combined with a merriment that never completely left his face. "I know when we do find him, we're supposed to go to where the lights dance. I saw it in my visions."

"Where the lights dance?" Kelat asked. "I do not know where this is, but perhaps Dmitri could tell us. He is sleeping now and so should you. You've been through a great deal already and you should take advantage of this calm before whatever storm Cadmus may bring to us."

Kallum nodded. Sleep was ready to take him this time. He went back upstairs with Kelat, who bid him a good day's rest and entered the room next to his and Ishtar's room. Kallum shuffled into the room and collapsed on the bed. His crash didn't faze Ishtar one bit, who was sleeping the slumber of contentment after having fed and made love. Kallum was asleep before his head hit the pillow and, this time, his sleep was dreamless.

CHAPTER 33
REQUIEM AND THE CONGREGATION

"And what glows warm behind us casts a shadow limp as sleep. It goes on forever or it seems that way. The words unspoken, the line uncrossed." ~ Shriekback "Evaporation"

When Eve entered the torture chamber Thiyennen had constructed and saw the King Vampyr lying on the floor headless and irretrievably dead, she cried out in great distress. The Vampires she brought with her to partake of the essence of mortation all followed suit, for the king of their Hive, the King Redemptor was no more.

"What have you done, you wretched creature?" Eve cried.

"What would you have me do, *pet*? I survived. Do what you will with me, but do not try to kill me or you will end up like your puppet deity, dead on the floor."

"How did you do it? What did you do?"

"Suffice to say, Thiyennen experienced firsthand what a child of dragons can do. It's not pretty, but it is functional and I will use dragonfire again if need be. Do not try to kill me or drain me to the point of death, Eve, or I swear I will burn this entire place to the ground with us in it. Redemptors far and wide will sing our requiem. For now, though, say your prayers over your King who, in his last moments, was clearly mad, more so even than Gideon, who at least saw relevant visions."

Eve had brought with her six Vampires who desired mortation. They gently removed the headless corpse of Thiyennen to a chamber adjacent to the dungeon. Eve turned the key of the construct one notch to make certain Cadmus was safely bound and, the dragonfire notwithstanding, posed no threat to the eager Vampires before him. One at a time, they walked up to him and bit into his mortal flesh, drinking his blood. Eve instructed them to take just a sip, for she was worried that Cadmus would react to a threat of death. And he would have. In fact, even though he felt no threat from these paltry beings, he was tempted to just spew forth the dragonfire and destroy them all. But no...let them have their mortality if that's what they wanted. For his part, Cadmus would have preferred being his old self instead of an eternal spirit trapped inside a body that was slowly breaking on this wheel of pain.

Cadmus watched the Vampires of the Hive of Redemption transform into their previously mortal selves and, despite their King lying dead nearby, they could not help but celebrate their freedom from a curse that plagued them like it did no other kind of Vampire. They fell to their knees and thanked god for this blessing that wrapped them in light and wonderment. How anyone would choose being mortal over that of the Vampire was beyond Cadmus' comprehension. True, he had never been fully Vampiric, aging as he did through the long years, but the aging process was so minimal, it was almost as if Cadmus had immortality. He had lived through centuries of human strife and triumph, pulling down the weak and the weary to feed his beloved chalice. He had shaped the course of history by forming secret societies and moving the chess pieces behind the scenes. His teacher was the best at such esoteric, being the dreaded Apostate, whose crown now rested heavily on Cadmus' bald head.

The mortated Vampires, three male and three female, approached Cadmus again, this time to kiss his feet and thank him for the gift of mortation. It amazed Cadmus and filled him with loathing for these trifling and miserable creatures.

"Get away from me," he spat. "You got what you wanted; now leave me to ponder my agony."

They quickly exited the chamber, leaving only Eve.

"I should end your agony right now for what you did to Thiyennen," said Eve.

"What about what Thiyennen and you are doing to me, hm? Hm? This is always the eventual path a Redemptor takes. Your self-loathing trickles out of you like a psychic stain and taints everything you touch, do, or say. How anyone who claims rights to what is holy or Godly can create a place such as this has either gone mad or is so hateful, it's no wonder they cannot find God. God does not reside in torture chambers. Only small creatures make these oases of agony their indwelling."

"What would you have me do, Cadmus? You took everything away from me when you converted me to Vampirism. You turned me into a child killer and a weak and worthless vessel available at any time for your pleasure. I became the Bride to the Beast and, until I took Thiyennen to heal, I led a life of grim solitude. Is it not right for me to mete out a little vengeance for all the woe you have caused me? Every gasp of pain you muster is one long year of my life as your Bride Inviolate. Every wrench of your body is a child gone missing because I had to feed. Tell me, if you were in my shoes, what would you do?"

"I am not in your shoes, as you say, and I care not for the petty unhappiness you felt because of your fate at my hands. You invited me in. In some small way, you know you wanted what I had to offer. Despite it all, after all these years, you still can't come to grips with the fact that you've loved me from the night you laid eyes on me. You knew I was dangerous. You were even warned by Marjoram Diamante, but you still invited me in. I did what I was meant to do. And what did you do? You did what you were meant to do as well and you know it. Accept your guilt and reconcile with it. Be a true Redemptor and take responsibility for your own actions. Then release me from this wretched construct before I die."

Eve's silent stare was clouded with large tears that pooled in her exotic Latina eyes. They dropped simultaneously and rolled down her olive cheeks and then to the stone floor.

"I did love you. I *do* love you. But I hate you too. I hate what you made me and I hate that, sometimes, when you would come to me in the night, I shivered with delight at being your Bride Inviolate. And I wished you would take more than just Blood. I wished you would take me and truly make me your wife."

"That was not in your destiny," whispered Cadmus. "Yours was always the path of purity and I could not take your maidenhead and maintain the level of purity I needed you to be for me. And now it's too late. Your hatred of me is all encompassing, compromising who and what you truly are. I have violated you by my mere presence, but that was always inscribed in my own destiny, now wasn't it? I stain everything I touch with the Blood of innocents."

Eve picked up on the tinge of regret she heard in Cadmus' voice and she stared at him in wonder. "You truly have changed, haven't you? Despite your protestations and pontification of the wretched and vile, you have changed. You are experiencing true emotion."

Cadmus looked away from her. "And with every emotion, I hear my own requiem being sung by those vicious angels in my head."

One of the mortated Vampires came back into the torture chamber.

"Excuse me, Eve?"

Eve turned her tear-stained face to the polite intruder. "What is it, Angus?"

"They're gathering, like they did when the chalice called out to the Hive. Dozens of Vampires are here, wanting to be given the healing blood."

"They will have to wait," Eve said in a clipped tone. "He's given too much blood tonight as it is. We don't want to kill him...yet. House as many as you can here and tell the others to find refuge until tomorrow night. In the meantime, I'll get his health back up and we'll transform as many as we can tomorrow night."

Angus nodded and left.

"The Hive of Redemption is going to bleed me dry. I would laugh from the irony of it, but it hurts to blink my eyes, much less attempt to laugh."

Eve stepped closer to Cadmus' stretched and naked frame. "I am sorry for this, but I will not release you. I will bring you some broth and juice, and tend your wounds tonight and tomorrow during the day. Then tomorrow night, I'll only allow a few to take your blood. I won't turn the wheel anymore, Cadmus, I promise.

But this is how it will end for us. Thiyennen built this construct with you in mind because of all the terrible things you did to him, and to us all. I will not sully his memory by letting you go."

"And I would not expect you to, so brainwashed you are by his Redemptor codes of honour, written in the heat of divine insanity."

"He was not insane. He was driven by his faith."

"He was driven by his faith in the oblivion that was the Apostate's counterfeit religion. How ironic indeed that the King of Vampires was snowed by the Apostate so thoroughly as to create an entire caste of Vampires that constantly keened and self-immolated in an attempt to cleanse themselves of their sin? Thiyennen was a fool and a lunatic without the merits of Gideon's insight."

"I have to go. I need to deal with the crowd that is gathering to take your blood and be healed of this curse."

"Go on then, poppet. I'll be right here when you get back, suffering in just the way you've always dreamed."

Eve gave Cadmus a wounded look, then left silently. The moment she left, Cadmus hung his head and groaned. There was no denying to Eve that he was in agony, but he refused to show it. The restraints dug into the flesh of his wrists and ankles, causing rivulets of blood that dripped down his body and onto the floor. This construct was indeed an ingenious device that did its job well. Thiyennen had delved deep into his heart of darkness and fell from grace as a result. No sane person, no person with a sense of right and wrong, would create such a tool of misery. Cadmus was glad his father was dead. His holier-than-thou sermons on how Vampirism could eventually be cured by way of the Christ both tired and irked the Pariah.

Thinking on that, he was suddenly very aware of the last magus' wreath of thorns that had merged painfully with his scalp. There was no tearing it off, not until Cadmus was dead. He had become the owner of the crown, just as the Apostate had been the owner. He wondered what powers he could wield as a mortal now, as a

Tarma. Closing his eyes, he focused on the crown.

Quite suddenly he saw Kelat and all the other surviving members of the Original Ten Upir. He saw what they were doing at that precise moment. Kelat was talking to Dmitri, Braecca was praying, El'Alan was rapturing a human, Danaewen was just waking from a long sleep after feeding, Treska and Orenelle were both in the congregation gathering around Cadmus, Moren'telah and A'sa were en route to Asheville. They would all gather and avoid Beholding one another, each of them hoping to take the blood of Cadmus and become mortal once again, to be free of the Apostate's eternal curse. He saw each of them, but it was Kelat to whom he was drawn. They would always have a bond, he reckoned. Ever since they connected psychically in the desert and especially during their conflict over the chalice, Cadmus was linked to Kelat.

She looked up and directly at Cadmus and the other Vampires disappeared from his vision.

Where are you? She asked him. *We are coming for you, but we need to know where you are. Thiyennen's geasa won't let me seek you out. How are you here before my vision even with the geasa unbroken?*

I am using the Blood Crown. I can see and apparently communicate with the Original Ten via the magick of this relic.

Stay connected to me and we will come for you. Are you in distress, son?

They are breaking my body one tiny turn of the wheel at a time. So it would be pleasant to have someone cut me loose from this construct.

We are coming, Cadmus. Be strong.

Cadmus was always strong. He was the epitome of strength and control. That is what he kept telling himself when the emotions tried to crowd into his mind and heart, and the fear of death lingered at the threshold of his sanity. He thought of the Vampires' filthy mouths on his skin, making bite marks so they could partake of his magickal blood and the urge to vomit overtook him. He leaned down as best he could and emptied his belly on the stone floor. It gave him a dark satisfaction that Eve would have to clean that up. Then again, she may get one of the placid Redemptors to tidy the torture chamber before the games began anew.

Eve and Angus returned with a thick broth and apple cider. Angus cleaned up the mess Cadmus had made while Eve plied Cadmus with the broth and cider. Cadmus would have none of it.

"Do you think you can eat at all?"

"I can only focus on maintaining my composure in such a state as this," Cadmus said as smoothly as he could. "If your vertebrae were bent at such an angle and your arms and legs were pulled to such a degree they were more a burden on the body than support, your appetite would not be very much in your thoughts."

"You need to build up your strength."

"For what? So I can be bled by your Redemptor clan and watch them drop to their knees and thank a god that does not exist for their mortality? I would rather die now."

His harsh words stung Eve, who felt increasingly guilty at Cadmus' state of agony. She truly was a good soul, the most pure spirit Cadmus had ever encountered, the female equivalent to Faust the Confessor. Cadmus intentionally softened his voice and said to her, "Set me free, Eve. I promise not to run. If you set me free, I will drink your broth and cider. I will allow the Vampires who want to be mortated to take my blood. I'll do whatever you wish of me, just set me free."

Eve hesitated, looking at Cadmus and his piteous state. This was not how she wanted to end it. She despised Cadmus for what he had done to her, what he had created in her transformation to Vampirism. But she did not want this. This was Thiyennen's vision, but Thiyennen was dead now, his soul reconciling in the afterlife. Eve was in charge now and she could not abide torture, even if it was of the vile and perilous Cadmus Pariah.

"Angus, help me take him down from this construct," Eve said.

"But Thiyennen – "

"Thiyennen is dead. I'm in charge now and I want him down. This is the only way we can keep him safe and strong to give the healing blood. Now help me."

Angus and Eve took Cadmus down and he rested on his hands and knees, breathing heavily and willing the tears away. His body felt stretched beyond breaking and his rib cage felt like it had collapsed. There was no way he could move to escape and his Vampiric Compulsion was gone from him. Cadmus had no choice as he was moved to a small cot in the corner of the room to lie down. He was still very much a captive of the Redemptors. His only hope was that his ability to heal quickly was still part of his nature.

Eve knelt beside him at the cot and fed him broth spoon by patient spoon. Cadmus was amazed at how good it was. All the food he had ingested since he was stricken with the mortal curse had been magnificent. He took all the broth and drank all the cider, lying back on his sorely abused spine and closing his eyes.

"Eve, I keep having visions of a mountain with ghostly lights that move and dance. Perhaps we should go there so the large group of Vampires can assemble more easily. You're going to get a great deal of attention here, if you haven't already. Do you know the mountain about which I speak?

Eve thought and was taken aback by what her memories brought her. "You're talking about the witch lights of Brown Mountain. It's about two hours east of here."

"I want to go there," Cadmus said, an urgency in his voice. "I need to go there...to fulfill the prophecy and end this dreadful curse."

Eve thought he was talking about Vampirism, but Cadmus was talking about the curse of mortality that was on him. He felt that if he could be close enough to Kallum he could pull from the Augury that he contained the secret to returning to his immortal self. There had to be a way to reverse it. Or perhaps Kelat would be kind enough to transform him. There had to be some way to get back to his former self.

"Cadmus, are you sure? I don't think you should move tonight. Perhaps we could start the journey in the morning. You and I can walk under the sun now...thanks to you. We can leave instructions for the hive to join us there. Word will spread across the psychic net of the hive and they'll assemble at the mountain beginning tomorrow night.

"That sounds perfect, Eve. Thank you for being so kind to me." Cadmus said softly. "You of all people had reason to leave me on that construct. Your goodness outweighs your instinct toward revenge. I find that amazing and refreshing. Thank you."

"You're welcome, Cadmus. You were right. I never stopped loving you. Despite it all, I will always love you."

She left the chamber and Cadmus lay on the cot alone focusing on his wounds, willing them to heal to no avail. He focused on the Crown and was soon watching Kelat again. She was brushing her hair.

Cadmus? What is it? He heard her in his head.

Eve and I are traveling to Brown Mountain tomorrow. I've had visions of the ghost lights on the mountain. A large congregation is gathering here in Biltmore, too large for the authorities to not soon notice. We'll be moving in the morning since we can both walk under the sun now. Everyone will follow in the night. Meet us there. Please. Bring Kallum.

We shall all be there. Dmitri will know the mountain of which you speak. We shall join you there, Cadmus. Are you fit to travel?

I hope I will be by morning. At least I'm not being tortured anymore. Your brother knows how to hold a grudge.

And you know how to kill people effectively. Kelat said flatly. *I know he was being beyond unkind to you, Cadmus, but you did not have to murder him.*

I'm sorry mother. That's still my first inclination, but I'm trying to work with different methods of...persuasion now. Forgive me for murdering your brother.

Kelat thought about what Cadmus said and nodded. *Over time,*

235

the wound will heal. I can understand your desperation and that's my only comfort in this sad situation to which I can currently grasp. Heal for now Cadmus. We shall meet you at Brown Mountain.

CHAPTER 34
BROWN MOUNTAIN

Not that there's anything much to blame, still you must wonder why everytime, the dead all look the same. We do a lot of thing all the time. We can be pragmatists, animat, or something along those lines. ~Shiekback "Load the Boat"

Kallum sat straight up in his bed. There was no point in trying to rest. Every time he closed his eyes, he saw Cadmus Pariah in amongst the ghost lights of the mountain. It was driving him to distraction. He opened his computer and began to do a search for lights on mountains. Almost instantly he came across Brown Mountain, a mountain not too very far from Asheville whose claim to fame were inexplicable ghost lights that roamed along the sides of the mountains.

It was a foothills mountain, only 2600 feet in elevation. Quite puny compared to the mountains the Vampires were currently in amongst. But it made up for smallness with its claim to fame ~ the lights. The lights seemed to be ancient, so much so that the Cherokee had old legends of them purporting that they were the spirits of fallen warriors.

Some people in Generation X knew the mountain as Witch Mountain for the book by Alexander Key and the movie from whence it was taken.

There were a plethora of explanations about the lights, but none of them seemed to hold credence for long. It would seem that the locals just accepted them for what they were and accepted their uncanny presence as a phenomenon they accepted and welcomed as yet another tourist trap. And there seemed to be so many in this part of the world. Kallum was growing increasingly fond of Western North Carolina.

He closed his computer and went downstairs because he knew that Kelat would be down there. She may say she needed to rest, but she was too wired to do so and Kallum knew this. Sure enough, she was in the room adjacent to the lobby. There were sofas and overstuffed chairs in here, as well as computers and an extensive library available to patrons. Kelat sat with her eyes closed, her brow knitted. When Kallum walked up to her, her large eyes opened and she bathed him her Atlantic Ocean gaze.

"Kallum, you cannot sleep?"

"No, Queen, I've been troubled by visions and I discovered what they are."

Kallum sat down beside her and opened his computer to show her the website about Brown Mountain.

"This is where Cadmus is going. He said that he and Eve were going to the mountain of the ghost lights, that he had seen it in a vision. It would seem that you and he are on the same page with your visions. This means something tremendous, especially since the Vampires are converging in Asheville again. Something momentous is going to happen, Kallum. Do you have any idea of what?

"All's I know is that once my work is done here, I get to return to my paradise, which pretty much means I will die again."

"Does Ishtar know this?"

"I've talked to her about it. She seems okay, if not a little sad, that I'll be leaving her behind, but I've assured her that we'll meet on the other side. That's just how the dice roll. Kelat..."

"Yes?"

"Do you know this melody?" And Kallum began to hum as best he could.

Kelat listened with great interest, but shook her head. It almost has a Native American cadence to it. Is it from the Augury?"

"Yes, and it's playing over and over in my mind, especially since I've been having visions of Brown Mountain. I believe we're supposed to go there and Cadmus and I are supposed to do something with this melody."

"You may not know exactly what it is until you're both there face to face. Perhaps it is the healing song mentioned in the Augury, the one the mortals sing to heal the Vampire curse. You'd' mentioned it before."

"I may have. Ever since I ingested the Augury, my personal short term memory is on the fritz, but memories I've never had before are right in my face."

"Memories of Gideon?" Kelat asked softly.

"Yeah, I guess you could say so."

"Can you share them with me?" Kelat asked almost shyly.

"I can try."

Kallum and Kelat turned in their chairs to face one another and Kallum touched his forehead to Kelat's.

They were suddenly in a dark and dingy motel room. The sink across from the cot-like bed was black with filth. He sat on the cot, a single tear dropping from his pale green eye. His hair was mussed and wild. He hugged his bony knees to his chest and pleaded to a god who could not hear him to make the visions go away. Taking a long nail on his right thumb, he dug into his own flesh and the blood flowed. Taking a small red stone, he rolled the jewel back and forth in the Blood until the Blood ceased. Gideon continued to roll the jewel, speaking swiftly in the High Tarmian, until all the Blood was dry and the Blood on the stone was fixed. Then he openly wept and cried out for a time that was gone an aeon ago. And he began to sing the same melody that Kallum had sung for Kelat. The words could not be made out, but the melody was unmistakable.

Kallum broke the connection and looked wide-eyed at Kelat. "You know, Kelat, Gideon wasn't mad. He was just weighed down by the undeniable weight of prophecy and he didn't know what to do with it. I find it amazing that something as expansive as his burden was, he was able to transform it into something so small as the Augury. Now, sometimes, I feel that weight myself, since drinking the Augury. Sometimes...when I close my eyes, the expanse of everything comes and weighs upon my heart to the point that I want it to stop. I think that's why I was destined to drink the Augury. I can take this weight that Gideon bore away to the place it was always supposed to be, to the realms of the holy. That weight will be taken from me as well and both Gideon and I can lay in repose in the sacred light of forever."

"You speak like a Tarma."

"I have a million Tarmi inside me at the moment. More than a million. Is it any surprise?"

"Hopefully, soon you can rest as Gideon is resting now. I must admit, though, Kallum; I will truly miss you, my little saint."

Kallum smiled widely and they got up to arrange for the trip to Brown Mountain with a local limousine service. The mountain was about two hours east of Asheville, near Morganton, so they would need to leave right at dusk in order to have any time at all. Kelat had the sneaking suspicion the Vampires that had congregated around Cadmus were readying themselves to make their way to the mountain as well, being told by Eve, who had unexpectedly aligned herself with Cadmus.

Or was it so unexpected? They were in a sense married in the Blood and, despite the harm Cadmus had caused Eve, there was no doubt that Eve loved Cadmus and she always would. The Glamour he placed on Eve had long faded, but the love was still there, just as it had been with Mary Magdalene. Kelat wondered if Cadmus knew how lucky he was to have not one, but two, women so thoroughly dedicated to him and his happiness. She doubted it, because Cadmus existed on a different plane that kept him apart from the normal mortal trappings of life. She did read his journal entry about Mary Magdalene and noted his slight sense of regret over her treatment and eventual death at his hands. Would he do the same to Eve? She doubted it. Eve had teetered on that edge of love and hate with Cadmus. She had seen a side of him that Mary Magdalene had never experienced ~ the side that caused children to have nightmares and mortals pull their cloaks around them in a moment of chilly fright. She had also met the seducer, the one who can speak words of nectar dripping from the flowers of adoration. This caused Eve to be conflicted in everything she did or said. She wanted Cadmus dead as much as she wanted him to love her instead of using her as a garden of Blood. Now that they were both mortal, Kelat reckoned that Eve might feel a little differently toward Cadmus, who was her captive in a sense and dependent on her in almost every way.

Kelat thought about the vision of Gideon that Kallum had shared with her. He had looked so gaunt and frail there – nothing at all like the tall, strong Tarma he had been. She remembered Gideon hauling great logs up to his mountain home and carving spirit faces into them, bringing out the whispers of the trees in forms of animals and human and Tarmi faces. The Native Americans of the Pacific still practiced this art in their totem poles. Spirit faces he called them. Gideon always loved the woods and the mountains of Welasia. He said the trees were each a living entity and that their spirits were often restless and needed to sing. This brought Kelat back to the present. What if the trees of Brown Mountain were restless and wanted to sing, so they sent out spheres of illumination in the hope that someone would understand their request and come sing the song? Was the melody Kallum was singing, the same one they heard in the vision of Gideon, an ancient song of the trees? Were the spirits of the trees of Brown Mountain somehow connected to the Vampires?

Trees were always associated with human beings. The Tarmi called them the Children of the Trees because they were arboreally-born. The Tale of the Budding Trees moon told that story unequivocally. Whether people wanted to believe it or not was not the issue; humans seemed forever bound to the fate of trees. Gideon was like humanity in that way. He contended that, if trees birthed humanity, they were living, sentient spirits that needed to be listened to always. Humanity hardly listened to them today, though, Kelat thought bitterly. They tore the trees down, creating great machines that not only cut the trees down, but shredded them as they passed through the ancient forests of the Earth. Humanity seemed to hold no regard for the trees that gave them life. There were some who knew the secrets of the trees, some who still sang their songs, but they were rare, and still the carnage raged on. It made Kelat bitter and sad to think about it.

Kelat seemed to be doing a great deal of thinking. Bidding Kallum goodbye as he drifted to the dining room, Kelat returned to the library and sat down, closing her eyes.

Cadmus can you hear me?

She got no response, but tried again. *Cadmus, if you can hear me, please speak with me.*

Still nothing. He must be asleep. She hoped beyond hope that he was no longer being tortured. It pained Kelat to know that Thiyennen's last moments involved torturing his only son. Sometimes, retribution is not the path to take, and that was something Thiyennen either learned to late or learned not at all. It broke her heart that her brother was dead, but it heartened her that he finally had the curse removed and tasted sweet freedom from it for at least a little while.

It was late afternoon and Kallum had enjoyed a large late lunch. His belly full of good food and his head full of Scotch Whisky, he made his way back upstairs and to the door of Rebekah and Mephistopheles room. They had been his Vampiric parents and he had always wanted to know about them. Now was as good a time as any, his Whisky told him, so he knocked a *shave and a haircut* and got a *two bits* before the door opened to reveal a beautiful black with a white towel wrapped around his face.

"Hey Bek, it's Faust...uh, Kallum. Get out of the shower!"

"Okay, just give me a quick minute Meph!"

"C'mon in, ex-child o'mine."

"Thanks, Mephistopheles."

"Oh, Meph, please. Why be so formal? We are family after all. Kind of." The man stepped back so Kallum could enter the room.

The room was a mess. It looked like a tornadohad hit it.

"You'll have to pardon the room, Kal. We can get rambunctious at times and, why not? We clean up afterward, just like when we feed. Never leave a mess you can't clean up, that's the key to being an effective Beast, which you wouldn't understand since you didn't get our Beast gene, or whatever it is that makes a Vampire a kind of Vampire, if you follow my logic."

It was hard to follow Mephistopheles' cyclic logic, but Kallum understood what he was trying to say and loved to listen to him explain it. He still had a soft Ethiopian accent just as Rebekah had maintained her Israeli accent over the years. It enthralled Kallum how some Vampires completely abandoned the accents of their origins, as Orphaeus had done, whilst others clung to that mortal aspect of their lives.

Rebekah came into the room, all toweled up and fresh-faced. The curtains were drawn to where no sun was allowed in, but the lights of the room were on, giving everything a Victorian yellow hue.

"Have a seat, won't you young Kallum?" Rebekah said politely. Anywhere will do.

"Thank you, and I'm hardly young."

Rebekah snugged his nose with two fingers and said, "You'll always be young to me, Little Dude."

Ire boiled in Kallum's throat at how Rebekah treated him. He was not a child. He was a prophet of Gideon, after all, and a resurrected saint to boot. He'd been around the block, and here this woman had the nerve to snug his nose and treat him like a boy. And what was with the "Little Dude" nickname? Just because he was mortal did not mean he was stupid.

"I'd appreciate it if you'd call me Kallum, and not Little Dude."

"Anything you say, Little Dude," Rebekah said playfully. "And to what do we owe this lofty visit from our Darkling turned Saint?"

Kallum took a deep breath and looked at the two Vampires, sitting on the bed across from him, still soppy from their shower. It was absurd.

"I want to know about my Vampiric family history. I want to know about the two of you and why it is you chose me to be a Vampire. And why you didn't stick around and show me the ropes before you left."

Rebekah's eyes widened. "Wow, you don't want much, do you?"

"I've wanted to know for years, for as long as I've been a Vampire. It's one of the reasons Cadmus got power over me, with the promise of telling me about the two of you. He lied, of course."

243

"Well that's what he does best, or so I've heard," Meph said. "To my knowledge, Cadmus doesn't know a thing about us. We're a bit of an enigma, Bek and I. That's how we like it.'

"Thus the humour, to cover up your underlying activity?"

"No we joke around all time," Rebekah said, drying her hair with a large fluffy towel. "A couple that laughs together stays together, and we've been together since the Crusades."

"My God!"

"I know. And you thought your silent film era was a long time ago. Kick back, I've got a story for you."

REBEKAH SPEAKS

Being a mortal product of my immortal father's tryst with a human thrall, my life was less than pleasant. I was ostracized, I had rocks thrown at me, and I was not allowed to attend temple with my mother. Oh, my mother wept and agonized over her Dhampir child, growing weary of her own outcast position in Jewish society. This was not the best time not to have the support of your community. Rome was waging war upon the holy land, trying to take it back as it had in the glory days before the Christ had come to get all rowdy and form pockets of resistance within Jewish society. It was Rome's actual task to get rid of all things having to do with Christ's real message and replace it with the more oppressive and Apostate-driven message of Paul.

Before you knew it, our community was overrun with conical-helmeted men in white tunics with a blood-red cross across their breast. They killed the men first then took as many women and children as they could for re-education in Rome; thus were the way of the Knights Templar. The last thing they always did was ransack the temple for treasure and sacred relics of our faith, often taking our cantor's Torah and the copies of the Kabbalah with them into the dust of their destruction.

My mother hid me well, bidding me to be silent for, if the

244

Knights had seen me with the glint of knowledge in my eye, I would have been taken to the Pope himself for special interrogation and teachings. It was then that she explained to me about my father, then known as Tien, a pilgrim from the Alpine villages of Switzerland. He had been anything but a pilgrim, taking his time to rend his clothing and pray at the Wailing Wall for the damages he'd done over the great expanse of time he had already lived. That night I ran away into the cradling night only to be met by the sister to my cowardly father, Lilitu Kelat of Judea. She took me in and taught me the mysteries of the world, telling me a very different story of how the world came to be what it was now, one of strife and fear. I asked Lilitu if my mother could join us at which time Lilitu told me the bad news that she had been taken to Rome to be a servant in one of the opulent homes scattered throughout the center of the Holy Roman Empire. I never saw her again. I was 13 at the time.

Lilitu Kelat took the next six years teaching me mysteries that seemed almost unfathomable to me. She taught me to read and had me memorize the Torah as well as study and understand the Kabbalistic mysteries. She even had me read the Apocrypha for they were of particular importance to the faith the Apostate was pushing. They were the books he did not want people to read, for they would seek out more knowledge upon reading the Apocrypha.

She catered to my strange food cravings, saying they were natural due to my genetic heritage, letting me have the blood of the lamb and cow as much as she would allow me to eat the raw meat. When I was finished with puberty, Lilitu came before me, as I was now 19 and extremely well educated and eager to go out into the world. She told me I was not yet ready to go into the world and it was then that she revealed the greatest secret of all; that I was the child of a Vampire and that all of my idiosyncrasies came from my Vampire father. I was as surprised as any one person could be and asked Lilitu Kelat to make me full Vampire so I would cease this vicious circle of never fitting in with the villagers of Jerusalem.

She did as I requested, teaching me the Way of the Vampire,

the code by which we were to feed, the hiding of bled bodies, the gift of the Glamour, all of it. One thing she did not teach me, but which pulled me to do nonetheless was the act of ripping my prey asunder and wallowing in the glory of his gore. This was a first amongst the Vampires and I was given the cognomen Ar'en El'meran, the Lion of Judea, the Tarmian for Lion of Judea, for indeed I was a predator living amongst the prey of Judea. Some of the older inhabitants warned of the dreadful spectre that left families torn and ripped asunder. They called me Beast in Hebrew...the word escapes me. People were happy to abide by the curfew set upon them by the Romans, for fear that the Beast would tear into their flesh and drink their heart's blood.

Lilitu Kelat was equally as horrified by my method of feeding and asked why I felt so compelled to feed in such a way. I had no answer for her. My instincts ran deep and I dreamt of the wolf wishing to burst forth and bay at the moon after I fed. It was at this time that I learned of the wondrous ability of Anubis. I began to hunt as a wolf, tackling my human prey and speaking to them as a person would, which would fill them with such fright the blood literally spurt forth from the wounds I inflicted their heart beat so fast and hard.

Eventually, Lilitu Kelat set me on the road and bade me travel the world to learn more of its wonders and horrors. I traveled south into Africa, killing and drinking the blood of both animal and human. I was not as refined as I am today. Eventually, I found myself in the heart of Ethiopia and found there a beautiful young man by the name of Kelile. In him, I saw my very mirror image, framed in the body of beauty, grace, and power. I approached him when the sun set, for he sat by his fire whittling a graven image in a large chunk of wood, much as I had heard the Makonde did..

"Hello," I said simply.

"Hello to you," he responded.

"The *others* have retired for the eve. Why not you?"

"I do not believe the rumours of a killer worse than the jungle cats waiting for my fire to die."

"So you are hard to persuade."

"Only when the rumours are spread on baseless information," he said to me, looking up *at* my pale olive complexion.

"You are Jewish," he said simply.

"You are observant."

"Come sit by my fire and rest your bones. I still have some meat, if you wish to eat."

"Are you not afraid that I am the great beast that people are in awe of and fear?"

"If you are, then I want to learn your secrets, dear lady. I grow weary of the ignorance of mortality. The disdain I hold for them is greater than this land, wider than the ocean I hear crashing upon the shore in great explosions of mist and brine, more endless than the Serengeti, more expansive than the sky. I wish to see the world. I want to walk in a state of strange blessedness. I would give anything to see the ocean."

"Come with me into the forest and I will show you the great oceans of the world. We shall learn all there is to know and bathe in the blood."

"Ah so you are a vandella," Kelile said, humour in his voice.

"If you must put a word to it, yes."

We talked all night about the Ethiopian ways and how they viewed the now world-renowned vampires. Even the African night was haunted with our myths and legends, it would seem. But Kelile was unafraid and, in fact, fascinated with what I had to offer, so offer it I did, and he became as vicious in his hunts as was I and all our children, barring Faust.

Such is our story, may it go on forever in Vampiric and, now, mortal circles!

"Why do you convert seemingly innocent people, like me for instance, into Vampirism? I was an insignificant artist making my way in the SoHo environment of Depression-era New York, a child of his conservative mid-Western upbringing. There was nothing special about me."

"Yet here you are, the resurrected saint of all Vampirism," explained Mephistopheles. "We all have our destinies and, even though Bek and I were unsure of your greatness, we sought you out because we felt you could do good as an artist, making a way for yourself and touching the lives of others. We may be Beasts, but we are supportive of the arts. Your sainthood and subsequent resurrection came as much as a surprise to us as anyone else in the room, to be honest. We thought you were special, but not that special, no offence, I hope. Nobody ever expects their child to end up being a saint. We figured you would become a great filmmaker rivaling that of even Orson Welles and Cecil B. Demille. Your Darkblood compelled you to become a priest and artist instead, which is fine by us, but we would still love to see what you could do with a movie set. Hopefully, someday, we'll get our chance."

"Hopefully so," Kallum said, not having the heart to tell them that his life was down to hours..

"What else do you need to know?" Rebekah ended her tale of love and blood.

Kallum was eager to get to Brown Mountain. He contended that all things of Vampiric importance would happen there. Agatha reminded him that this was the contention when everyone converged upon the lonely cabin in Swannanoa, only to be disappointed by a brief psychic interaction between Cadmus and Kelat and the subsequent destruction of the Order of the Crimson Cup.

"It was, needless to say, anti-climactic, not to mention I lost my partner in the fiasco," Agatha said flatly

"This will be different, I promise you. All three relics are present. Trust me. It'll be worth writing about in your little *fiction* novel about the Vampires. I think you'll be more than satisfied.."

"What exactly is supposed to happen?" grilled the ever-imposive reporter.

"A lot of the Vampire clan will return to mortality and will be at a loss as to what to do. They'll require mentors to live in this century. Others will choose the path of the immortal and their road will be tinged with the blood of innocents, for they shall be the hardcore Vampires, prepared to take the blood as they see fit. You will need our protection when this happens. All mortals will. They will be the Beasts of the clans, the Vrakshatha, the monsters who feed without regard and wallow in the gore of their victims. Vampirism will take a dark turn, but those Vampires who wish to be healed of the curse, will certainly be a barrier of protection between their bestial brethren and the mortals there to witness the magick that will transpire. You'll have plenty of fodder for your novel, of that I promise."

"And what of our enemies?"

"I led them to the forests and, ever since, they've been running through the jungles in which humanity cloisters themselves, be they the dwindling jungles of the Earth or the steel jungles the humans erected with the mistaken belief that they are safe in their high rises," Kelat said woefully. "All it takes is a simple press of the button to go up to one of the many condos and turn it into a blood-drenched vessel of carnage the police are good at leaving Kallum almost speechless...almost.

Cadmus had to take a limo with a handful of transformed Vampires and Eve, who could have easily followed them to Brown Mountain, but opted to stay close to her ward and the man she loved unconditionally. During the ride, Cadmus opened his laptop and decided to write about his experience so far.

> I have been made into a mortal...a miserable, weak, incompetent mortal. I have to depend on Eve for everything from Eve. She seems more than ready to help me with whatever it is I might require. My bodily functions such as hunger, nausea, and illness have crowded in on me like the groupies for Magnificat used to do, clamouring for just a touch of my dark fabrick as I quietly entered the car that would take me off to an undisclosed

location so that I might feed and rest at my leisure. Those days are gone.

Now all I have to suffer are Blood groupies from the Hive of the Redemption clamouring for just one sweet sip of my mortal blood. I hate them all. I hate the stirrings of uneasiness and panic they inspire. What if my bodyguards falter and I am left exposed to the ranks of hungry Vampires? Would I collapse under their weight, being bitten and drained right there on the street for any mortal to see with disgust? It jangles my nerves, which is not pleasant since I've never before had my nerves jangled in such a personal way.

I've asked the driver to take Eve and myself to Brown Mountain. He said wearily that the trip would be over three hours. I prompted him by saying his payment would be beyond anything he could imagine. He thought I meant money. His payment will be the spilling of his blood as out-of-control Redemptors lick it from the grass blades, if I can muster it. Granted, he was as dull and dry as any one limo driver could be, but I was eager for anything to eat, even this bag of indifference. The limo driver looked increasingly more tantalizing as we passed through the sacred city of Asheville and out into the Eastern countryside, heading for the decayed ruined castle never fully built that now served as the monument to the strange graveyard that contained the answers to his questions. Even though I might not be able to drink blood anymore, it would hearten me to see the Redemptors fall upon him in their religious fervor. My raven-haired companion is looking at me sidewise. More later.

What do you want, Cadmus Pariah?" asked Eve quiely.

"I want our limo driver dead. And I want resolution... completion...the answer to my questions," confided Cadmus before he thought better of it. Eve made him comfortable, to where he felt he could answer questions without judgment.

"And you think you'll get it at the final resting place of your biological father, the King Vampire Thiyennen?

"I believe that, if I bury the sacred chalice with him, the curse that binds me to it will finally be broken and I can live out my now brief life in peace. Asheville is where I shall settle, with you at my side if you will, for all the good it does me now, I will come to some sort of resolution, I do not know what. At least with his final burial, it will not come forth in response to Kelat's Blood, long gone from its present bowl. It simply is a cup, and an accursed one at that, to be buried and forgotten.

He helped dig the small hole into which Thiyennen's ashes would be interred and, as he placed the chalice within the hold, a voice called out.

"Do not bury the sacred chalice!"

Cadmus looked up to see Kelat emerging from a taxi, Kallum at her heels. "Do not harm my chalice, Cadmus!"

"It's nothing but a cup, now Kelat, Cadmus argued.

"No, it contains your Blood. It's very important. Now give it to me."

Cadmus looked up at Eve and shrugged. What harm could it do to give Kelat a cup that had residuals of his mortal blood encrusted within?

He handed Kelat the cup as she approached the grave of Thiyennen.

"He never wanted this..." she whispered. "He never wanted any of this."

"What did he want a great ceremony for burial?"

"He never wanted to be lost to obscurity, like all us Tarmi. No

251

one will know that a magickal being is buried here, someone who taught the people how to sing plants to live and weave blankets with poetry. Now he is eternally forgotten, a mere hint of a legend amongst the Pagan circles around the Earth. I grieve for him, Cadmus, truly I do."

Cadmus felt his heart tighten at the sight of Kelat's tears. His first inclination was to stand and hug her to him, to tell her everything was going to be all right. However, he refused to succumb to such display of affection, no matter how wrenching it may be. He was in the dirt, burying her freshly-cremated father, how could she not be emotionally distressed? But he refused to be. He felt nothing for Dmitri but dismay and lack of respect. Kelat on the other hand, had been nothing but kind to him and he relised he did not want to cause her any pain. It was then that Cadmus realized that he had a genuine affection for Kelat. The feelings were always under the surface of his thick skin and, with every positive emotion he felt, he inclined to lash out.

"Oh, Mother Kelat, always there to clench her claws at her breast and keen for the ones you've lost. If I didn't know better, I'd peg you for a Redemptor."

"Your words do not affect me, Cadmus Pariah. I know you are only trying to avoid what you are becoming. Well, son, the time has come. Here on Brown Mountain, the reckoning will be had. The two of you, get into the limos. Cadmus, you're in mine. Eve, take the other one.'

"What about our clothes, our belongings?"

"We'll pick them up later, Eve. Now, hurry!"

Eve immediately got up and rushed to the second limo, where she was greeted by Agatha and Rebekah. Dmitri and Kelat beckoned Cadmus to the first limo.

"We're going further up the mountain, Dmitri explained, "where the lights are most often spotted. It's sure to be a sight for the tourists to see tonight if we're right and the lights are connected to Vampires."

"They aren't connected to Vampires, you fool," Cadmus

groused. "They're connected to anything that will help them find a way home. This time, it happens to be Kallum and my strange connection to him and the chalice. I don't see how it could be connected to anything, really. I'm woefully mortal now and the chalice has lost its Blood charm."

"No it hasn't, Cadmus. Your Blood is the blood inside it now, traveling from bottom to rim, waiting for fulfillment. But, if the song is any indication, the chalice won't be needed after tonight. All souls may go home if they wish."

"I personally think the whole thing is a bunch malarkey. Magick died when the chalice of Kelat was drained by that little ant, Kallum."

"We'll see," said Kelat. "Certainly the hold it had on Upirdom was broken, which was a blessing in and of itself, but I don't think that's the only magick it contained. I think that, with the three other relics, one of which still resides in part in the chalice, we shall behold a miracle tonight."

"Well, now that I can truly laugh, you'll pardon me if I laugh in your face when this becomes yet another disappointment pre-thought and perpetrated by the Apostate, may he crumble in horror in the catacombs of Rome.

"This is no trickery," Kelat said, resting her cool hand on Kallum's warm one. "We're almost there."

Her words seemed more ominous than hopeful as the two limo drivers hit a dead end on the bumpy forest road. Kelat gave them large tips and send them on their way, commenting that non-Vampires would have to hike down the mountain, but it wasn't very high and at least they weren't having to climb it. She noted that everyone had sensible shoes except for Eve. For some reason, she felt that Eve probably wouldn't need them, being the Atlantean bride.

"Listen up, people. We're at the heart of where the Brown Mountain Lights tend to dance. "Now we can stay in this clearing or we can go into the forest where there won't be too much notice. I see other Vampires are gathering as we speak, scaling the shallow mountain with a religious fervour. Meph and Bek, it's up to you to protect Cadmus, Kallum, and the chalice. Killing Vampires is not forbidden. If they insist and attempt to take Cadmus for their own, tear them asunder.

Dmitri, Ishtar, your wards are Agatha and Eve. The same rules apply ~ there are no rules. The Vampires are coming here to be reconciled of their curse. They will, by any means necessary, take measures to insure their state is altered before morning light. We have five hours.

They trudged into the forest, at first all brambles and briars, which didn't bode well for Eve, but she trudged onward with the help of Cadmus of all people, lifting her over the thick brush, then back down onto mossier paths. They stuck to the mossy paths when they suddenly stopped behind Dmitri, who was studying a tree with fascination, fear, and wonderment.

"What is it," Kelat asked him.

"Look," and he pointed at the word **CROATAN** on the tree. "There has to be some connection between the Brown Mountain Lights and the tragedy that happened on Roanoke. That word, why that word?"

"Perhaps we will find out tonight," Kelat said quietly.

"Perhaps we'll find out dying," Orphaeus retorted.

"Do not be so hasty in your judgments, loved one. All will be revealed when the Reckoning is to be had."

Again, their journey into the woods continued, deeper into the older part of the forest where only moss and fern could be found on the floor and the trees stood like great sentinels of time. Every other tree had the word **CROATAN** carved into its bark and this clearly agitated Dmitri.

"What could it mean?" he asked aloud. And that is when the first light appeared, huge enough fit a large SUV inside, glowing yellow but, at its heart, it was a constant barrage of all colours.

We are the Croatan, the keepers of light, the harbingers of souls.

More lights converged on them, illuminating them from all

angles. *It is holy tongue for "little angels." We help those who cannot carry on to the worlds beyond. Do you wish to pass on?*

"No, it's nothing like that. My companion here saw the word carved on a tree on an island far from here and he had often wondered what it mean. We have brought with us thousands of Upir, waiting to be healed of a curse that was not of their making. Can you help us?"

"The song must be sung."

"Song?" Dmitri asked.

"What song?" Kelat said, perplexed.

"Is it this song?" Cadmus stepped forward and began to hum. The lights began to dance in a rhythm only pure light knows.

"But there were words, too. Holy words."

Kallum stood forward and, at first, began to chant:

U sa dorken na'aalor kenropfehli
Na'aaulor ter'a sa
Rhos'a rhos tema rhos
Meneterah rhos berran
U sa dorken na'aalor kenropfehli
Na'aaulor ter'a sa
Rhos'a rhos tema rhos
Meneterah rhos berran

"Yes..." Cadmus said, moving closer to Kallum, their voices mingling like they were always supposed to sing together.

U sa dorken na'aalor kenropfehli
Na'aaulor ter'a sa
Rhos'a rhos tema rhos
Meneterah rhos berran
U sa dorken na'aalor kenropfehli
Na'aaulor ter'a sa
Rhos'a rhos tema rhos

255

Meneterah rhos berran

U sa dorken na'aalor kenropfehli
Na'aaulor ter'a sa
Rhos'a rhos tema rhos
Meneterah rhos berran
U sa dorken na'aalor kenropfehli
Na'aaulor ter'a sa
Rhos'a rhos tema rhos
Meneterah rhos berran

With each verse, their song became more frantic and Kelat could see the giant cone of power stretching far into the sky. This was going to be glorious and terrifying.

U sa dorken na'aalor kenropfehli
Na'aaulor ter'a sa
Rhos'a rhos tema rhos
Meneterah rhos berran
U sa dorken na'aalor kenropfehli
Na'aaulor ter'a sa
Rhos'a rhos tema rhos
Meneterah rhos berran

U sa dorken na'aalor kenropfehli
Na'aaulor ter'a sa
Rhos'a rhos tema rhos
Meneterah rhos berran
U sa dorken na'aalor kenropfehli
Na'aaulor ter'a sa
Rhos'a rhos tema rhos
Meneterah rhos berran!

And with that the cup crumbled into dust and the crown on Cadmus head broke in two and fell off his scalp. There seemed to be an explosion and everyone within a five mile radius of Brown

Mountain either fell, or felt the jolt coming from the Witch Mountain. So, too, did the two Vampires who had sung the prophetic song. Ishtar cradled Kallum's head in her lap just as, surprisingly, Eve did the same with Cadmus.

It took a few minutes before her composure allowed her to do so, but Kelat crawled over to where Kallum lay in Ishtar's gentle lap.

"Is there anything you can do?" cried Ishtar, whom she noticed was once again mortal.

"Nothing but comfort you in knowing that he has gone home to his paradise and awaits you there."

It was little comfort, but that was all she had. Moving on to Eve and Cadmus, Kelat found a very different situation. Cadmus was alive, but dying. He had aged twenty years and deep lines framed his face from nose to lips, giving him a look of sophistication he'd never before possessed.

"I am dying, Mother. Have you the magick to stop it?"

"I'm afraid not, Cadmus. What's done is done."

"May I taste your Blood just once before I go?"

Cadmus looked askance at Kelat, then realized what she meant. She was no longer a Vampire, but a Tarma with the star of Kessilon on her brow and the bear claw mark of Artanis on her left cheek.

"Yes, I see you understand. We were not given a choice in the matter, thanks to the redeemer and the redeemed. Our hearts decided for us. You delivered us and Kallum blessed us. We can live out our lives now without the curse of the Apostate trailing our every move. Thank you, Cadmus."

Cadmus blinked his vast eyes slowly and he breathed outward in pain. "I have lived my life in such wretchedness, I know nothing else. When I die where will I go?"

"You will go to a place of blessed respite. You have earned a lofty and celebrated place in the Summerland."

"Mother, I am afraid."

"I know you are," she said, slicing her finger open with Cadmus' dragon claw blade and pressing the wound to his lips. "We are always afraid when we are to make a blind leap into the great unknown. But know this, my child. You are beloved of the Tarmi of Meybhelahn and of Earth. You will not be remembered as the Pariah, but as the Redeemer. I will tell your story to the Tarmi as will Agatha tell it to mortals. As you live in bliss in the Summerland someday, so shall your memory live on. For now, life calls you and Death sings his lullaby."

"Mother..." Cadmus said and he reached one trembling hand up to touch the star of Kessilon. "Mother, I see – "

And he was gone. But in his eyes, which had always been all-absorbing, there kindled a light. Knowing that her only child's new life was just beginning, Kelat closed his eyes and kissed Cadmus upon his pale brow.

Eve looked up at Kelat with mortal eyes. "My curse is gone too. Despite my sins, I believe I can open that portal to Avalon if you and your remaining clan wish to go."

"This is a world wrought by the Apostate. If we were to stay, we would be cloistered in some underground bunker, interrogated, and tortured in the name of science. No. Even now, I feel the remaining seven making their way up here to us. We will leave this land to the Child of the Tree and hope that the children don't completely forget our teachings before it is too late."

Kelat turned to Dmitri, who was just getting up from the blast. "Behold, Dmitri, our Atlantean Sibling is able to open the doorway to the blessed Isle of Apples. Won't you – "

And then she saw...Dmitri was still a Vampire. He could not go with her into the land of youth, not as a creature of darkness. Tears fell like rivers from Kelat's eyes. "Are we ever meant to be together, Dmitri? Ever? I know I've sinned and rendered our connection before, but must we always be punished by separation?"

"It seems that our paths just aren't the same, yet, love," Dmitri said in a kind of drawl. "When it's time for me to cross over, you know I'll be right there by your side. In the meanwhile, go in purity and love. Your mother and siblings await you there. Your father and all your friends. They're all there on Meybhelahn. Do not disappoint them because you want to stay with a Vampire who still believes there's mystery to be discovered on this beautiful planet of ours.

A trail of cured Vampires walked single file up the mountain and to the portal Eve had created. Kelat looked at their hopeful faces, their beatific expressions, and she began to cry.

"Will I ever see you again?"

"That's a silly question to ask a soul mate, don'tcha think?" Dmitri said, trying not to get choked up himself. If he cried, then Kelat definitely would not leave.

"Well then...until we meet again, my lover...my friend. My soul mate." And Kelat entered into the portal without looking back because she knew if she had, she would never have entered Meybhelahn without Dmitri.

The Vampires who remained with the curse, willingly stayed on the Earth to continue drinking blood and making the magicks of the night slowly began to withdraw from the mountain as the sun was soon to be rising over the crests of the Smokies. Orphaeus, Rebekah, and Mephistopheles were among them. Dmitri turned and followed them off into the dusky light. He returned home and collected Dare from his sweet neighbour, giving her a hefty chunk of money for watching the dog. He turned on some music which seemed incredibly appropriate for the moment, though he couldn't remember the name of it. It was by Annie Lennox, though. Her voice was inimitable. Dmitri lay there, his eyes pooling with tears as he ruffled the thick hair around Dare's neck.

"So it's just the two of us." Dare thumped a grateful tale in response, just being happy to have her human back.

EPILOGUE

"Did you ever get an invitation? A little window to another life?"
~ Shriekback "Sea Theory"

It has been prophesied throughout time that an End to All Things is inevitable and that a redeemer will be instrumental in bringing about a new beginning for those whose hearts follow in that soul's footsteps. Humans throughout time have long held these beliefs and take hope and comfort in these prophecies, taking heart that the cycle of all things will bring about a renewed and better world. Vampires, too, hold these hopes close to their own secret faiths and collections of foretellings, as revealed to them by Tarmian turned Upyr, Gideon the Mad.

His utterances were treasured and passed on by rote by those who heard them until there came a time when he went silent and appeared only rarely to those he felt worthy of his secrets and insanity.

Two he graced with his madness. Two and two alone. Both were murdered by the monster that Gideon often foretold, the one with whom he seemed so obsessed in his later years. Looking back upon them, one guardian of Gideon's Augury was to keep it hidden until the time of its revealing. The other, the one destined to redeem and bring about a new age for Upyr kind, knew the Augury's song and held it as a precious melody until once more his soul was reunited with the collection of prophecies, complete and ready for revelation.

Only one prophecy, known only to the Queen Upyr, was that mortal kind would save the Vampires and that the redeemed was to bring forth the true saviour of Vampire kind, through Blood, suffering and, eventually a kind of personal redemption that may kill or cure.

This redeemer only Gideon knew and this was the only thing he never told a soul. But one soul knows who the Redeemer is and he is determined to bring forth the saviour told of old.

Agatha looked at the intro and seemed very satisfied with it. She would use it to tell the whole story from beginning to end, of how the Vampires lived and died on this planet of wonders. Hearing a rumble of thunder in the distance, she imagined that it might be a dragon coming to humanity's rescue, but she doubted they'd be that lucky, at least not yet. She closed the lid to her laptop and placed it on the floor beside her bed, turning over for some fitful sleep, if she got any at all.

Furtive eyes peeked through Agatha's window. They were familiar eyes, older, yes, but still endless and all-absorbing. Let her write her stories, the owner of those inexplicable eyes thought to himself. People would think they were fiction unless they happened across one of the characters in her novels. Cadmus Pariah, reborn into the Hive, a true Vampire now, watched with amusement. He smiled, truly smiled, at the reception the books would receive, and he felt a certain glee at coming in contact with an avid reader. How would they feel meeting the villain in the book they read? How would they feel when his teeth sunk into their ample flesh? He looked forward to finding out in his new undead Vampire skin. So much fun would be had with this, he knew it. Laughing gleefully, Cadmus whisked away, his laugh becoming the lonely *peent* cry of a nighthawk. And then, following him, came blessed oblivion.

FIN

THE AUGURY LEXICON

- <u>Ambrosciata:</u> The act of Blood exchange between two or more Vampires. A form of lovemaking.

- <u>Anubis:</u> Those within the Great Hive who can transform into other forms. Origin of the Werewolf. They are named after the dog-headed Egyptian God of the Dead.

- <u>Beholding:</u> When two or more of the Original Ten lay eyes upon each other and begin the process of self-destruction because of the horror that they see.

- <u>Banshie:</u> A vampire who wails in horror at having leeched or bled a host. All Banshies are Redemptors.

- <u>Apostate:</u> The one to whom Vampires attribute the conversion of the Original Ten. Also known as The Dread Magus.

- <u>Bleeding:</u> The act of killing a mortal by taking the blood.

- <u>The Blood:</u> Vampire Blood. Affiliation, as in "I am of the Blood."

- <u>Bloodbath:</u> The act of smearing the body with the victim's blood and viscera.

- <u>Bloodlust:</u> Feeding frenzy involving the rending of flesh and occasionally the Bloodbath.

- <u>Conversion:</u> Transformation of an unwilling mortal into a Vampire. Usually, but not always, accomplished through magick instead of Blood transfer.

- <u>Darkling:</u> Name or title used by many Vampires, particularly in the Dark Blood Hive and the Hive of the Beast.

- <u>Dhampir:</u> A mortal child of a vampire. Usually born with canines, which soon fall out after birth. Almost always,

262

these children have some psychic ability. Dhampiri will crave a mixture of blood (as from steak) and milk, probably a subconscious re-enactment of their conception.

- Eleftherosi: The Tarmian tribe from which the Original Ten come. Thiyennen was chief of that tribe and Kelat was the Tarmian Mother of Memory, the tribal shamaness.

- Felling: The killing of a mortal without Bleeding.

- The Great Hive: That which all Vampires call their social order. Divided in smaller subhives, which are:
  - Dark Blood Hive: Classic Vampire Society eschewing guilt over what is considered a Natural State. Most Dark Bloods are Incubi and Succubae.
  - Hive of the Beast: consisting of those prone to Bloodlust and the revels of the flesh.
  - Hive of Purity: consisting of the Original Ten and their first Children.
  - Hive of Redemption: consisting of those of Blood who strive to overcome their predatory nature.
  - Tribe of the Tomb: the handicapped ones. The undead. The shamblers.

- Incubus: A male Vampire who feeds by sexually stimulating his victim in order to encourage the heart to literally pump the blood out of the victim into him. He always kills for food.

- Inferno: A method of Vampire suicide involving the telekinetic combustion of the Blood. This act will kill any Blood relative of the suicide. Done only once, the deed decimated the Great Hive by two-thirds and destroyed one of the Original Ten.

- Infusciata: A term, first used in Ancient Rome, to sum up the act of turning a mortal into a Vampire, which involves the transfer of blood.

- Leeching: The act of taking the blood without killing the

host.

- <u>Libation:</u> In the Order of the Crimson Cup, it's the act of drinking Blood from the chalice.

- <u>Moritada:</u> The death of a Vampire.

- <u>Mortation:</u> Vampire myth of being transformed from Vampire back into mortal. It has never been accomplished.

- <u>The Original Ten:</u> The very first Vampires. Also known as the Ancestors. Said to have been converted in or around what is now Wallachia in the days of prehistory.

- <u>Rapture:</u> To kill a mortal by Bleeding during orgasm.

- <u>Seizing:</u> The exsanguination and death of a Vampire at the hands of another Vampire. A form of cannibalism.

- <u>Succubus:</u> A female sexual vampire, using the same feeding methods as the Incubus; however, she need not kill.

- <u>Tarmi:</u> Non-human inhabitants of ancient Earth. Most-likely the origins of the modern conceptions of Elves and Fairies.

- <u>Thrall:</u> A mortal Blood-bound to her/his Vampire mentor.

- <u>Thralling:</u> The taking of a mortal to service a Vampire. *Always* involves the conception of a Dhampir if the Vampire is male and the thrall is female. The thralling of males also makes them eunuchs. The thralling of a female by a female Vampire gives the thrall the gifts of Sight and Allurement.

- <u>Tithing:</u> In the Order of the Crimson Cup, it's the act of giving blood to the chalice.

- <u>Undead/Nosferatu:</u> Shambling zombies and ghouls of the Tribe of the Tomb. Another name others in the Great Hive is Unfortunates.

- <u>Upirdelak:</u> Ancient Vampires. The Ancestors.

- <u>Vampiri:</u> Vampires of average power, having to feed every night, but never having to kill.

- <u>Vampyr:</u> Old European vampires with much power. Must only kill occasionally.

- <u>Vrakshatha:</u> Eastern European Vampyr, almost all of which are Beasts. Prefer Bleeding.

www.ingramcontent.com/pod-product-compliance
Lightning Source LLC
Chambersburg PA
CBHW070850250626
47159CB00003B/1016